FORGOTTEN WISHES

DJINN EVERLASTING BOOK TWO

LISA MANIFOLD

To all those who read Tibby's story,
And demanded Xavier's.
Xoxoxo

1

livia

"*I* don't know why you're picking on her. She's a good kid and a good worker. She just wants to learn, and I know she looks up to you. That's a good thing, Liv, but trust you and your mom to make it something bad!"

The slam of the door marked his exit.

I couldn't speak. I stared as though the door could give me answers. What had gotten into Royce? He'd stopped by to talk to me about plans for the evening. I was in the process of filling out paperwork to end the internship, and when he'd asked me what I was doing - we'd ended up fighting.

I didn't understand why. We had interns every summer. If they sucked, which didn't happen often, we got rid of them. Politely, and completely legally. Why was he all up in arms about this one? For that matter, how did he know her?

A thought snaked through my head, one that I stomped on and shoved into the trash. I had work to do, and I needed to call the university and let them know this intern would not be returning after Friday.

I forgot about the girl, Suzan, and everything else after calling the school. I had a mountain of paperwork to get through for our next proposal.

When I got home later that night, Royce was making dinner.

"Hey, are we all right?" I asked as I came in, setting down my purse.

"Why do you ask?"

He didn't sound angry.

"Well, you were pretty mad about the decision to let Suzan go." I kept it light, and vague.

Royce shrugged. "I think you're a tough employer, but you're right, if people can't do what we need them to, they need to go."

He turned his back to me to stir something on the stove, so I felt free to raise my eyebrows and just watch him. He never agreed with me anymore. Everything became a fight. This felt…weird.

I didn't want to ruin what seemed like a moment of olive branches from both sides.

avier

I raised a glass. "To Seth and Tib!"

Bryant and Seth raised up glasses, and we all drank. The waitress, who'd been hovering, scooted over.

"Another round, guys?" She gave me a little toss of her hair.

"Yep." I ignored the hair.

I caught the eye of the other two. "Hey, we're not driving. We have someone to do that for the rest of the night."

"Some of us have to work in the morning," Bryant muttered.

"You're not going to work. Don't even kid yourself," Seth patted him on the arm. "You'll be the only one in the office, so give it up. The world won't collapse if you and Tibby aren't in for a couple of days."

Bryant sighed, looking down into his empty glass. "What the hell? You will have to explain to your bride why we're all hungover as hell tomorrow."

Seth laughed. "I'll tell her the truth. It's all X's fault!"

"Hey! So much for fraternity and all that!"

That made the two of them burst into laughter. Honestly, she'd be pissed at all of us, but not really. Other than Tibby, I didn't have close friends. Because of her, I'd met first Bryant, and then later, when she told us she was getting married, Seth. I liked both of them.

It had been hard for me at first. With Tibby being my oldest, closest, and as previously mentioned, only friend, I'd been jealous of sharing her. But Bryant was awesome, and in spite of my initial reserve, Seth, the guy that Tibby was marrying in two days, was pretty amazing, too.

She deserved it.

"It's all right. She'll yell at me most, figuring that I was the ringleader."

"She'd be right," Seth and Bryant said together.

That made me laugh. "Can't let my reputation go to shit, then, can I?"

We got another round.

"*W*here are we?" I leaned into Bryant, trying not to lean too far. It felt like I might fall on my ass, and that would not be good.

"Cobalt. Best. Club. Ever." He leaned against the wall, closing his eyes.

I could feel the thump of the base against the wall, even though we were outside. "Dance club?"

Bryant nodded, eyes still closed. "My favorite." Then he opened his eyes and pushed off from the wall. He went right for the bouncer. I couldn't tell what he said, but he pointed at Seth and me. As he walked back, the bouncer called someone from inside the door to take his place. He followed Bryant to our place in line.

"You XTC?" The guy asked.

I nodded. "Every day."

He shone a flashlight into my face. "Holy shit, you are! C'mon man, I'm sorry, get out of the line!"

I looked up, brushing at my head. It still kind of hurt to look into the sun, even though the bachelor celebration had been two nights ago. But I was used to working with a hangover, although this one seemed to be lingering. Old age, my mind whispered. Can't hang anymore. I ignored it.

It wouldn't do to take pictures with my best friend on

her wedding day with bird shit in my hair. I couldn't see a bird anywhere, but I'd felt something hit my head. What the hell? I brushed my head again, definitely not looking up at the sun this time.

"X!" Tibby's voice broke into my thoughts. "Cake!"

"Coming, coming, Ms. All-that-and-the-bag-of-chips," I muttered.

As I approached her, she tucked her arm into mine. "I heard that, jackass."

"It's Mrs. All-that now," Seth leaned around to grin at me. "No more of this Ms."

I matched his grin. I liked the guy. He'd appeared almost out of nowhere, at least to me, anyway, and he and Tibby had gotten married so fast I had to ask her if she was knocked up. She laughed, not offended in the least, and told me that they knew it was right. After hanging out with him, I knew she was telling me—and more importantly, herself—the truth.

I'll admit, I'd been skeptical. Sure. *You just knew it was right.* I had any number of ex-girlfriends and one bitter ex-wife that said otherwise.

However, nothing I'd seen from either of them showed me that my skepticism had merit. In fact, I felt like the grumpy asshole uncle, glaring over a cheap beer, waiting for something bad to happen. Every time they met one another's eyes, they both glowed.

I was happy for Tib. She deserved it. She'd worked hard to get away from her past, and I admired and supported hard work more than anything. That was what got me away from my past. As bad as Tibby's past had been, mine was worse.

I shook my head. No need to dive into that crap right now, or ever. I watched as the two of them cut the cake together, and carefully, tenderly fed it to one another. No face smashing here. While some of the guests catcalled their disappointment, I didn't mind.

Tibby had found her happily ever after. I had nothing but happiness for her.

Why, then, did I feel a pang of...something, I didn't know what—every time I saw how they looked at each other?

I shook my head again. Time to see if any of the guests were single and in the mood for bad decisions.

Two hours later I stood with a drink in hand and not one bad decision in sight. Tibby and Seth were getting ready to leave on their honeymoon. Since they'd held the wedding at the club of the marina where Tibby kept her boat, she and Seth went back to the boat to change so they could leave. I'd laughed to myself about the fact that it seemed to take them a long time. But now, they were ready to go.

Tibby stood with Seth, Bryant, her law partner and other best friend, and me. It struck me that this was more than a simple good-bye.

"Thanks, guys, for being here for me." Tibby had an expression that almost looked soft on her face. I don't know when I'd last seen that kind of happiness and peace on her.

"Of course," Bryant said before I could answer. "Where else would we be?"

"Oh, I don't know," a scowl made her eyebrows furrow. "Maybe at a bar?"

Seth, Bryant and I looked at one another, all three silent for a moment, and burst out laughing.

"It's not my fault!" I said, trying to control my laughter. "All I did was take us out to Barrel."

"Where they serve very good whiskey," Seth added.

"That was both good and bad," Bryant said, which caused all three of us to laugh again. The rest of the guests were looking at us; Tibby was glaring and the three of us laughing like fools.

"It really isn't his fault," Seth started and stopped when Tib turned the glare on him.

"Yeah, he can't help getting phone numbers, and hook-up offers wherever we go," Bryant snickered.

"I also got the bill!" I protested. "I don't think we really drank seventy-two shots of tequila, but you never know."

All of us except Tibby laughed harder.

"Which bar?" She hissed.

"Um, Barrel was nothing major. The rest is Bryant's fault." I threw him under the bus without a second's hesitation. "What?" I spread my hands as Bryant gave me a mock glare. "I wasn't the one who chose Cobalt."

"Didn't stop everyone there from getting a drink on you and giving you their number," Seth put in.

"Not helpful, dude."

Bryant tried to keep up the glare but lost the battle. He bent over with laughter. "Tib, you should have seen it. X had enough to drink that he didn't even blink when guys were stuffing numbers in his pockets. Even when I tried to whisper—"

"There was no whispering," Seth said.

"That X was just there, and not looking for anyone."

"Well, my manager's already pissed," I said cheerfully because I had to admit, I liked pissing him off. "Apparently, there are pictures, which there always are, and some rag contacted Marcia—"

"Classy name for a total bitch," Tibby muttered.

I ignored her. Not that she was wrong. I liked that she disliked my recent ex-girlfriend as much as I did. Solidarity was a good thing. "And she was quick to tell them that XTC, hard ass and mean-to-women rapper is like that because he's in the closet, and so sad that he won't come out."

I made a face at Tibby, and she finally laughed. "As if anyone who knows you would think you're gay!"

I shrugged. "I don't care. Press is press."

"Next time, you keep your damn driver," The laughter faded from Tibby. "I don't need to pick your drunk asses up at three in the morning, whining about food."

I grinned at her. "Maybe. You'll live. Besides, that's not really why you're mad. Admit it. It's because we made fun of your car."

She made a noise that sounded a hell of a lot like a snort. "At least no one puked in my baby."

How Seth responded without laughing, I'll never know. "Yeah, it would be a shame for the flying lime to be out of commission."

That set the three of us into laughter again. Tibby had this ancient Volkswagen Thing, painted lime green that she wouldn't part with for love or money. I'd told her I'd buy her whatever she wanted if she'd just retire the ugly ass thing.

No joy. When she loved something, she loved one hundred fifty percent. I realized that this now included Seth, and a part of me felt sad that my best friend had someone. Not that I felt sad for her. No, it was more selfish and asshattish—I felt bad for me. I couldn't believe I struggled with envy at her wedding. But I did.

Seth leaned in and kissed her, and the glow I'd seen on her all day came back in a flash. Then both of them looked up, brushing at their heads. I saw them meet one another's eyes, and then almost as one, turn and look at Bryant and me.

Seth's eyebrows went up, and Tibby shrugged. It all happened very quickly. What, exactly, had happened?

Something had. I could tell.

"Shall we, Mrs. McKay?" Seth held out a hand, which Tibby took.

"Yes. I leave you with these two jokers, who knows where they'll drag you off to this time." Her words held no real heat, and Tibby gave the pair of us a fond look.

They moved away as one, and I felt the pang again. I glanced over to see Bryant watching them as well.

"I'm happy for her."

He nodded. "Me, too. She deserves it." He didn't speak for a moment and then turned to me. "So, you up for going out again tonight?"

$\mathcal{T}$ibby and Seth had finally said their goodbyes to everyone else and were standing with Bryant and I once more. I'd arranged for a limo to take them to the airport. One last thing I could do before she officially became someone else's charge. I could see it heading towards us from the marina entrance.

Tibby put her arms around us both and hugged tightly. "I am going to miss you guys."

"No you're not," Bryant laughed at her. "You're going to be preoccupied. Or at least, you'd better be."

Seth kissed the side of her head with such tenderness that the pang watching them on and off all afternoon increased to almost painful.

"I'll take care of her," he said to Bryant and me.

"We know it," I answered.

Tibby glanced at Seth, and I was surprised to see that there was a shit ton of communication in their look. When had that happened? It was the same thing I'd seen before

—that look where a lot happened in a very short amount of time.

"Listen, I need to tell you guys something," Tibby said.

The tone of her voice made both of us pull back a little to get a better look at her. She glanced at Seth again, and while I didn't see anything, he must have given her encouragement, because she went on.

"If anything weird happens, you know, while I'm gone…just go with it, okay?" She looked first at me, and then Bryant.

"What the hell does that mean?" I asked.

The Tibby I knew came back instantly. "It means that if something out of the ordinary happens, just go with it. Stop being an ass and take some well-meant advice for once in your life!"

Bryant cut the moment short. Thank God. "Get in the car, Tib, and shut up. We're gonna be fine, even without you here to boss us around." He gave her a one-armed hug as the driver held open the car door for them.

Tibby pursed her lips and shared another one of those looks with Seth. "I love you guys. Always." She stepped close and kissed Bryant and then me.

With a few more steps, she and Seth disappeared into the car and were gone. I wished I had someone to whisk off into a limo with to somewhere fab. But I didn't.

So it looked like hanging with Bryant, maybe some bad decisions if I got lucky, and the inevitable confrontation with my manager it would be.

Could be worse.

Why didn't that cheer me up?

 livia

I stared at the papers in my hand. "What is this, Royce?" Maybe if I didn't look, it would go away.

"Don't make this worse than it needs to be, Liv. You know what it is."

I struggled to keep the tears from spilling over. Crying wouldn't make this any better. "I thought we were going to talk about it." God, did I sound whiny?

He sighed. "What is there to talk about? We're not happy—"

"You mean you're not happy. What's her name, Royce?" I threw it out to see what he'd say.

He sighed again that put upon '*I'm such a victim*' heavy sigh that made me want to brain him with the nearest heavy object.

"It doesn't matter, Liv. Look, just take them to your attorney."

"And what happens in the meantime?" We had a house, a life. It pissed me off that he didn't even deny that there was a *her*.

"Well…" For the first time, he looked unsure of himself. "I think…I think you should get a hotel room."

"What? You hand me divorce papers, and want *me* to leave?" My voice rose. How had I married such an insensitive jerk?

"I think it would be best, don't you?"

I couldn't hear anything for the roaring that began in my head, getting louder with each breath. "I think you need to leave. Right this minute, Royce." I did my best to keep the roaring under some control.

Royce seemed to have managed whatever hesitation he'd had. "No, Olivia, I am not—"

I rose and slammed my hand on the table in front of me in one swift motion. "Yes, Royce. You. Are. Leaving."

He opened his mouth, and then closed it. Whatever he saw in my face convinced him that he needed to stop arguing. Without another word, he turned, and I heard him mount the stairs, and then a lot of steps above my head, and he thudded down the stairs again.

"I'm leaving, but…"

I slowly turned to look at him. I still stood where he'd left me when he went up to pack some of his shit.

He shut his mouth and disappeared from the doorway of the kitchen. A moment later, I heard the click of the door as it shut behind him. Only then did I sit down, head in hands, and let the tears come.

I don't know how long I sat there, hunched over the table, tears falling on my hands and the Goddamned papers. The tears slowed and then stopped. Finally, I sat up. The cup of coffee I'd gotten right before Royce handed me his good news still held some warmth. I wrapped my hands around it for a moment, needing warmth from something.

None of this would help me. Only one thing would, now.

I pulled out my cell and called my momma.

She answered on the second ring. "Sugar! How are you?"

"Like shit, Momma."

Her voice changed. "What's wrong?" I could hear the steel in it.

"Royce…" Damn it. I couldn't get the words out because tears choked me.

"That bastard." She grasped the situation immediately. "I'll be there in a flash, sugar. You kick his ass out and lock the door." She hung up.

How had she known instantly? The thought made me cry harder.

I hadn't moved from the kitchen table when I heard her let herself in. The cup of coffee had gone completely cold although I still had my hands wrapped around it. I watched Momma pocket her keys. Royce had hated that my mother had a key. One of the arguments that never got solved.

"Where is he?"

"I told him to leave."

"Good."

"He wanted me to leave, Momma."

"He was never anything more than trash."

"Momma! Not helping."

She came and put her arms around me, and I had the sense of being enveloped. She always had that superpower —making me feel supported no matter what.

"We're gonna get through this, honey. Now, what has he done?"

I reached a handout and pushed the papers at her. She took one arm from around me and inspected them.

Momma, in addition to being kick-ass awesome, is also an attorney. Together, she and I ran a talent agency. I work with our clients, and she makes sure they don't do anything stupid legally. I felt her inhale deeply as she read.

"That sonuvabitch."

"That bad?"

"He wants alimony."

"What?" I sat up, leaning back to look at her. "How can he ask for that?"

"Apparently, sugar, you are the breadwinner in the family."

"With a business that he complained about constantly." The irony felt like a hot knife cutting me to the bone.

"Well, he's not complaining now." Her lips tightened.

"He's got someone else."

She looked over the paperwork at me. "He told you that?"

"All but."

"That man always did have one foot in the gutter. I'm sorry, Olivia, but he did. At least now you can shake the shit from your shoes."

Momma doesn't mince words. It's why I work directly with our clients.

"I thought we were going to work on things, Momma."

She set down the papers and hugged me again. "You are a good girl, Livvie, of course, you wanted to make things better. Can't get blood from a turnip, honey. It takes two, and you've been one for a long time."

"How is it you haven't said anything about this?"

"I don't hold with interfering where I'm not invited. Now you invited me." She patted my shoulder. "We'll take care of this. I'll get Lloyd on it."

Lloyd was her "work colleague." He was also my de-facto stepfather. He and my mother had been dating for a number of years, but she wouldn't admit it, and she wouldn't marry him. She had loved my father dearly, and when he'd died in a car crash, she stated she was done with marriage. Lloyd made her rethink a relationship, but she wasn't budging on the marriage thing.

Like Momma, Lloyd was an attorney, although he practiced family law.

"How could he do this, Momma?"

"Because he's a dumb ass, sugar. Can't see what he had. Dry those tears now." She moved away to the counter and brought back a box of tissue.

"It would be nice to have some sympathy," I glared, but it's hard to be imposing blowing your nose.

"That's all well and good, but he's got a head start on you. You don't have the time for tea and sympathy. He's after your business, the house, everything."

"Why would he do this?" I knew we had problems. They didn't seem worthy of a divorce and the taking everything from me, though. I reached across and looked, really looked at the filing papers.

Momma kept silent as I read. She wasn't exaggerating. He really did want it all.

"She must be poor as dirt." I looked up to see her with crossed arms, fingers tapping out an impatient tattoo as she waited for me to finish. "He needs to feather his new tacky nest." Funny how her accent got stronger when she got mad.

"Why do you think that?" I couldn't keep up with her at the moment.

"Because what real man would make these kinds of demands? He's no gentleman."

"I don't know, Momma."

"Who's pluckin' this chicken, sugar? You or me? I'm the lawyer. Let me handle this." She stepped away, pulling out her cell.

"Lloyd, honey, what are you doing? I need you over at Olivia's." She stopped. "This is an emergency. I need some papers filed today." Another pause. "Yes, indeed. Maybe put in a call to Judge Martine, while you're at it. Let him know you're filing a response today." She turned to look at me.

Then she smiled at whatever he said. "You, too." She ended the call.

"Momma, it's okay to tell him you love him in front of me. It's not a secret."

"That is my business, missy. Now, what are we gonna do with you?"

"What do you mean, Momma?" I felt very tired. Her energy sapped whatever I had left.

"You are going to leave this to me—well, to Lloyd and me. We'll have Royce trussed and bagged before he knows what happened. But you, you need to get out of town."

"I'm not going anywhere, Momma." I started to put my head back on the table.

She yanked me up before I was able to. "Oh, yes you are. I shall stay right here, and make sure that Royce doesn't try anything, and you will go somewhere and get yourself together. What's on the schedule at work?"

"I don't know, Momma! I can't even think straight right now!" Her pushiness stirred me to anger. Couldn't she be a normal mother and be nice and get me a Cosmo, or something? Let me cry in peace? It had been all of five minutes since I found out that I'd be a divorced woman soon.

"I know, sugar, that's why you called me. Let's see," Momma walked away to open my laptop, one finger tapping her lip. "Where can I send you? It's important that Royce have to deal with only Lloyd right now."

"Whatever," I finally got a chance to put my head down.

"I have it! You're going to see Liz!!"

Oh, God. My mother, a southern woman, was obsessed with The Red Door spa in New York. Why she couldn't have an obsession with something here, in Nashville, I didn't know. But I also knew I wouldn't win an argument once she dragged Elizabeth into it. That would be Elizabeth Arden, by the way. Whom my mother calls 'Liz'. Like she knew the woman or something.

"Whatever, Momma." I had no energy to argue.

I ignored her as she muttered to herself, making reservations.

The doorbell rang.

Momma looked up happiness all over her. "That'll be Lloyd. You go and shower, and pack. We'll take you to the airport."

I didn't speak as I made my way upstairs. What in the world was there to say? My marriage was over before I'd even had a chance to fight for it, and now I would need to essentially put on a suit of armor to get through this. I supposed it made sense to go to a spa first since I knew the dismantling of my life wasn't going to be easy.

Maybe going to Elizabeth, as Momma would say, and letting her sort it out would be the best thing. Since I felt like I swam in thick water that didn't allow me to move, and couldn't seem to think straight. Since she hated Royce and would be happy to scalp him for me. I hoped I wasn't making a mistake, but as it took everything I had to put one foot in front of the other, maybe I'd best let Momma handle this. I hoped I wouldn't regret it later.

2

$\mathcal{X}$avier

$\mathcal{I}$ leaned back on the couch, glaring at the spot where my phone landed. My ears felt like they were ringing. I'd cut off Preston, my manager, in the middle of the ranty bullshit he delivered to me. Still not happy about the night out at a gay club. Rather, not happy about me being out without a thousand bodyguards who broke cell phone cameras for fun.

Yeah, he was a little behind the times. You can't do that shit. People sue, and I end up paying. Press is good; lawsuits are not. Christ. Wasn't it his job to tell me that kind of thing?

I wondered how Tibby and Seth were. I flew home last night, and honestly, didn't expect to hear anything from them. I told Bryant to call if he needed anything, but that came out lame even to my ears. I dragged my feet coming home, and I couldn't figure out why. I loved New York, loved that I got lost in it, and loved my place.

So what the fuck?

I ignored the phone ringing. I knew Preston wouldn't let it go, and felt the need to call back and bitch some more. To hell with him.

I dialed Bryant.

"What's up?" He answered on the second ring.

"I hate my manager. He's a prick. I need new management."

"You know we do shipping, right?"

"Yeah, but Tib always looks over everything for me. She vets it, makes sure I don't overpay, whatever. She found me the web people."

He sighed. "Okay. But only because you're family, even if you are a giant pain in the ass. Why now?"

"Preston can't get over himself. For whatever reason, he thinks it's his job to yell."

"You sound about twelve, X. I almost feel sorry for the guy."

"Don't. I pay him enough to learn to work with me. It's not that hard. I'm not a complete asshole."

"I shouldn't help you at all. I think I'm still hungover."

"Lightweight. Ask around, okay? You can dump it on Tib when she comes home. She'll be thrilled."

"I'm sure. All right. Don't get fired yet, okay?"

"Got it."

We hung up. One thing sorted. I'd find someone else, and get rid of the nag.

Something fell on my head, and I reached up to brush it off automatically. What the hell now?

I looked at my hand, and it had glitter all over it. Looking up, I saw…I don't know what the fuck I saw. A cloud of glitter. It looked like a crazy craft fairy had exploded above me.

What the hell was all this doing in my apartment? If I called maintenance, maybe they'd still be around. Even though I owned the building, I kept a maintenance crew. I wasn't up for dealing with all the things that went wrong in older buildings in New York. Was there a leak or something? This was the day for dealing with the bullshit, apparently. I reached for the phone when the glittering cloud landed in front of me.

"Are you quite over moping around and feeling sorry for yourself?"

I rubbed my eyes. Since when did glitter talk? I glanced at the glass of tea I'd been drinking. I hadn't added anything to it.

"This is not a hallucination, and no, you are not drugged."

All right. What. The. Fuck?

The glitter cloud shifted around, and I found that a guy sat on the couch with me. And what a guy! He had no shirt on, which…oh hell. Did someone get ideas from our clubbing the other night?

"Hey, pal, whatever it is, I'm not into it. Just leave now, and I won't call the cops."

The guy sighed. "You don't need to call anyone. I'm here to help you."

"Right, pal. That's what all the nut jobs say." I edged away, wondering where the fuck I kept something that could be used as a weapon. I hadn't had a stalker since… since that weird chick – what was her name? Tommie? She thought she had a career in music, and I was just the guy to help her get there. I'd had to take out a restraining order on her. But she hadn't been a problem in a couple of years.

It's why I lived in a building with security. No need for weapons.

I wished I had one now.

The guy leaned back, and I hoped like hell his paint job wouldn't rub off on my couch.

"I am here to help you, although you're rather an ingrate," He said.

"How the hell am I supposed to be grateful for the glitter fairy breaking into my place and messing it up?" I shot back.

"I am not a fairy. I'm a djinn, and I'm here to give you something you want if you could get out of your own way, boy," he said.

Right. A djinn. What the hell is that? "You're a what? What's your name, glitter boy?"

He rose from my couch, and when I say rose, I mean floating. Full on ghost liftoff. I didn't often find myself speechless, but I couldn't say a thing. My mouth tried, but the words wouldn't come out.

For the first time, I felt fear. What the hell was going on? This went way beyond normal stalking crap.

"Close your mouth, and open your ears and more importantly, your mind, Xavier," the man said. "My name is Dhameer, and I am here, as I've said, to offer you help in attaining something you want. Not give, you'll note. But help." He crossed his arms and glared at me.

I gauged the difference from where I sat to where he… floated…above my couch. Took a deep breath, and pushed off. Maybe I could…

I fell onto the couch with such force that I bounced off and landed at the other end. I looked up and saw Dhameer had risen higher up, and still glared at me.

"I know you're not stupid," he said. "But you're intent on trying to show me otherwise."

I rubbed my head. That fucking hurt.

"You're not going to be able to hurt me, Xavier. But we can play this game until you wear yourself out and are ready to listen to reason. Or I could just leave."

I opened my mouth to tell him to get the fuck out when something Tibby said yesterday came back to me.

We'd been standing together waiting for the limo.

"If anything weird happens, while I'm gone...just go with it, okay?"

"What the hell does that mean?" I asked.

The Tibby I knew came back instantly. "It means that if something out of the ordinary happens, just go with it. Stop being an ass and take some well-meant advice for once in your life!"

I'm not a big believer in a lot of hocus pocus shit. It has no place in the real world, for me. But there was glitter boy hovering around my place, basically laughing at me while offering...something. I didn't know what. And after Tib suggested going with anything weird that happened.

How could she have known?

I rubbed my head, negating my concerns on that front. She didn't. It was a coincidence, and the universe conspired to pass on a message I would listen to. I generally only listened to my manager and Tibby.

Okay. So maybe this guy is real. "What the hell is a djinn? And do you have to spread the glitter shit all over my place?"

He hovered closer to me. "There. Wasn't so hard, was it?"

"Don't push it. Can the glitter please stop?"

Now he looked offended. "No. It's part of me. As for me, I am a djinn. That's also another name for a genie."

"Where's the bottle?" The Aguilera song immediately went through my head.

The guy rolled his eyes. "No bottle. I'm going to have to make this simple, aren't I?"

The sense that I was fucking something up hit me. It didn't happen often, but when it did, I'd learned to pay attention. I held out my hands. "Okay, okay, wait! I'll listen. You're a genie, so what? What are you doing here?"

That must have been the right thing to say because the pissed expression left almost right away.

"I am here to offer you the chance to find what it is you want, Xavier."

"What the hell—I mean, what does that mean? I have everything I want."

He didn't say anything, only raised a single brow at me.

"Okay, sure, I don't have everything, but no one does. What's your name again?"

"Dhameer. And why can't people get what they want?"

"Because the world doesn't work that way," I shot back. Shit, even I could hear the bitterness in my reply.

Dhameer shook his head slowly. "But you could. You just need to get out of your own way. What have you wished for—" he held up a hand, "I mean, really wished for, something that is at the core of you and what you want?"

That stopped me. How could he know that I'd wished for something like Tibby and Seth's relationship only twenty-four hours ago?

Dhameer nodded. "It's coming back to you, isn't it? I heard your wish at the wedding yesterday."

"You were there?" I did sound stupid.

He smiled. "I like to see people happy, so I happened by. I could hear your wishes."

"You're a mind reader?" Oh, shit.

"No. I don't have the patience for that kind of curse.

No, I hear wishes. Real wishes, wishes that come from the soul. You had one of those yesterday."

I didn't know what to say. I took the safe route and kept quiet.

"So I am willing to help you achieve that wish."

"What's the catch?" Nothing came for free, ever.

"I'll give you exactly what you want. That means there may be things that aren't always positive."

That sounded more like it. Everything too good to be true usually is.

"So what are you giving me here?" I still didn't understand how this helped me.

"What do you want, Xavier? And don't be your normal self. Tell me what prompted that wish so strongly yesterday. That's what caught my attention." He'd dropped down to the point that he looked like he sat on the sofa.

I got up and sat in a chair across from him. "I want someone who looks at me like Seth looked at Tibby." Damn, that sounded pathetic as hell.

"What about how you look at someone else?"

I started. "I've never met anyone like that."

"Yet you want someone to behave that way towards you?" Now both eyebrows raised.

I didn't like the feeling that I'd give the wrong answer. I didn't give wrong answers. If they weren't right, I made things happen, so they were the right answers.

"Well, yeah."

He sighed, and looked away from me, out the window. "That wasn't exactly what I hoped to hear. Your wish yesterday…well, that doesn't matter. I have offered to help you, and so I shall."

I held up a hand. "Wait, what the hell are you talking about?"

He shook his head and waved his hand—and more

fucking glitter—at me. "It doesn't matter. I do not go back on my word. You wish to find someone who will look at you the way you saw your friends looking at one another. Very well. You shall find her."

"What? When? What, you just wave your hand, and it happens? That's it?"

Dhameer sighed. "Pretty much. Djinn are designed to make things happen. Here's the deal. You'll meet someone who, if you don't get in your own way, which seems to be a struggle for you, will look at you the way you wish for. Within the next month, or so. That means you'll need to pay attention to those around you, Xavier."

What the fuck? "I pay attention to everything around me. How do you think I got to where I am?"

"Alone, scores of broken relationships behind you, and only a few friends? I'm not sure I'd call that success."

I could feel my temper rising. First, he breaks in and makes a fucking mess, and then he insults me? People have been beaten down for less.

"You'll need to be aware of the new people around you. Can you manage that?"

"Why can't you just magic her here, or something?"

"Because humans don't value the things that are given to them, unfortunately."

"You have a low opinion of the people you're helping, then. Why bother?"

Dhameer sighed. "I love humans. I was created to help them. Being free to do what I want doesn't change that. So I still help them. On my terms, however. I've been around long enough to know that outright gifts are not the best choice. So you must be part of this and earn it. She'll be in your life. It will be up to you to keep her there."

This didn't make any sense. "It's not really giving me anything at all, is it? The world is full of maybes and possibles. I come across women all the time who could…be the one. How is what you're offering any different?"

"You'll have to take my word for it that it is different. Are you willing to try?"

He would have been a good negotiator. He didn't give an inch and matched me glare for glare.

I shrugged. "Sure, whatever."

Dhameer looked at me, and I could swear that for a moment, I saw sadness cross his face. But I blinked and figured I must be imagining things.

hameer

*I*t felt wrong to gift anything to this spoiled manchild. He had indeed made a wish from the heart yesterday. Even Dhameer had felt a pang at seeing Tibby and Seth together. So it didn't surprise him that her best friend would feel something similar.

However, for the first time in a while, he wondered if he'd made a mistake. Tibby had been a joy. The real feeling, the emotion he'd felt from Xavier yesterday had spurred him to make the offer. The fact that it was one more wish from the heart, a wish that counted against the ten thousand—that hadn't hurt. When he'd met Tibby, he'd had no idea that she would help him reach his goal as well. He was so close. He sighed. He'd help this wish to happen, at least, as best he could.

Xavier was not as he expected. Now, unlike yesterday, the man acted as though a little boy. Spoiled, unwilling to do anything to help himself. He knew from Tibby that

Xavier worked hard, and came from nothing, depending only on himself and his abilities.

So where had that fallen off?

"How will I know?"

Xavier's voice broke into his thoughts.

"How will you know what?"

"How will I know that the woman is the right one?"

The man had no shame. He wanted the love of another handed to him like something on a platter. Gave no thought to what it took for someone to give that—had no sense that it was a gift, an exchange. Normally he didn't let the foolishness of humans bother him, but this man did. Only his honor as a djinn, the fact that he knew he'd given his word, prevented him from vanishing and removing all memory from this ingrate shell of a man.

"You will know. The question is, Xavier, will you see it to know it?"

Xavier rolled his eyes and expelled his breath in an impatient huff. "Man, you are talking all kinds of crazy."

"Well, we shall see, won't we?"

Xavier stood up. "Look, if you're just playing games, get the hell out. I have enough going on without you coming in here, making a damn mess with your glitter and shit, and handing out riddles like they're candy!"

Dhameer waved a hand. Xavier stilled in mid-rant.

"You will remember, but forget," Dhameer spoke softly. This would be the best way out of this. He'd do what he promised—put a woman in the path of Xavier that would be the relationship he longed for. But since the man had arrogance enough to carry ten men, he'd make him forget this conversation. If Xavier was so observant and so aware of things, let him prove it.

Sometimes, like now, his temper got the better of him.

Dhameer stopped—was this the right thing to do? But then he remembered all that Xavier said and did in the short time since he'd arrived, and how badly it irritated him.

There was nothing wrong with teaching the man a lesson.

He waved a hand, and Xavier fell back onto the couch.

"So be it. You are truly on your own, young man. In spite of you, I wish you luck."

The honest sentiment didn't stop him from making sure more glitter than normal fell to the ground as he left.

Xavier

I woke up rubbing my eyes. What the hell? I didn't normally nap in the middle of the day, and I felt groggy, almost like I'd been drinking recently.

What had I been dreaming? Something that I wished I could remember. Something I needed to remember.

Whatever. I got up, still rubbing my eyes. I looked around my loft. "What the hell?" It looked like someone had started a party in here. Glitter everywhere.

The housekeeper was fired.

Olivia

I gazed out the window of the car, not really seeing anything. Momma had been as good as her word. Within mere hours, she'd gotten me booked on a plane, and in a hotel, and every service Elizabeth Arden had to offer. I also had firm instructions not to come home until I'd met her personal shopper, Pilar. All these years, and I had no idea Momma had her shopper.

"What am I going to do in New York, Momma?" I spoke quietly.

She didn't even look at me from the driver's seat. Probably a good thing, if I thought about it. "You are going to be pampered as that ass soon-to-be-ex of yours should have been doing all along. When you're not engaged in personal improvement, you're going to go to museums, and galleries, and sit in Central Park and be a tourist. You're also going to flirt as if your life depended on it."

I stared. "What are you talking about? I don't want to talk to anyone, much less flirt with men!"

"Men are half the human race, sugar. God willing, you'll find one who deserves you, and make a better choice next time."

"Momma…"

"Sweetheart, you chose a bad horse. Made a bad bet. The nice thing about life is that there's more than just one race. So look around, see what the other stables have to offer. No one's sayin' you have to choose the next horse right this minute, but it will be good for you to see what else is out there. Look at it as practice."

"I'm still married, Momma." I couldn't handle her easy acceptance that my marriage had ended.

"Not for long, and by the time you get back, Lloyd and I will have things close to settled. Royce won't know what's hit him."

We'd left Lloyd at my place, drafting my response to Royce's divorce filing.

"I'll also get my PI on him. See exactly why it is he's trying to take all your hard work."

I knew this to be a sore spot with Momma. She and I had started the business before Royce and I got married. He'd been invited to be a partner but declined. I found out later he didn't think it would fly, nor was he sure we'd last. Well, he got that one right.

She'd never forgiven him for doubting us. The fact that we had become very successful, to the tune of me making more than he did in IT, didn't help. At least regarding my marriage.

Maybe Momma was right. I'd backed the wrong horse.

It felt like shit to put it in those terms. To simplify my marriage down to the idea of "backing the wrong horse."

"All right, sugar. Here you go. I booked you first class on both legs. I am sorry, though. You'll have to transfer in Washington. I do hate Dulles! They always have your flights on opposite ends of the airport!"

"Momma, it'll be fine. Thank you. I love you."

She kissed my cheek, and then kissed me again. "I love you too, sugar. It's gonna be fine. I promise."

I nodded and got out of the car before tears showed up.

The flight from Nashville was uneventful. First class was nice. I didn't usually fly it because, in spite of my business success, I wanted to keep costs low. Additionally, Royce…I thought about it. He got jealous if I used any perks that came with being good at my job. I represented talent, and at times, that meant that I got tickets to shows, or some fun thing because of my clients. We were always "busy." What that meant, in reality,, was that I worked to assuage Royce's ego.

Is this what Momma had seen? Is this why not only was she not surprised but she encouraged me to move on? Because he'd been the wrong horse for a long time, and shit on me with alarming regularity?

Shame washed over me. He had been actively shitting on me. I'd been so accustomed to it I didn't even notice. That was all me. Much as I'd like to blame Royce. What a lowering realization.

Lost in my thoughts, I made my way from my plane to the one headed for New York. Momma was right. It was on the other side of the terminal. Or so it seemed.

I settled into my seat, pulling out my earbuds. I didn't want to think about how I'd had a hand in the mess I found myself in. Watching videos or reading would allow me to pretend all the thoughts I'd been realizing were back in a box behind a closed door somewhere.

The flight attendant moved down the row. He leaned in toward me across the empty seat. "Can I bring you anything? I'll be by again after we take off as well."

I shook my head, and he moved on. I hoped the seat next to me would remain empty. On the flight from Nashville, I'd sat next to a man determined to converse. Only by turning to the window and blatantly ignoring him did I make it clear I wasn't interested. I'd thought I'd heard a muttered, "Bitch" but I ignored that, too. Who cared what some jerk I'd never see again thought?

I would never again be at the whim of a man, not even to be polite.

Unfortunately, as the attendant was going through the small cabin and closing the overhead compartments, I heard heavy footsteps. A very tall man threw himself into the chair next to me. He had a hoodie and sunglasses. He also had, I noted, really nice, high cheekbones. I'm a sucker for high cheekbones.

The hoodie and glasses suggested he wanted peace and privacy as much as I did. I turned my shoulders towards the window and my attention back to my tablet. The airline offered free Wi-Fi, and I clicked on YouTube and made sure my earbuds were secure in my ears. Hopefully, all this body language would save me from being called a bitch again.

A video popped up by my favorite artist, XTC. I know, I know, what's a nice southern girl doing liking a foul-mouthed bad boy, and a rapper to boot? We're all supposed to be fangirls of the Grand Ol' Opry, and nothing else.

Or so Momma says. This is one of the things I ignore from her. I loved the guy. I loved that he yelled out his anger, or frustration, or whatever it was that he felt at the moment. I realized that I envied it. That freedom. Whatever it was, I loved XTC's work.

That thought slid dangerously close to in-depth thinking, and I wanted none of that. My seatmate stopped the attendant as he walked past our seats.

"Can I get a whiskey? Best one, whatever you have, please."

I could hear him even over the music of the video. Whiskey sounded good.

"Make that two, please!" I said before I'd even had a chance to think about it.

Hoodie turned to me. "Good choice."

I saw a wide grin with white teeth. Full, red lips.

"I'll need to wait until we reach altitude," the attendant said apologetically.

Hoodie waved. "No worries." He pulled large headphones from around his neck and situated them on his head, all under his hoodie. His glasses didn't move either.

Impressive. Then I realized that I was staring at him. How embarrassing! Hopefully, my mouth wasn't open. I ducked my head down quickly. Thank God for electronics. I stared at the tablet, feeling my face flush with warmth. The next video in the feed opened. Another XTC song.

Trying Again. That song had so little in common with the rest of his stuff, but it was one of my favorites. The lyrics seemed particularly meaningful now. I'd have to learn to try again, once I made it through whatever happened in the next six months.

Oh, God. The thought of what would happen next made me lean back in my seat. I had no illusions of Royce and me being able to sort things out in a civil fashion. He would hate Lloyd as my attorney, and hate Momma's involvement. It would make him meaner and nastier to me. Add that in with his request to be supported—I couldn't even get into my indignation over his nerve—and this would be ugly.

Which only made me want to slap his face until his head spun. This whole damn thing promised to be a downward spiral into the messiest thing possible. Why would he want such a thing? How could he, if he loved me?

Because he doesn't, a hateful whisper came back. *He hasn't for a long time.*

It felt like something hit me across the solar plexus. How long had that lack of love been there? How long had I ignored it?

I could feel tears pooling at the corners of my eyes. It sucked to be handed divorce papers. It sucked even worse to realize that you couldn't just blame it on your asshole soon-to-be-ex and be done with it.

For the first time, I hoped Momma and Lloyd found something really good on Royce. Something that would move this process along, and let me blame him like I wanted to.

I felt a tap on my arm. I pulled out an earbud and looked over to see that Hoodie had his headphones around his neck again and held two drinks in his hands. He rattled them invitingly when I looked at him.

"Here you go." He handed one towards me.

"Thanks," I took the glass and drank a large swallow.

His smile widened. "Didn't think anyone needed the drink more than I did right now, but guess I was wrong. You want me to get you another?"

Yes, I wanted to say, but I didn't drink hard liquor often, and I still needed to be able to navigate when I got off the plane. "No, I think this will do. But thanks," I added.

I wish he'd take off the glasses. I'd love to see if the eyes matched the rest of the face.

"Let me know if you change your mind. I'll probably have another." He smiled, and the lips/teeth combo flashed at me again.

Then he leaned back in his chair.

Okay. I guess the conversation is over. Probably better that way. I put my earbud back in and hit replay on the video.

*X*avier

*T*he woman next to me is hot. She is also on the edge of crying. I'd been around enough crying women to know when it was coming. At least this time the tears weren't directed at me. Which made a nice change.

Women like her didn't drink in the middle of the day on airplanes. I might have a slew of car-wreck relationships behind me, but I knew that fact as well as I knew myself. She was on the edge of something.

Normally, I didn't notice this kind of thing, but ever since the wedding, I'd been seeing people—especially women—differently. Like, with more interest in their lives. I didn't know what to make of it.

Back to the hottie next to me. I let my eyes slide over to her. She stared at her tablet, where she watched a video of…oh, holy fuck.

Me.

A fan. She's a fan of XTC.

I'm not sure where that falls on the scale of good versus bad. All my relationships usually begin with meeting a fan. But, in the spirit of being honest, the women that make up my exes probably are not the most stable, or put together of women. Neither am I, if I'm still being honest.

This woman, however, looks like a professional. She's dressed casually, but her clothes are still professional. She doesn't look like a groupie.

Not enough skin is showing.

I let my eyes come to rest on her face. Whatever I might have done is cut off by seeing her take another swig of her drink, and sort of choke as she does.

Some shit is going on here. I let myself relax into the seat. Do I really want to get involved, even for something as trivial as talking on a plane ride? This sort of thing is how I have an ex Mrs. X, and numerous bitter ex-girlfriends. I don't have a good track record, and my judgment seems to fall straight out of my ass when a nice face smiles at me.

Tibby got mad at me once and told me no amount of groupies would fix the fact that my mom is crazy, and failed me my entire childhood.

I shook my head a little. Christ, I didn't need that right now. Just peace, and my drink.

I snuck another glance at the woman. She's a fan. Do I tell her it's me? This could be a bad decision, but so what?

She hits replay on the *Trying Again* video. Rubs at her

face. That makes what? Two? Three times? Ah. That's it. She's on the rebound.

I'm single. Not particularly fucked up about anything at the moment. I can handle a little shit from someone else. And I'm feeling all whatever after seeing my best friend get married.

Not to mention I'm annoyed and restless. In spite of Bryant's warning, I'd flown out to Los Angeles, and fired my manager. We weren't a good fit.

The good news got around. I'd noted at least ten messages on my phone before getting on the plane.

I slide my headphones down, put my drink on the tray table in front of me, and hand her my little napkin. I can see tears coming down her cheeks even though she's not making any noise.

She looks up, her expression startled. Then her eyes move to my hand, holding out the napkin, and she slowly reaches up and takes it.

She dabs at her eyes and pulls her earbuds out.

"Thank you. I'm sorry to disturb you."

She's from the south. I can hear the accent, even though she's speaking in low tones.

"You didn't. I just happened to see that you were in need."

"Oh? Are you in the habit of rescuing damsels in distress?"

I grinned. "Not at all. Not even close. But I'm not a complete ass."

"I'm surprised you can see anything behind those dark glasses." Her tone sounded better, less I'm-about-to-throw-myself-off-a-cliff.

"Oh, they're necessary," I leaned in towards her. She didn't pull back.

"Really?" Now she leaned in. "Why is that? Are you in disguise?"

I had decided to talk to her because she's hot, but she's witty, too. I like that. Maybe being stuck on a commercial flight wouldn't be so bad after all.

I pulled down my glasses for a minute, gazing at her over the top of them. "I might be. I don't usually fly commercial."

Would she recognize me?

Would it be worth it to let her know who I am? The indecision was not an emotion that I experienced often. It made me decidedly uncomfortable.

What the hell? What was the worst that could happen? Without warning, I heard my ex-manager Preston's voice in my head.

She could go to the press. She could tell everyone that you're desperate. She could say you asked her to be a beard for the fact that you were finally caught doing what you wanted at a gay club.

I shook my head a little. Shut the fuck up, Preston. I didn't need this shit. It's why I just fired him. I'd kept my word to Bryant—*I* hadn't gotten fired.

I watched Hot Chick next to me. Saw her eyes dart back and forth across my face and…did she just look at my lips? She might have, and then color flamed up her cheeks. Just as quickly it drained away.

She looked down at her tablet and then back at me. "You're him! Oh my God!"

Thankfully, she spoke just above a whisper.

"What are you doing flying with…with…"

"With the general public?" I leaned in, taking off my glasses at the same time. I enjoyed the fact that her eyes widened and the color returned to her cheeks. It had been a long time since I'd seen a woman blush because of me, and it felt…nice.

Innocent. Everything I didn't have in my life anymore.

"I had to go fire my manager. After we spoke, I got the first flight—or flights out of there I could. I didn't want to hang around. Besides, no one sees what they don't expect to see." I shrugged.

If she felt disconcerted by me, it seemed to have faded. I could see the humor in her eyes. "Probably because it's not dark yet. No one expects that you'll actually be up."

I laughed quietly. "Touché, smart ass."

"Didn't I just see that you…um…"

She'd seen the press on hanging out at Cobalt. "Came out?" I helpfully finished her sentence.

She nodded. "Or is that just another means of getting press?"

"You want the truth?"

"Sure."

"I was out with my best friend's fiancé, and we ended up there."

"What?"

I could see her trying to make the connection. She wanted to ask questions but didn't want to be rude. I took pity on her.

"My best friend is a woman. I was out with her fiancé, and her best friend. Her other best friend is gay. The three of us went out together, and we let Bryant choose the club. Being slightly intoxicated, he picked one that he liked personally."

She stared at me for a moment and then started to laugh. "So you ended up there under no choice of your own, and now you're a gay man? That's hilarious!"

"My manager, well my former manager, doesn't think so, but…" I stopped for a moment, thinking. "I think I need to make a nice statement in support of those who are." Christ. Look what happened when people thought I might be gay. It was like the end of the world or something. No wonder Bryant kept his private life private. Here I thought it wasn't a big deal, but society was proving me way wrong.

"I think that would be nice." She looked over at me, and I could tell that she wanted to know what I was thinking, but was too polite to ask.

"Hey, don't mind me. I tend to get lost in my own shi— I mean, thoughts regularly. So if I go quiet, it's nothing personal. I'm just thinking."

A look of relief flashed across her face. "No problem."

"So what's your story? Who are you? I'm Xavier."

"I'm Olivia. I'm from Nashville."

Her face dropped, and an expression of such sadness showed on her face. "I'm going to take some time for myself in New York."

Ah-ha. This is the rebound thing. Let's see if she tells me.

"Been a rough week?" I took a sip of my drink, not making eye contact.

"You could say that. My…my husband handed me divorce papers a couple of days ago."

Oh, *shit*. Rebound was one thing. Divorce was something else entirely. Lots more baggage from a dying marriage than from just a breakup.

Shit, shit, shit. I was stuck next to her for at least another hour. I would need to keep up the conversation, keep it light.

"Did he tell you why?" This seemed the safest direction.

"He just said it was over, that we knew we were having problems, blah blah blah." She sounded impatient. "Who knows? It didn't sound very original, and he was sure to make this my fault. Even though I think he's got something on the side."

Her accent got more pronounced as she got angry. That was…hot. Stop it, jackass, I told myself. This is more than you want to deal with.

"Did he tell you he has a girlfriend?"

She shook her head, and her dark curls moved around her face in a manner I could only describe as charming.

"It's just the way he talked to me, all smug. He's found something he thinks is better."

"Do you know who?"

"No, I…" She stopped. "I think I do, actually. If it's who I think it is, he's a stupid fool."

"Well, he's that already."

Her head whipped towards me. "What do you mean?"

"He let you go. What a dumbass."

The color moved up her cheeks again. I couldn't believe how much I liked seeing that.

"Thank you, that's kind of you to say."

Now it was my turn to shake my head. "No. I'm not kind. I'm brutally honest. I don't get anywhere otherwise, so it's moved to all parts of my life. You're a nice woman, and getting out of a relationship by cheating is just a jackass move."

"What, you've never cheated?" Her eyes narrowed. I could tell she thought I had.

Fair enough. All kinds of shit was written about me every time a relationship imploded. It didn't help that generally, my exes were rather bitter.

"Nope. I just tell 'em it's over. Which brings out the nasty side in most people. People would rather be lied to, or let down gently. I don't do either."

"I would rather know this way. He didn't pull any

punches. I'll give him that. But I think he's lying, and he wants me to support him."

"What, like a sugar momma?" I couldn't help it. This was interesting, not your normal divorce case.

"I own my own business. I make more than he does. I always have, because my mom and I are good at what we do. And now he wants alimony for life since he is claiming he helped support us as we built the business."

"Did he?" Women usually didn't give a man much, if any credit for anything when shit went south. I wanted to hear what she'd say.

"No. We gave him a job and offered him a share in the company. He thought it was a loser idea, and found another job, and refused shares. He figured we'd fail, and he didn't want to be tied to the business, or," her voice got very bitter, "Me, if things failed. But now that we're successful, all of a sudden he was part of that. Damn that man!"

"You gonna fight him?"

The anger faded immediately as she looked at me with a grin that looked evil. "My momma is. She is a bitch on wheels when crossed, which I love. I'd love to grow up to be like her. And she has a boyfriend who is one of the biggest divorce shark lawyers in Nashville, so Royce'll be lucky if he gets away with his boxer shorts."

I laughed. "His name is Royce? Are you kidding?"

"What's wrong with that?"

"C'mon, Royce? That's such a…" I wanted to say something really rude.

"It's not manly?" She covered her mouth with her hand.

I could tell she wanted to laugh, too.

"Not like Xavier."

"Or XTC?" Her brow arched.

"Take you to awesome, baby," I grinned. That was my tagline when I first started. I didn't do drugs, though. Booze was more than enough for me. But people liked the play on words with the drug reference, and I got a lot of shit for promoting an illegal substance.

All of which kept my sales going. Kind of the point, moral discussion aside.

"I think you're a little hard on him," she started.

"Oh, you want to cut him some slack?" I shot back.

Her eyes widened. "Touché."

"So what are your plans for New York?"

She sighed. "Momma booked me the everything package at Elizabeth Arden."

"What the hell is that?"

"It's a spa. A famous one that my mother adores. It's her cure for everything."

"I love spas," I confessed, hoping like hell she wouldn't head straight for the tabloids. It might kill my manager. Ex-manager. I'd need to work on getting him out of my head. I hadn't realized he was so far in there. "I always feel lighter and younger."

That made her laugh. "You're not old, Xavier!"

"I work sixty, sometimes seventy hours a week. I wake up thinking about lyrics, and fall asleep thinking about the shit I gotta get done the next day. In between, I try to keep time for my creative production and put out fires."

"You need to hire better employees to help you with that," she said firmly.

I nodded. "I've been thinking the same thing, but it's hard."

"Poor little rich boy?" Her tone mocked me.

"Actually, yes. I need someone to trust with my finances, my personal shit, the people who are important to me—there aren't many, but I'd die for them," I said, thinking about Tibby, and Seth, and Bryant. "It's hard because someone is always trying to game. The unfortunate fact of my business. So finding someone I can actually trust—yeah, it's hard."

"I'm sorry. That was pretty nasty of me."

I shrugged. "No biggie. It's part of the job. When you're famous, and you have a lot of cash attached to that fame, and career, you attract assholes. I've learned to carry a big asshole swatter."

She laughed. "I can see why your lyrics do so well. You talk like you sing."

"Kind of the point, isn't it? Sell yourself, sell your brand. So what else do you have planned?"

Olivia shook her head. "I don't know. I hadn't gotten that far."

This was the perfect time to ask her for a date. The question is, did I want to?

While I thought about it, the moment passed. It would have been awkward now. She wasn't as much of a wreck as I'd suspected, and in some ways, she was. She was strong. And hot. And funny. And a hard worker.

I could forgive a lot for hard work.

But she had a business with her mom! What the hell?

That was it, wasn't it? What the hell?

"So you wanna give me your number? Maybe while you're there, we can go do dinner or something." Holy fuck. Did that just come out of my mouth?

She blushed. "That would be nice. You're not expecting anything else, are you?"

I sure as hell didn't expect that. Talk about fuckin' brutal honesty. "Why would you even ask that?"

The blush deepened. "Because you live in a different world than me. I don't have the same anything that you do in my life. I have no idea if what I read in the papers is true or what. I certainly don't want to operate under any false expectations. Since you've been so nice to listen to all my bullshit, and not run away screaming or ask to move seats, I figure I ought to be honest with you."

Listening to her say 'bullshit' in that southern accent made me wish that I could toss out some insane expectation and have it be met. Goddamnit. I always did this to myself. Got attracted to someone that I needed just to smile, wave, and move on from.

"I have no expectations," I said instead. "It's just dinner."

"Well, all right then."

"Here, give me your phone."

She dug into her bag and handed me a phone. I opened it, and went to her contacts, adding myself to her list. I used 'Xavier.'

"Text me, and I'll add you to mine."

"Isn't this a little cloak and dagger?"

I could tell she wanted to laugh.

"Maybe, but you get used to seeing the worst. I'd hate for people to take advantage of the fact that you and I sat here and had a nice conversation."

She looked around, and I could see fear move into her eyes. "People would do that?"

"For a couple of bucks, people will do almost anything." I didn't even try to disguise the bitterness in my voice.

"Okay, I'll text you then." She tucked the phone back into her bag.

I didn't know if I felt disappointed or relieved that she put her phone away. If she were just being nice, this would solve a lot of my concerns, wouldn't it?

If she were a plant for a news rag, I would just have to change my number again.

There was generally no downside to this. Well, maybe a small one, thinking about how I found her intriguing and wouldn't mind getting to know her better. Even with the mountain of baggage that I could tell came with her.

Shit. I had to ask. "So, where are the kids?" Because of course, a woman like this had kids.

She shook her head. 'No kids. We weren't ready for them—well, when I was, he wasn't. And we just couldn't seem to get on the same schedule. Probably for the best," She looked out the window. I could see that the lack of kids made her sad.

But good for me, right?

Sometimes I really was an asshole.

Olivia

I wished he hadn't asked about kids. While Royce hadn't said a thing, I figured that was part of the problem. With a newfound bitterness I didn't entirely like, my first thought was that he'd blame me for that too, even though both of us were better off not having to deal with parenting kids from a failed marriage.

I pushed that out of my mind for the moment. Plenty of time to go over and over my own lapses and failures. Right now, I needed to focus on the fact that XTC, who asked me to call him Xavier, as though we're friends or something, had given me his phone number.

Was it cool that I didn't text him right away? I didn't want to look like a sixteen-year-old who had no control. I'd seen him watch me as I put my phone away.

This whole flight had the air of the surreal. Things like this didn't happen to me.

"Well," Xavier said, "I think I'm sorry? I don't know what to say."

He couldn't have chosen anything better to say. I smiled, letting my pleasure show. My reward was seeing those red lips curve into a smile.

What kind of hussy was I? I wasn't divorced, only served with papers a week ago, and here I am watching another man's lips?

Then I thought about how Royce and I hadn't had sex in...I didn't even know how long. I was busy with work, and he always seemed distracted. It didn't help, my awareness of his mood. I struggled with the feeling that I wasn't quite right. That there was something wrong with me. Otherwise, wouldn't my husband be attracted to me?

"Thank you," I said. "I think not having kids when you want them is sad, but it's obvious this wasn't the person I should have had them with." I took a deep breath. "Enough about me and my sob story. What's your deal?" I plastered a non-gloomy expression on my face.

"You want another whiskey?" He asked.

I could see the flight attendant coming down the aisle again. "I'm good, thanks."

He ordered another, and I waited to see if he'd remember that he hadn't answered my question.

He did.

"I was, as I said earlier, at my best friend's wedding. She and her husband left on their honeymoon, and after Bryant and I—Bryant is her other best friend I mentioned before—took Seth out for a guys' night, my manager nearly had a heart attack. He also kept calling like the world's nosiest mom," he had a weird look on his face like he'd just smelled something bad. "So I went out to California, fired him, and now I'm running like hell home. This was the quickest way to do that."

"Oh, you live in New York?"

He nodded. "It's a great place. I've been there a long time, and I love it. I have a loft, and my studio and office are on the first and second floors of the building."

"Well, you don't have far to commute. That's pretty nice." I didn't know what to say. It felt if I asked too much, I was heading into crazy fan territory.

He laughed. "I bought the building a couple of years back after my first album took off. I'm lazy as fu—I mean, I don't want to have to travel a lot to get work done. Plus," he looked up, and nodded at the attendant who handed him another glass, "it's easier to keep my mom out. She was a problem for me at first. I'm sure you've read about her?"

Now it was my turn to nod. Xavier's mom made nightmares look good. She'd abandoned him as a kid to various relatives. With a jolt, I remembered some of the interviews I'd seen with him. He said it was his one friend growing up that had saved him, along with their family. That must have been the best friend he'd been talking about— the one who'd just gotten married.

"I have. I'm sorry. Your mom always sounds as though she's challenging." I struggled to be politically correct. She was a nut, but you didn't say that about other people's mothers.

"She is. Now that I'm grown and independent, and not to mention, well-off, and she doesn't have to do shit, she's right there when she can be. You also get the occasional crazy fan, so having all my shit in one place means less hassle for my security."

"I don't know that I'd want to live like that."

He shrugged. "Been doing it so long, I don't even notice anymore."

The seatbelt light came on, and the captain's smooth voice told us that we were about to land. Where had the time gone? I busied myself with getting my things tucked away. I was so excited to meet someone I'd been watching for years, but this felt a bit awkward.

It hadn't initially, but it had gone that way, and I didn't know how to change it.

Xavier put his glasses back on. "I'm not trying to be a dick, but I'll say goodbye—for now! Before we get off the plane. I don't want you to get hassled because people see us talking."

"You can't be serious," I started.

"I am. You wouldn't believe some of the things people will do." He adjusted his glasses, looking around. "Listen, I know you just put all your stuff away, but shoot me a text real quick."

I hadn't decided if I was going to, and with things being weird, I was leaning toward not contacting him. However, Xavier asking me to text outright, while he sat there, looking at me...I didn't feel like I could refuse and not look like a jerk. So I pulled out my phone and texted the number he gave me.

He smiled when he read it.

'As you wish'

"Princess Bride fan?"

I nodded, feeling more at ease. "Absolutely."

"Awesome. Listen, I have a busy week, and I don't want to be in the way of your spa thing, but can I text you?"

I nodded. Maybe we were just weird because...sometimes things went weird.

"I'll do that, then. See if we can hook up."

Oh dear. I hoped he didn't mean what I thought he meant.

As the plane landed, we didn't speak. He stood up when the door opened, and turned to me, one last time, leaning in and speaking quietly.

"I'm really glad I sat next to you." He reached out with his hand and grabbed mine, squeezing a little.

The light touch sent a thrill through me I hadn't felt in ages. "Me, too. I certainly didn't expect something this nice to happen."

I got to see his grin again, and the thrill raced down my spine. Good lord, his smile should be a lethal weapon. I'd been so worried about not coming off like a crazy stalker fan that I hadn't looked at him much once he'd let me see who he was. What a waste of time on the plane! I could have been drinking in the beauty of him. He was beautiful. Hotter than a goat's ass in a pepper patch, as Momma would say.

She would, too. One of her favorite sayings.

I follow him off the plane, admiring his behind. It's quite nice. The muscles moved smoothly as he walked. Everything on him is nice and Xavier himself, even more so.

I hope he texts me. I hadn't been enthusiastic before, but his touch fired something within me.

Maybe that made me shallow. I don't know.

I know I have a stupid grin on my face as we walk down the ramp. Without warning, Xavier disappears. Woah. How did he manage that?

I don't like to admit it, but I feel deflated with him gone. Why did I get all shy and stupid when I had a chance to talk and interact with him?

I'm still kicking myself as I gather my luggage and

head out to the hired car area. Momma told me she'd booked me a car.

I spot a guy with my name on a card, and he leads me over to a limo. Momma. Of course. He whisks me off to the hotel, and I check in with no problem. The clerk hands me an envelope from The Red Door.

Within an hour of checking in, I'm at the spa, face down on a massage table, and getting the most amazing hot stone massage I've ever gotten in my life.

I should be thinking about my marriage, or how I screwed it up, or how to navigate the fight I just know is coming, but all I can think about is meeting Xavier on the plane.

I hope he texts me soon.

---

*F*our days later, I'm packing for my trip home tomorrow. The only people I've talked to since I've been here are nice strangers in the museums I go to in between spa appointments, and Momma and Lloyd regarding the state of my legal affairs.

Xavier has not texted me. Not a peep.

I even looked him up on Google, to see if there was anything in the news about what he is doing.

Nothing. Other than the pictures from the club he'd told me about. And lots of speculation about him. Along with some nasty interviews with a couple of his exes.

As well as a statement from him: "I am disappointed to see all the crap being said about me going to a club. For the record, I had a fantastic time. I've also heard some less than kind talk about the fact that Cobalt caters to a diverse clientele. Let me be clear—I support that wholeheartedly. To see all the negativity being spread around due to some stupid idea of intolerance is not only disheartening; it's wrong. "

The club, in response to this statement, mentioned he would be their guest the next time he came in. A social media thread between Xavier and the club followed that was hilarious.

I loved that he made a statement, but I hated that he hadn't texted me. It felt like I was a balloon and each day that I didn't hear from him, I deflated a little more.

Damn it. I'm so annoyed with myself; maybe that's why I can't sit still.

Finally, I have everything packed, and there is no reason to prowl around my room anymore. I don't feel like heading out, not even down to the bar.

I get into my PJs and go to bed. Might as well get home and back to my real life.

3

Xavier

I can barely look at my phone. Fuck. I haven't texted Olivia, and it's been three days. I've picked up the phone and even started to text her, and then I stop.

I can't explain why.

Nor can I explain why I keep thinking about her.

When I took her hand on the plane, I wanted to pull her closer, kiss the shit out of her, and drag her off somewhere that I could be with her naked, private, and not come out for days.

It scared the fuck out of me.

I wouldn't admit that to anyone else, but I couldn't deny it. Her touch both shocked and scared me, and I ran with all my might.

Didn't stop the fricken phone from glaring accusingly at me every time I looked at it.

And I was well aware of how damn insane I sound, thinking a phone is glaring. But it's better than owning the shit tons of guilt I felt every minute I let pass that I didn't get in touch with her.

I hadn't asked her how long she planned to be here. I didn't ask where her hotel was. All I knew that she was spending serious time at Elizabeth Arden.

When I couldn't take it anymore, I Googled it and called the spa. The snotty receptionist told me they valued their patrons' privacy and she would neither confirm nor deny a patron's presence at the salon.

Well, fuck.

I did my best to ignore it, and let two more days pass. Each time I looked at my phone, it felt like a giant mosquito bite that I couldn't stop scratching.

So six days after I met Olivia on the plane, I texted her.

'Hey Ms Olivia'

And waited.

For over an hour.

Fuck this.

Since I couldn't sit still, I shoved the phone into my pocket and went down to the studio. I didn't expect to find my favorite engineer, Markus, working on his own.

"Hey, man, what are you doing here?"

He looked up, sliding off his headphones. "Just doing a little more clean up. You know how it is, man."

I smiled. "Yep. That's why I won't work with anyone else." He is a genius at what he does. I pay a shit load to keep him working mainly for me. He's freelance, which means he can work wherever and with whoever. He chooses to work mostly for me. He likes to tinker with the sound. We'd come to an agreement years ago that he could come in at will, and do his thing.

"You need anything from me?" I ask.

He shook his head, eyes on the board. "Nah, we're good. You happy with the sound?"

"I haven't heard it yet. You know I don't listen until you're done. Then I listen, and decide." I take it up to my loft, and go into my sound room, and listen with a pad of paper, taking notes and going through each track measure by measure.

"You gonna drop this at the next show?"

I shrug. "Maybe a couple. Listen, you around if I come up with some new stuff? I got a lot of ideas rolling around." Maybe if I wrote, I'd take my mind off Olivia.

He nodded, the hint of a smile lifting the corner of his lips. Markus is low key, and very laid back. Being around him was calming.

"Yeah, sure. You got something?" His eyebrows went up.

"No, actually, I came down to work. I can't seem to focus upstairs."

"I hear you," he turned back to the board, slipping on the headphones once more. "Paper's over there," he indicated with his head.

I went to the file cabinet where he'd gestured towards and found some of my notepads and paper. I did better when I wrote down my lyric ideas. I know, I'm all old school and lacking in modern technology, but habits die hard.

I sat at the desk in the back of the booth and tapped my pen on the pad.

'X's and O's

Whoa. Holy fucking whoa. Where did that come from?

I dropped the pen and ran my hands through my hair. At this rate, I might as well text her, and end the fucking agony. X and O. Xavier and Olivia. What the hell am I thinking?

An apology. A *mea culpa* from me, because I am a giant asshole.

We smile
We meet
We share the same seat
Can you see it
Do you want it
Xs and Os

The words are out of my brain and onto the paper before I even realize it. I let my head wander like this. But normally, I'm not in a twist about the subject.

I read over the lyrics. Okay, what the fuck? I sound like Lionel Ritchie. Not that he sucks, or anything, but that is not my sound. I toss the pen down again in disgust; only I can't figure out what exactly I'm disgusted about most.

Maybe that I just fell into a vat of super sappy shit and I can't even breathe?

Dude. Just fucking text her. Again. If you were her, you wouldn't text back right away. Her feelings are hurt. Maybe she's spa-ing. Or home. Or working. Something.

I pull out my phone.

'Guess you're workin. Text when u can'

I set the phone on the edge of the desk with the screen down, and pick up my pen again. I want to do this, but my way, not Lionel's.

I touch your hand
It's like you leave a brand
I can't shake it
Good or bad
Now you're gone
What do I do
All I want is you
O O O Xs and Os.

No. That's not gonna work either. Fuck. I hold the pen, ready to cross the lines out, but I hesitate.

What did I feel when I met her?

The phone buzzes on the desk. I grab it, feeling nervous. I hope it's her, and I also hope it's not. She's well within her rights to tell me to fuck off. I would if someone ignored me for a week after asking me out.

'Surprised to hear from you.'

Oh shit. Those five words say it all. I feel shame wash over me. Like I was a dick, and probably didn't need to be.

Okay. I was a dick. I need to find a way to make this better.

'I'm sorry. Things got in the way. You still in NYC?'

Her response is a lot faster than the past hour and a half.

'No. I flew home yesterday.'

'Dammit. I'm sorry Olivia. I had things I had to do. How was spa?'

'Amazing. Hate admitting my mom is right, but she is.'

'I get that. What's going on with other stuff?'

I want to ask her how her dickhead ex is but don't know how else to ask. I haven't been this nervous about a woman in I can't remember how long.

'Other stuff? You mean divorce stuff?'

'Yeah'

'R dug heels in. Fighting with my lawyer.'

'Dick'

Like I should be calling anybody else names, but what the hell? Nothing ventured, nothing gained.

'Agreed. He wants to set himself up, so he's going to push back hard.'

'I'm sorry.'

'Thanks. My lawyer is enjoying it too much. I didn't realize how many people didn't like R. Would have been nice to know before I married him.'

With that, I can feel the pain in her words. All the things she believed have been pulled out from under her like a rug. I don't have the same response when people are assholes. My rug got pulled away years ago. I'm only surprised when people don't try and pull the rug. But I've never forgotten how it feels.

'At least you're not 60 and wondering what the hell?'

She doesn't respond as fast. Shit. Did I just step over a line? I curse under my breath and look up to find Markus watching me.

"You okay, man?"

I nod. Honestly, I don't know what to say. I'm trying to fix a fuck up, and I'm sweating over a chick? Most of the people I work with hate all the women I date, so they'd roll their eyes. I don't even know if there's anything with Olivia, much less a thing, so I don't want to talk about it.

'There's that. Still feels terrible.'

Oh man. I am a dick. I decide to be honest, and whatever happens, happens.

'Sure it does. But at least he showed himself to be an asshole now, rather than years in. You still have the chance to make life the way you want it. This sucked even when my marriage ended, and we both wanted it to be over it sucked, but it had to happen. I think this needs to happen for you. I don't know you well, but from what you told me you deserve better someone who will support you.'

I hesitate and then hit Send. It's a big step for me to be

that open, but something tells me if I'm not, I don't have a chance in hell with this woman. That's even if she can forgive me for being such a jerk about not calling.

I don't even know if I want a chance, but I feel like I'd better make an effort. I've been kicking my ass all week. If that's not a sign, I don't know what is. Normally, I ignore this kind of thing with women, but…something is different. I can't tell what it is—the phone buzzes again. I look down, feeling like an addict, wanting to know what she says.

'Wow. That's what I needed to hear. My mother hates R. She said the same thing that he never supported me, but it's different hearing it from someone who doesn't know any of us.'

Without thinking, I pump my fist in the air. It feels like I've won something, although I can't tell what. But the fact that I ignored her for a week is not the killer I thought it would be.

Markus glances over at me, and I shake my head.

'So what is on your week?' I text fast, so she doesn't disappear.

'I have to get back to work and figure out what comes next. You?'

'I'm in CA this week. Benefit show.'

'Benefit for what?'

'I do private shows for the Y for their donors'

'You do? I've never heard that!'

'I keep it quiet.'

'Why?'

'Not everything needs to be about publicity.'

One of the things that saved me, in addition to Tibby and her family, when I was growing up was being able to go to the Y. One of my teachers suggested to my mom, at a parent-teacher conference, that maybe I could take swim-

ming lessons at the local Y. Mom must have been in a
decent place because she signed me up. First and last time.
But I kept going to the Y. Once the people there figured
out my situation, they made sure to invite me to the free
events and give me a place where I could be when Tibby
wasn't around. I had a soft spot in my heart for the Y. I
don't know what would have happened to me without
them.

'That's fantastic, Xavier.'
'Thanks. They're a good group.'

I didn't want to get into my reasons. This felt like
enough of a risk as it was but it still felt…unsettled. I
needed to make this more solid. Not for her, but for me.
Which still means I'm a kind of a dick, doesn't it?

'I'm sorry I didn't get in touch before now'

Her response is fast. **'I was disappointed.'**

Shit. That says it all, doesn't it? But wait. Why do I
need to take this on? I toss the phone down onto the desk.
It's not my fault she's disappointed.

Markus turns around. "What is going on, X?"

I shake my head. "Just trying to sort some shit. And I'm
working on something, and it's not coming out smooth."

"Why?"

"I dunno. I was thinking about a new song, and I'd like
to get it together for next week, but I don't know if I can."
I switch gears. "What else do we need to do still?" Before I
went to Tibby's wedding, I'd been finishing up the
next album.

"You're good for a while. I need to go through all the
songs again, and then you can listen, and see if you want
to make changes."

"So you're good if I want to mess around with this
new thing?"

"Sure."

An idea is forming. I know that I hurt her feelings. I haven't even got anything going with this woman, and I'm already behind. I want to do this song, and get a preliminary recording down so that I can do a video. So she can see it.

Why is it I can't just say something to her?

I don't fucking know. I don't want to think about it right now.

livia

*M*aybe I shouldn't have been so blunt with him. But it's true. I *was* disappointed. A lot more than I would let on. I didn't see any sense in pretending otherwise.

He finally responds. Thank God he can't see me, sitting at my desk, hanging onto my phone, waiting to hear from him.

'I know. I'm sorry. Feel like a dick.'

He has somewhat of a salty mouth. Lots more cursing than I am used to. I laugh a little to myself. I guess I'm more my Momma than I thought.

As though hearing my thoughts, Momma glides into my office. "What are you laughing about, darlin'? Not that I'm not glad to see you smile." Her face is warm as she looks at me.

I set down the phone, flapping a hand. "Nothing. I was just reading something on Facebook." I hadn't told anyone about meeting Xavier. I felt shy, and then when each day went by, and he didn't get in touch with me, stupid.

"Whatever it is, good. Listen, Lloyd called. He's

coming by with some paperwork for you. We got a response from Royce and his counsel."

"What does he want now?" The thought made me tired.

"I don't know, sugar. I did hear the sound of glee in Lloyd's voice, so perhaps he's browbeaten them into sanity."

"Okay. I've got time today."

"Speaking of which, I need to go over some of the clauses from the Lowens account."

Momma is one of the best multi-taskers I've ever seen. It's why we're so good together, in spite of being mother and daughter. I'm good at explaining the hard things to clients, and Momma finds the hard things for me to say. Usually, because people want things they really can't have. You know, due to the law, common sense, that sort of thing.

It's part of what is so frustrating with this whole Xavier situation. Outside of my husband, I can manage almost anyone. I'm a fumbling mess with Xavier. Just this texting thing is making my heart race.

Oh, no. I haven't texted him back.

Once Momma sails out, I grab my phone.

'Sorry. Client stuff. Didn't mean not to reply.'

'Work? Like an office. I'm sorry'

'Not all of us can laze around while the maid brings in coffee!'

'Sitting at a desk in the studio working. Made my own coffee this morning smart ass'

I laugh out loud.

'How's your day going? I'm putting out fires.'

'Frustrating. Trying to get something out of my head and it's not coming easy.'

'I understand.'

'Do you? Nice to know I'm not alone.'

Interesting. He's having one of those days, too. It does
feel good to know I'm not the only one feeling put upon
and frustrated.

'Course I understand. I work with people.'

'No thanks' His response is fast. **'I like working
alone, and I have a good crew that works with me,
but that's it.**

'You find a new manager yet?'

I want to recommend someone to him, hell; I want to
recommend myself, because I'd sort him out toot sweet,
but…I can't. You don't sleep with clients—where the hell
did that come from? I drop the phone, shocked at myself.

**'No waiting on my BFF to get her lazy ass off
her honeymoon and help me find one. I'm not
gonna die. I had her partner deal with the legal
side of the breakup LOL.'**

Oh. I'm dying to ask more, but it's not my business,
and I already know I have some conflict of interest with
this one. Even if he doesn't. I can't remember if I told him
exactly what I do. I decide to move away from this topic.

'When do you leave for CA?'

'3 days'

'Is the show public?'

'Gonna stalk me on youtube ;)?'

'Not that I'd tell you. Your ego is big enough.'

I find that I enjoy texting him. The awkwardness I felt
with him in person is slipping away, in spite of the fact I
felt rejected for nearly a week. He probably did have to
work. I look at my desk, and I see all the things that piled
up while I was gone. He runs a bigger business than I do. I
sigh. I have to take his word for it, but that doesn't mean
that I have to throw myself into this, or him. I don't need
to be hurt again if he goes all squirrelly on a whim.

I wish that I knew if he was a nice guy underneath all

those layers. His press shows a guy who takes no shit from anyone and is pretty private, so while there's a lot written about him, you don't get a lot of him from a personal standpoint.

It's frustrating as hell. I'm contemplating doing a more in-depth Google session into him when Momma comes back in, followed by Lloyd.

'I have to go, Xavier. The meeting is here.'
'Later, biz tycoon'

God, he's funny. Like I'm a tycoon compared to him. God, I hope he really means this, whatever the hell this is.

"Darling, Lloyd has some wonderful news!" Momma beamed at me.

"Well, don't keep me waiting. Sit down and share," I say.

They sit in the chairs across from me.

"I heard back from my investigator. He followed Royce while you were gone. We know where he's staying at the moment."

Oh. I'd wondered about that but hadn't given it much thought what with my own Xavier obsession going on. "Where?"

"He's staying with some girl. She interned here, can you believe it?" Momma looks indignant.

"Suzan, isn't it?" I ask. In that moment, everything— the divorce, Royce's behavior toward me lately, even his showing up in the office—crystalizes. Royce took up for her because he is involved with her. And when I tried to fire her, he fought for her. Sort of. But then he backed off. I remember wondering why at the time. It was odd for him —he didn't back down from me about anything.

Now I see why. Royce was sleeping with that snide, snotty little girl, and needed to get her out of his wife's business. Then he plotted to take as much as my business as possible.

I banged my hands on the desk and pushed myself up, turning to the window behind me. I crossed my arms, trying to control my rage. I could also feel tears of anger forming, and it made my throat hurt.

That son of a bitch. Momma called it from the get-go.

The thought of him plotting this with that sneaky trashy little snake of a girl made my blood feel like it boiled. I took a deep breath. I didn't know that he'd done anything of the sort. Jumping to conclusions wouldn't do me any good. All I knew at the moment was that he was sleeping with her. Perhaps the grab for my business was just his selfish greed.

"How did you know her name?" Lloyd asked.

"Because Royce took up for her in a big way when we decided to fire her. He took up for her even before then, telling me to stop picking on the poor girl, that she only wanted to learn, that sort of drivel. I thought it was odd at the time. He didn't normally take up for anyone here, not even me," I finished bitterly. I didn't turn around. I didn't want to see the expressions of pity I knew Momma and Lloyd would both be sporting.

I had a hard time catching my breath. While I'd had a brief flash of concern about this before, hearing that my suspicions were correct hurt in a way I didn't think it would.

But wow, did it hurt. Like a punch to the gut. All the joy, all the happiness I'd felt from texting back and forth with Xavier—gone.

"That rotten bastard," I said.

"Honey, don't you worry," Momma came around the desk to where I stood, arms nearly wrapped around me, trying to keep upright. "We'll get his ass. He is not going to have a leg to stand on, not with this."

"We also have affidavits that he has been seen there before this week," Lloyd added, his voice soft.

I could tell he didn't want to upset me. I appreciated it, but nothing was going to make this any better.

"What does this mean for my case?" I asked in a tone of voice I didn't even recognize. Harder, more stern and foreboding. I wanted Royce to feel the same kind of pain, the same depth, and intensity that I did.

Why, *why*, did this hurt so damn much?

Because I'd stayed faithful. I knew we had problems. The abortive attempts I'd made to speak with him about it showed me that. He brushed me off, telling me that he felt it was fine, just fine. That he was tired, hungry, stressed, whatever.

That Goddamned liar.

I whirled around to face Momma and Lloyd. Momma was right behind me, and my sudden movement startled her.

"I want him to pay for this. I want him to go away, and just leave me alone. If he's done with me, that's fine. But he doesn't get jack shit from me. Not one thin dime, Lloyd. I'll split the house—I don't want the damn thing anymore —but either we sell it, or he buys it from me."

"Even if he moves her in?" Momma asked. She watched me with an expression I couldn't decipher.

"I don't care what he does with it as long as I get my fair share of the value. I don't want it anymore. Let him move an entire harem in there. He'll just need to pay for it. What do you think is going to happen with his request for alimony?"

Lloyd smiled, laughing a little. "He's not going to get far with it. Courts in this county, this state, don't often award alimony unless there's a big difference in income. You make more on paper than he does, true. But that doesn't take into account that you are a business owner, and subject to a greater tax burden than Royce, as a W2 employee, will ever be. With that, you make quite a bit less. I filed to negate claim and showed that you are the lower income half of the marriage, and asked for alimony for you."

"He'll never agree to that," I said with a slight smile, the anger of just a moment ago lessening at the thought of how this request would hit Royce.

"No, probably not. But the court could award it. If you don't want it, or say," He raised his brows suggestively, "Want to force the sale of the house, either to a stranger or that he buys you out of fair market value? This could be a nice bargaining chip."

"Always ask for more than you want, sugar," Momma interjected. "Then you can let the other side think they're winning something while getting exactly what it is you want."

I hugged Momma. "Thank you. I don't know what I'd do without you both."

She beamed, first at me and then at Lloyd. "We love you, honey. And we're not going to let that cheatin' swine get away with trying to make you pay for his mess ups."

"It's okay to use stronger language, Momma," I said, amused by her terminology.

"I'd rather not. It's more ladylike," she sniffed, sounding prim and proper.

"Except when you called him a sunuvabitch the other day," I teased.

Now I felt lighter, and could laugh. The blinding rage of realization had passed. Which was weird, because I hadn't felt that sort of anger, that level, before. But

Momma and Lloyd were so clearly on my side, so sure that I didn't deserve this—it made the pain of being cheated on easier.

Well, kind of.

I'd still need to see Royce at some point. Let him know what a piece of slime he was. And Suzan!

I shrugged then because she wasn't anything to me. Or me to her. I was just her mean employer. But she had worked here—she knew that we were married. She had been a snotty little know-it-all, however. Sure that her way was the right one. It had been a problem with a few clients. I'd chalked it up—then—to a lack of real-world experience.

I gasped. "That's what he wants," I said.

"What?" Momma and Lloyd said together.

"He wants everything so he can give it to her," I breathed. I'd bet Royce told her she could run things better, and that he'd help her get what she wanted. But to think that he'd planned something like this with her? It nearly took my breath away.

He'd get rid of the pesky old wife, and get a new young thing, and keep the same financial position, the same life-style. Through MY company, my hard work.

At that moment, I made up my mind to let the university know that she was involved with her former employer's spouse. Petty?

Probably. But I would hate for another company to hire her, even to bring her in as an intern, and have this snotty, rude, selfish child upset things in their organization like she'd done here.

She didn't do anything more than expose what was already there, the snide voice in my head put in.

I hated that voice.

"Surely not?" Lloyd asked.

"At this point, I wouldn't put anything past him," I said, feeling my jaw clench. A burst of pain shot up toward my head.

"We'll find out, and if that's the case, he won't even have his greasy underwear left," Momma said, putting an arm around me.

This had to be the worst day of my life, and yet I felt strong, and able to handle it. Thank God for the two of them.

$\mathcal{T}$he next day, I got up. I hadn't been good for anything after Momma and Lloyd's visit, so I went home early, took a bath, drank three glasses of wine, and went to bed. I didn't even text Xavier because I didn't want to be whiny, or burden him with my anger. Even I recognized that it sat squarely on the potentially irrational line.

But today was different. I would—

The ringing of my cell phone startled me.

I looked at the number. It was Royce.

I answered it. "Hello?"

"What the hell is this shit, Liv?" He didn't even bother with pleasantries.

"Well good morning, Royce. Which shit are you refer-ring to?"

"This pile of crap your pet lawyer daddy sent over yesterday! Do you want the house? Or the money from the house? That is—"

"It's jointly owned," I interjected, feeling a smile cross my face at his anger. "I no longer wish to retain the asset. Therefore, we can sell it and split the proceeds. Or you can buy me out of it for fifty percent of fair market value."

"I'm not giving you shit, Liv!"

"Olivia," I said.

"What?"

"Olivia. Liv is for my friends, and you've made it clear we're not good friends anymore."

"Not now, not after you're trying to take everything!"

"Or not after you started fucking Suzan?" I asked, making sure to keep my tone level.

He didn't answer right away. Boom, asshole.

"You have no proof of that. It's just your irrational thoughts."

"Oh, I have proof, Royce. Plenty of it. How could you think otherwise?"

"You don't have shit," He growled. "And I'm not giving you a penny for the house! If you want this to be over in any sort of timely fashion, you won't fight me! We wouldn't want our clients to know," his voice turned sly.

"Did you read the response, Royce?" I asked, breathing deeply to keep my temper. I could hear the nasty tone of his voice, and he knew—he knew—how much I hated it. How easily he could win an argument with me when he used it.

"I read enough."

"I don't think so. If you'd read it or listened to your attorney and not your girlfriend, you would see that your request for alimony has been answered, as has your request for two-thirds of the marital assets. My attorney feels good about our chances in front of a judge. He told me that he requested a speedy hearing, as well. Like a wait list or something," I added far more breezily than I felt. "if an opening comes up, we're ready."

"This is not going to happen, O-livia," he said, stressing my name.

"It's not going to happen the way you envisioned,

maybe, Royce, but it's going to happen. You started this. I'm going to finish it. There's no going back."

"You think I would take you back?" He burst into mean-spirited laughter. I could almost hear the hate in his voice.

When had that happened? When had Royce begun to hate me?

Just as when I'd heard that he was cheating, and with that tart Suzan, this hit me as though a punch to the gut.

"No, I wouldn't think such a thing," I said, struggling to keep my temper. "I'd have to want that, and I want nothing to do with your dog tired ass. Don't call me again. Anything you have to say goes through my attorney. I'm sure yours has his number."

I hit 'End' on the phone.

Bastard.

I wanted to hit something. Hard.

I picked up the phone again.

'If you're there, please talk to me. I don't want to go to jail for murder.'

God, please let him be there. Please let him be willing to talk to me.

In thinking about this, I had to wonder why I didn't text someone else.

I didn't have anyone else, other than Momma. My friends from college—they were gone. We'd drifted apart. Royce and then the business had taken me to a place where I had no room for anything else.

I'd let him.

That was the worst thing of all. I had let him.

So here I sat, madder than a wet hen, and no one to tell about it. I could call Momma, but lord knows, she didn't need any more reason to hate on Royce. She was out for blood as it was.

Thank sweet baby Jesus, the phone dinged.

'You need an alibi or a getaway driver?'

I burst out laughing. I had not given texting much credit as far as a communication tool, but this was fun.

Even when mad as a wet hen.

'Both, if my stupid ex calls me one more time.'

'What'd the ass do now?'

"Admitted he did and is cheating, that he hates me, and he's going to take me for all he can. And had the hellish nerve to call me names and be nasty as could be.'

I felt like a crybaby, but I had to get this out.

'Well, that's what douches do. Act like douches.'

'You have a way with words, Xavier.'

'Kind of my job'

I laughed again.

'You're right. He's a douche.' I hit Send quickly. I didn't use this kind of language normally.

'What are you doing right now?'

'Talking to you, silly.'

'Always the wise ass. I mean, what's on your schedule the next week or so? You're the boss. Wanna take another vacation?'

My heart sped up, beating fast and irregular. I could feel my cheeks warm at the thought of what he was asking. What I think he was asking.

'To do what?'

'Come with me to Cali.'

'Isn't that a little fast?' I hated asking it, but I had to ask.

'Yeah, maybe. I'm mad at myself for not getting in touch with you earlier, so I don't wanna have to kick my own ass again.'

I sat back, feeling stunned. He was not letting any moss grow on him.

'Hello?'

'I'm thinking.'

'What's to think about? Me, sun fun. Win all around.'

'You have a high opinion of yourself.'

'I'm kind of a douche too, but I'm a lot nicer about it. I figure if I have a nice feeling, I better act on it before my douche self takes over.'

That gave me pause. One thing Momma told me, and I didn't listen to, was to hear what men said. If they told you something, you needed to listen to them.

Xavier was telling me he was a douche.

'That's not exactly enticement.'

'It's honest. Do I get any points for that?'

'Maybe, but telling me you have to fight off the douche side of you might outweigh it.'

'Well, shit.'

I couldn't help it. I laughed again.

'What will happen if I say yes?' I felt my heart jump again, and I found I held my breath waiting for his answer.

'I'll show you how someone should treat you.'

I believed him.

'Can you hang on for a few?'

'Yep'

I got up, and took three deep breaths, willing the air all the way to my toes. Dialed the number fast, before I chickened out.

"Momma?"

"Sugar bean, how are you? I've been worried, but I wanted to give you your space."

"Thank you, Momma. I love you for that. I have a favor to ask you."

"Anything."

"Can you cover things for me for another week at work?"

Her voice immediately went business. "What is going on, Olivia?"

"Momma! Can you or can't you?"

"Of course I can. What a question. The point is, I want to know why you want another week off."

Stay strong, I told myself. Be honest. This was crazy, but it felt right. "I met someone in New York, and I want to spend time with him."

It didn't happen often, but I managed to stun Marguerite Meroux into speechlessness.

"Momma?"

"You're…what?"

'I'm going to go play hooky with a man, Momma."

"What? Who is this? Have you lost your mind? Where are you going? You know you're still married?"

I laughed, and I couldn't believe how freeing this felt. All that she said was true.

"Momma, you are right, on every count. But my husband called me, let me know he's been fooling around since that bitch interned here, that he hates me, and thinks I owe him. So when a nice man I met while in New York—"

"You didn't tell me about it!"

"Because I was taking things slow, waiting to see if this was someone worth talking about."

"Is he?" Her voice went soft.

"I don't know, but I would like to find out."

"Did you sleep with him?"

"I didn't even kiss him. But I talked with him, and I'm still talking with him, and I like him."

"Does he know your situation?"

I stifled a giggle. "He does. He refers to Royce as a douche."

Silence, and then Momma roared with laughter.

"Can't fault him for accuracy, can you? Livvie, honey, I will help you any way you want. But this makes me nervous. Who is this man? What if he's not what he says?"

"He is, Momma."

"How can you be sure? Ted Bundy was nice looking with nice manners, and look what happened to his dates."

"Momma, I will leave you his number, and the hotel, and the event he invited me to."

"You're going away with him?" Her voice rose to nearly a shriek.

"I don't know, but when I do, I'll tell you everything. Deal?" I wanted to get off the phone, so I could tell Xavier yes.

"Okay. But you'd better spill it all, missy!"

Oh, she was pissed at me. I only got called missy when Momma's temper was roused.

"Promise. I love you."

"Love you too, sugar bean. Go be a hussy and call me later."

Laughing, I hung up with her.

'I got work covered.' I didn't want to tell him that I'd had to ask permission from my mom.

'Nice being the boss, isn't it? So when do you get to come and play with me?'

'What exactly is the agenda?'

"How about we boot this whole flying with a crowd thing and I'll pick you up at your place?"

What? **'We're driving?'** This could potentially be bad.

'No. My jet is back in commission. Can you be at the airport tomorrow morning?'

'And then?'

'Out to San Fran. I have the party thing for the Y, and I planned on being there for a couple of days. We can see Alcatraz, or whatever tourist shit you want to do.'

'Why Xavier, what a compelling offer. Of tourist shit.'

'Well, it might be shit. I don't exactly get to go out like other people. I don't want you to deal with my life. But we can spend time together.'

In spite of his flippant tone that was apparent even through text, I could also feel the hesitation. He was worried. I couldn't understand why. As if anyone, even me, the not-yet divorcee, couldn't say no to him.

I wondered if I should be worried about being another notch on his belt, as it were. Then I thought about his smile, his lips, and the way that the mere touch of his hand sent my entire being up in flames, and decided that I wanted to see what could happen.

'You could make up for ditching me all week and make sure I eat well.'

'Done'

'Tell me where to meet you. I don't want to miss my ride.'

'No way I'm leaving without you, Ms Olivia'

'Well since you offered me a nice ride, you'd better not. I won't have a man who won't keep his word.'

I couldn't believe I flirted with him. Momma was right. I was a hussy.

I didn't care. If this was a week of my life, and a week with him is all I'd ever get, I wanted it.

I wanted that fire that he made flare up in me to happen.

Xavier texted me where to meet the plane, and what hotel we'd be at.

'I got two rooms for us with a suite.'

At that text, I burst into tears. Here I was imagining kissing him, and he came out with this. He had no expectations. Or if he did, he knew better than to assume.

I immediately called Momma.

"Okay, Olivia Anne, you tell me what is going on right this minute! I thought I could wait, but I can't. I was just about to call you."

"I met a man named Xavier Reede, and he is going to a big benefit for the YMCA in San Francisco. I'm flying out with him tomorrow morning, and we are staying at the Ritz Carlton there. He got me my own room." I knew she'd appreciate that.

"Well, he's a gentleman, then. He knows what ought to be done."

"I think you're right, Momma." I couldn't stop the smile that came over my face so wide I thought my face might split.

"Well, all right then. You call me when you get on the plane, and when you land, and when you get to the hotel. Then I won't worry so much. You hear me, girl?"

"I hear," I said.

"Now, what are you gonna wear? You spend time with a man, you need to look good."

"You want to go do some shopping with me, Momma?"

"Do I? Let me sort these fools here and I'll be by to

pick you up. Go look and see what you have, and we'll go get the rest."

We hung up, and I raced up to my room. I ignored the first closet door and went to mine. We had two walk-in closets which cost the earth when we had the house built. Now I was glad that we'd done it—I didn't have to see the space where my old life used to be.

Let Suzan deal with Royce and his wardrobe. He was her problem now.

Part of me knew that I was merely putting a band-aid on the hurt that had been done to me. I would need to deal with it, and it promised to be painful and crappy.

You know, though, a band-aid helped to heal. It didn't fix the problem—only time and natural healing would do that. But a band-aid helped things along.

Xavier was one hell of helper, as band-aids went.

Momma got to me faster than I thought and we spent the rest of the day shopping. To my surprise, she didn't fuss, or carry on.

Dear lord. How bad had my marriage looked to the outside? No one other than me seemed to be mourning all that much for it and I was nothing to write home about.

When Momma left that night, after having gone through my suitcase, closet, and bathroom, and packed me up, I went to bed. I couldn't stop thinking about Xavier. How excited I was to see him.

He'd caught me watching one of his videos on the plane, but he didn't know how big of a fan I was. I'd been a fan of him in high school, listening to him when Momma was at work, and couldn't catch me. She knew I listened to him now, having caught me dancing around the house to his music, and she didn't think highly of him.

His lyrics were pretty raunchy. I'd given her his full name, even though he didn't use it. Hopefully, she was

impressed enough with his action so far as to not google
the hell out of him, and I'd have a little peace to see what
might happen.

The phone buzzed at me.

'Can't sleep. I'm excited to see you.'

'Me either. I don't want to oversleep.'

**'Told you I wouldn't leave without you. I'd hate
to have to drag you out of the house.'**

**'I'd hate to see you beat to a pulp by my neigh-
bors. They're rather protective.'**

**'Get some sleep, Olivia. I want you bright-eyed
for our trip.'**

'Good night, Xavier.;)

I stared at the phone for ten more minutes, but apparently, he was done.

I was doing a lot of waiting around for this man. It was
part of what had brought me to Royce, I realized. Royce
had come into my life like a whirlwind and told me where
we were headed.

I'd let him.

That was the kicker of all this. I'd let him. I had to
make a promise to myself, right this minute. I couldn't
allow Xavier, or anyone else, to lead me like that
ever again.

I needed to lead myself. I did it for business. Royce had
pooh-poohed my dreams, told me no one would come and
seek out the help of a consulting and management business
run by two single women.

He'd even told me that getting married would be better
for our business. I'd pissed him off something fierce when I
kept my maiden name. I figured I built my business as
Olivia Meroux, and that was how I'd keep it going.

I woke before my alarm went off. Raced out of bed
and straight into the shower. I'd dragged my suitcase

downstairs the night before. I made breakfast, and managed to get it down, in spite of the fact that an entire field of butterflies had taken up residence in my midsection.

A knock on the front door startled me so bad I almost dropped my cup of coffee.

What in the world? Please don't be anything that would delay me, I thought as I headed down the hallway towards the door.

When I opened it, a man in a black suit stood there. "Miss Olivia? I'm here from Xavier to drive you to the airport."

"Oh, um, I wasn't expecting you. I'm just finishing breakfast," I said. He hadn't said anything about a car.

"I'll wait in the car. When you're done, just come to the door. No rush, ma'am." He nodded, and turned and went back to his car.

I went straight back to the kitchen and dug my phone out of my purse.

'You should have warned me.' I wanted to see what he said.

'About what? Did the car not get there? He left in plenty of time.'

So it was from him. **'You didn't tell me you were sending a car.'**

'I'm sending a car.'

'Smart ass'

'Have you left yet? Got a plane to get out of here.'

'Finishing my coffee. Leaving shortly.'

'Hurry'

I smiled. I liked to see that he had some excitement over this too.

I rinsed out my coffee cup and headed for the door.

The moment I opened the door, the man in the car jumped out.

"Ma'am, ma'am, let me get your bag," He came up behind me as I pulled my bag out the front door.

"Thank you," I let him take it and turned to lock up.

"Oh shit," I stared at the door.

"Ma'am?" He'd heard me.

"Nothing, nothing, I'm fine. Let's go." I locked the door and followed him to the car. I slid into the back and pulled my phone out again.

"What?" Momma didn't like being woken before she decided to get up.

"Momma, I need you to stay at the house."

"Why are you callin' me this early, sugar?"

"Because I'm on my way to the airport and I realized the home would be here, empty, and I don't want Royce in here."

"Okay, darling, fine. I'll get someone over there today to house sit while you're gone."

"Thank you, Momma."

"You're welcome. Now let me get back to sleep. It's the only thing that slows the march of time."

She hung up without another word.

I tucked the phone away. Now I felt like I could go and not have to worry.

The airport came into sight, and the butterflies fluttered back into life within.

Oh my God. Had I done the right thing? There was no turning back now.

The car pulled up to a small, sleek jet. As the car purred to a stop, the driver ran around and opened the door for me. He held out a hand, and I took it, afraid that I'd fall on my face otherwise.

I looked up, and Xavier appeared in the door of the

jet. I could see, even in the shadow of the hangar, that he wore a wide smile. The effect was more striking now that I could see him without glasses.

And he wanted to go out with me.

Stop it, I told myself. Stop that nonsense right now! Of course he does, in spite of the millstone you're currently sporting, and in spite of all the other stuff that might come with that.

You're worth it. Don't you forget it. I heard that last bit in my mother's voice.

I lightly ran up the steps, and he held out his arms and pulled me into a hug.

He smelled so good.

I wanted to bury myself in him, and it surprised me how strongly he affected me. I couldn't remember the last time I—no. Stop it. Don't think about that now, while you're with Xavier.

His body felt warm and hard. There was no fat on the man. I couldn't help it, and I gave him a little extra squeeze.

He kissed the top of my head.

"I'm really glad you decided to come." His voice warmed me, flowing over me like warm honey. So different than what I heard when he sang.

"I'm really glad you asked me," I said. I didn't want to spill my guts, but I wasn't going to lie. I wanted to be honest with him. I would be, as much as I felt it was safe.

"Well then let's get going," he said, grinning at me.

He stood back and let me enter. I'd never flown on anything other than commercial flights, so a private plane in and of itself was a treat.

The passenger area had only six seats. The driver came on behind us with my bag. A man appeared from the cockpit area and took it, and the driver from the car was gone.

"Have a seat. You hungry?" Xavier asked.

I sat down, and he sat across from me.

"No, I had something before I left. I have to ask, is this yours?"

"No, I share it with a couple of other people. Keeps the costs down, you know?"

I laughed. "You're a bargain hunter?"

"Damn straight."

He seemed a little off-kilter. I hoped it wasn't because I wasn't what he remembered. I almost asked, but his look of…surprise? Made me feel shy. Instead, I opted for a smile and tried to let myself relax.

4

*X*avier

I couldn't believe how good she looked. Why the hell had I waited before? I must be stupid. Seriously.

Even though I was used to women tossing panties—women of all ages, I have to add—at me on a regular basis, I still couldn't believe this woman was willing to take a chance with me.

And she was a fan. Which meant she probably had seen some of my shit choices in the past.

When she hugged me, the urge to kiss her until she couldn't breathe nearly knocked me over. I think I covered it, but I'm not sure. I'm a Goddamned grown man! This is not supposed to be this hard.

She crosses her legs and runs her hand through her curly dark hair. I feel like this is a habit, maybe a nervous habit? I hope so. I hope I make her nervous. It'd be nice not to be the only one.

"Can I sit next to you?" I ask, hoping I don't seem like a creeper.

"Sure," her smile is nervous and something else. I hope it's a good something else.

I sit down and feeling brave, I take her hand in mine. The cabin steward comes through.

"We're taxiing shortly, Mr. Xavier," he says. "Coffee for you ma'am?"

"That would be nice," she smiles up at him. "You want something more? They can make the fancy shit," I add.

"Café au lait?" She asks. "Is it too much to hope for Community coffee?"

"No, I'm sorry we don't have that particular coffee, ma'am," he smiles at her. It's hard not to. Hers is infectious.

"We'll get some, won't we Byrnes?" I ask.

"Absolutely. We'll have it on the trip back."

He leaves the cabin.

"So explain your private timeshare jet," Olivia turns to me.

"I know it's seen as a joke, but having a private plane of any kind is expensive. These in particular," I gestured to the plane. "So I was bitching about not wanting to fly commercial because you can't get any privacy, and eventually, a couple of guys decided to go in on one together. We bought it used, and we share the expenses. None of them are asses, so it's pretty easy with scheduling." I shrug, but I'm lucky. I work with decent guys. Not everyone in my business is decent.

"That's a good way to do it. My momma would approve."

"Is she thrifty?"

"She loves to shop, and as I told you, loves her Liz spa, but she loves a bargain, and hates to pay full price for anything."

"Just because you have money doesn't mean you have to blow it. So many guys in my industry don't manage their shit well or have crews that help them spend all their money, and then they have to tour just to make the mortgage."

Olivia nodded. "You need to have people you trust to tell you, *No*, to give you a budget."

"Remember Hammer? That's what happened to him. Too many moochers, all encouraging him to spend, and no one on his ass about saving."

"I don't think it's only your industry," she said, sadness coming across her face. "That is one of the problems Royce and I had. I made all the money, and he wanted to spend all of it."

"That's a recipe for divorce," I said. I got that. My exes —all of them—had the same problem.

"I didn't think so." Olivia's voice was small.

I leaned in to look at her. "Are you okay with this? I know it seems kind of soon."

She turned then, and her dark eyes looked at me, and I couldn't see any lies in them. "It is soon, but that's okay. It's weird— the things I think are going to bother me about getting divorced aren't bothering me at all, and the things that I don't even think of pop up and hit me in a soft spot."

"It'll be okay, promise."

Her mouth twisted, and I forgot everything for a moment as I focused on her lips.

"Sure it will. My ex is being bitter. It will be better when the legal wrangling is over."

"Trust me, toss enough lawyers at a problem, and things get better."

"Spoken from experience?"

"Abso-fucking-lutely. I have a lot of practice in protecting myself from those who would leave my ass in a cardboard box under a bridge somewhere."

She laughed, and the mood lightened.

"Let's talk about something else. I remember reading that you had a good friend you grew up with—was that the one whose wedding you just went to?"

I nodded. "Tibby. She's great. We've been friends since elementary school."

The memory returned. I had just moved with my mom. It was the most recent school for me. We usually moved two or three times a year, depending on how many times Mom got evicted. Or broke up with her boyfriend. Or whatever.

I went to lunch with the rest of the class. I didn't have a lunch because I'd been out of school for a while, and Mom wasn't up to date with the school schedule yet. Not that there was a guarantee she'd ever get up to speed with the school schedule. But on this particular day, she'd forgotten to make me anything. That was assuming we had anything for lunch.

I sat at the end of the table, some of the other kids watching me and whispering. I could feel my face heat up, which meant it was turning red. Add that to my red hair, and I looked stupid.

Which I hated because that meant the name-calling of 'tomato boy' or something equally clever wasn't far behind.

Someone slid in next to me. I didn't want to look. I'd been in trouble for fighting at the last school when some of the boys in my class refused to leave me alone. I made them, but at a cost to me. So maybe if I ignored the person next to me, I'd be able to stay out of trouble. Mom beat me when I got into tro—

"You want half of my sandwich?" A small voice said next to me.

I snuck a look. A little blond girl, tiny, with an almost-smile, held out a sandwich.

"Sure," I said.

"I forget my lunch sometimes, and I hate it. I guess you forgot yours too." She smiled for real this time.

I ate the sandwich, and a friendship started that day. It was still the most significant relationship of my life.

"Tibby offered to share her lunch with me on my first day of school," I said. "My mom forgot about things like lunches, so…" I stopped. I could feel the wash of bitter anger that thinking about my mom usually brought.

Olivia squeezed my hand. I'd forgotten that I had taken hers originally. "I'm sorry," she said. "I had a great momma. I still do. But we lost my daddy early, and now I know Momma could have gone bad, real bad, after that. She didn't."

"She sounds great."

"She doesn't like you," Olivia said in a rush. "I told her your legal name, but nothing else. So I hope she doesn't google or anything. I'll never hear the end of it." She sighed.

I felt a hot stab of jealousy. I'd love for a mom to fuss at me. Without hitting me, or trying to put out cigarettes on me. But there was no place to say that kind of thing. Nor did I want to.

"Oh, no! Xavier, can I make a quick call? I need to check in real fast."

'Uh, sure." I wasn't sure whether I should be offended that she was checking in or not. It's not like I wasn't a completely public figure.

I stopped myself. I was used to women who couldn't

wait to be a part of my world. Olivia wasn't like that. She was normal, even if she was a fan. I needed to chill out.

She pulled out her phone and hit a number.

"Hey, Momma. I'm on my way. I'll call you when we get there, and give you the hotel info, okay?"

She listened for a moment, and I could hear the tones of someone who was giving a lecture. Those tones all sound alike.

"I will, Momma. Love you." She ended the call and smiled at me.

"Better?"

"I know it's a pain, but Momma is one of my best friends. It's why I can work with her, as well as being related to her."

"What do you do?" I asked curiously. She'd mentioned the business more than once, and the ex was trying to get a piece of it. It must be good.

"I'm a consultant."

"What does that mean? I hear that all the time – consulting for what?"

"We do what you'd call PR or personal consulting. Helping people navigate sticky situations, or how to handle changing brands in business. With that, we'll do a lot of market analysis, see what's trending. Basically, we're a personal advice company."

"I'm not trying to be rude, but people actually pay for that?" It seemed a bit out there to me.

She nodded. "Oh, yeah. You'd be amazed at the people who don't know how to handle their press, or worse, that screw it up every time they try to do anything."

"So you work with all the Opry stars?" I teased.

"Some of them. Momma is an attorney, and she's a specialist in contract law, so she will also go over contracts, suggest where things are not quite right, and I help people figure out what will and won't work with their contracts. There's pretty much no limits to the types of people that we see."

I nodded slowly. "That's interesting. I can see where that has a lot of possibilities."

"No one thought we'd make a go of it, but there are tons of people who are just desperate for advice and to be told what to do." She grinned. "Momma and I are just the people to tell them."

"Maybe I need to talk to you," I joked.

"Oh, probably not. You don't look the type to take anyone's advice over your own."

I leaned back a little, surprised. I hadn't expected that.

"You're right. How can you tell?"

"I size up potential clients all the time. Some people know but aren't sure. Some are completely sure, even if they might not know the best way to get whatever it is they are trying to accomplish done."

"Are you saying I'm overconfident?"

"Don't you have to be in your business?"

She asked the question with complete seriousness, and no sarcasm or teasing.

"Well, yeah. I guess." I looked towards the front of the cabin, thinking.

My train of thought faltered when Olivia laughed softly. "See? Not such a flighty business concept after all. But this is so serious! Let's talk about something more fun."

"Don't you think business is fun?" I asked.

"I do, but I want to know you outside of the business you. What's your favorite thing to do?"

I hadn't been asked that in a long time. I'd been in the public eye long enough that no one asked me anymore.

"Walk down the street unrecognized."

"Does that happen often?"

"You didn't recognize me on the plane," I pointed out.

"Yeah, I failed the super fan test. I was far too preoccupied with my own stuff."

"Well, I am glad you made time for me," I said, my voice going husky.

The way she looked up at me made me act without thinking. I leaned in and touched my lips to hers. Tentatively, hesitantly.

I surprised her because she didn't react right away. Then she kissed me back.

I thought my head might actually explode, and my dick woke up, wondering what the hell was going on.

With one hand I pulled her in closer to me, loving the feel of my hand in her hair. Then the other hand snaked around so that I cradled her head.

She wrapped her arms around me, scooting closer.

Swiftly, I stood a little and pulled her up and into my lap. I caught a flash of her eyes. Then I kissed her again and forgot everything else.

Every instinct in me said to take her to the back and take her clothes off, piece by piece. Spend the rest of the flight getting to know her body, every inch of it. In detail. Until she sobbed my name with a voice hoarse from crying it out.

The image was so strong it left me weak.

I couldn't remember the last time I felt desire this strong for anyone.

I might have been able to control my raging libido but for one thing.

Olivia gently bit my bottom lip.

livia

*O*h my God. OmyGodohmyGodohmyGod. Everywhere his hands touched me, and they hadn't even gone below my neck, my skin exploded. Or felt like it did.

I couldn't get close enough to him, so I wanted to weep in relief when he picked me up from the chair and settled me in his lap. I could feel his hardness beneath me, and it excited me. A lot.

Basic desire and instinct for a strong man warred with my thirty-one years of being a proper young lady. I wanted to rip his clothes off and spend the rest of the flight naked.

But instinct aside, women who did that often ended up being the woman of the week. I know I'd thought I'd be okay with just that, but now, in his arms. I didn't feel so sure.

He made a small sound in his throat, and I felt the answering wetness between my legs. Oh my God. This man hit every good thing I'd ever even thought about physically.

I bit down on his lip.

If I'd thought he'd been passionate before, I'd thought wrong.

No sooner than had my teeth closed onto that full bottom lip, he lifted me up from his lap, wrapping his arms around me.

In answer, I twined my legs around his hips, not wanting to lose the delicious feel of him between my legs.

I couldn't remember the last time I wanted sex so badly it hurt.

But it hurt right now.

"Oh God, woman…" he murmured against my lips. He walked a few steps holding me. We ended up next to the wall of the passenger cabin, and he propped me against it, taking the opportunity to grind himself into me.

I wanted to cry, it was so good.

"We…" I started.

"Are not going to make it a week," He finished.

Well, not quite what I'd been planning to say. But it would do.

He leaned away from me with a sigh.

"Much as I want to, and holy shit, you have no idea how much I want to—"

"Oh, I think I might," I said, gazing at him from under my lashes.

He closed his eyes and inhaled deeply. "I'm not going to do this on a plane. Where we're on full display. Think you can contain yourself?" He let me slide down the wall until my feet rest on the floor.

"It's hard for me, such a good boy, to deal with this," he said in an aggrieved tone.

"Oh, stop it," I rolled my eyes.

"I am right now," his voice dropped to a whisper that went right through me. "But only for right now."

He led me back to the seat—the scene of the crime, as it were.

"Well," I said. "I didn't expect that."

"Disappointed?" He asked.

"Only in that we're sitting down again." Another from-under-the-lash look from me.

His nostrils flared. "Patience."

"Oh, one of your strong suits, is it?"

A bark of laughter greeted my comment. "Not at all.

But I get the feeling, Ms. Olivia, you are worth the wait. Any wait." He brought my hand to his lips and kissed it.

"That feeling is mutual, Xavier," I said.

At that moment, the steward came back in.

Oh, that's right. We'd ordered coffee. Maybe he had delayed…oh God. No wonder Xavier stopped. Because we were on a plane, and if the steward had waited for us to finish whatever we were doing, it meant that we were monitored.

I could feel the blood in my cheeks. I hadn't felt the heat from a blush like this in a long time.

How embarrassing. Not that I was with Xavier, nor even that I might only be his young lady for a week or so; no, it was that we weren't alone.

We both sat silently as Byrnes served the coffee, and then he took himself from the cabin, almost like a ghost.

"That's what you meant by not being on display," I said.

I couldn't look at him.

I felt his fingers lift my chin up and he was right there, putting a gentle kiss on my lips. "I'm sorry. I'm used to it. I've forgotten how hard it can be at first."

"How do you get used to this?" I kept thinking how we must have looked, panting and tangled together against the wall.

He shrugged. "It takes time. And you learn that everything you ever knew about privacy is something you have to relearn. Whether you like it or not. That's why most people only date others in the biz."

"Is that where you normally meet women?" I was curious.

"Usually. The women I come across know the deal."

"Oh," I said, feeling uncomfortable. I wasn't naïve, but I don't know that I could be termed as 'knowing the deal.'

"Hey," Xavier leaned over and turned my face toward his. "I'm glad you're not in the biz. I like that you're not."

I smiled, feeling better.

His confidence was compelling.

*X*avier

I looked into her eyes, seeing the confusion and the insecurity fading. Good. That's what I wanted to see.

Didn't I?

I didn't like that I was questioning myself. Part of me felt like someone like this was too good to be true. And something else hung around the back of my consciousness, wanting to be recognized, but it was slippery, and I couldn't get a grasp on it. There was something about Olivia, something that I knew, or ought to know. But I couldn't get hold of it.

"Well, that's good," she said, with a smile that looked genuine. "I can't change who I am any more than you can."

I leaned back, letting go of her. "Who would want to change all this?" I asked sarcastically. At her look, I laughed.

"I'm astounded you and your big head fit through the plane door," she said, laughing as well.

"I'm not a total ass. But always being confident is part of the job," I said.

"What, you're not always one hundred and fifty percent confident?" She teased.

"Not always, no. But I don't let anyone else know that,

so you need to keep your mouth shut," I said, mock-frowning at her.

That only made her laugh more.

"I'll keep your secret, I promise."

The sight of her laughing stirred me again, making me want to say to hell with my conventions, and I leaned over and kissed her lightly. "Good."

She reached up and stroked my cheek. "You know, I'm not normally—"

I held up a hand, stopping her. Then I put my hand on hers. "It's fine. I'm not normally the type to invite strange chicks on my plane. It's new for both of us." As I spoke, I surprised myself with the realization that I was telling the truth. I wasn't above inviting a woman up to my hotel, with no intentions beyond twenty-four hours in the future. But my plane—that was part of my life, my permanent personal life. I didn't bring groupies on the plane. I normally didn't invite anyone to the charity things I did, either. This was new for me.

She exhaled, obviously relieved. "I'm glad I'm not the only one who is in strange territory."

"You're not." I kissed her again, and then sat back in my seat, reaching for my coffee. But I reached over with my free hand and twined my fingers with hers.

"It's strange. I don't really know you, but we've spent so much time texting, I feel like I do."

I nodded as I took a sip. "I agree," I said. "But let's talk about something more fun." I didn't want to talk about whatever this was. Too many new things too fast. "What would you like to do in San Francisco?"

"I haven't been. Usually, when I am in California, I'm in Los Angeles."

"Do you have a lot of entertainment clients?" I asked.

She shook her head, smiling. "Now I'm not gonna tell you that," she said. "I don't talk about my clients."

"How old are you?" I asked.

"Thirty-one," she said.

I was surprised. She didn't look very old, but she carried herself like someone a lot older. "When did you start the business? Or get married?" I asked before I could stop myself.

At that, she laughed. "Do you know the south at all? My momma wanted me to get married the moment I graduated, although I did notice that after Royce and I announced our engagement when I was still in college, she told me more than once I could wait," Her brows furrowed as she stopped, thinking. Then it cleared, and she looked back up at me. "It's amazing and pretty embarrassing, to see how many people really didn't like your husband when your marriage finally breaks up."

I shrugged, wanting to keep this light and not wanting her to focus on the douche. "Everyone hated my ex, too. Actually, most of my exes were disliked by the people around me."

"Your friends?"

"My friends, my manager, my crew, everyone. I've always figured I was the one who had to put up with them, so the opinions of others didn't count. But I have to admit, when Tibby doesn't like the person I'm dating, I should just listen to her." I sighed. Not that I would admit that to Tibby. I'd never hear the end of it.

Olivia smiled. "I feel the same way about Momma. I should, for the most part, just listen to her."

"What's that like, being best friends with your mom?" I asked.

"It's not always easy. We're both adults, and we're part-ners, but she's always my mom. Thank goodness she can put that aside when we work because it wouldn't inspire a lot of confidence to have the person you hired be fussed at by her mother. So we have an agreement that we never disagree in front of clients, and we discuss all cases behind closed doors."

"That sounds smart. But how did you decide to go into business?" She was young to have a business that her husband wanted to fight over. I'd have to ask Tibby or Bryant to look up her company, later sometime.

"I thought we were talking about what we were going to do in San Francisco," she said with a smile.

"We are, but I'm a diverse conversationalist," I said. Part of me, in spite of my nearly overwhelming desire for her, was nervous. I hadn't checked her out. I didn't Google her, or look her up, or set a PI into looking into her—what if she was a total flake? What if her ex wasn't a douche, but running for his life? I actually felt a bead of sweat run down my back.

Even though I'd fired Preston, my nagging manager, I could hear his warnings in my head. Maybe he'd had more of a point than I gave him credit for. Which made no sense, as I didn't care that there were rumors I was gay floating around. Why did I care about this all of a sudden?

Because I really liked her. I would be crushed if she was crazy pants. The thought made another bead of sweat slide down my back.

"Momma was looking for something else to do, as the main partner in her firm passed away, and she didn't like the other two partners. I went to school for communications. Momma also had a client that could not get out of his own way, and she was telling me all about it one night because he'd called her at home. It came out of that," she finished, waving a hand.

I could tell there was more, but she didn't want to share. That was OK.

"Did your ex want to work with you?" I felt like I needed to know a little more of what might be going on with her divorce. If this thing with us kept going, I might end up being pulled into the court case. That kind of shit happened all the time. People saw my name and saw money, or influence, or something that would help whatever their agenda was. I was used to it. I didn't want to interrogate her, but I wanted a little info so that I had something to give my PI.

She shook her head. "We asked him, well, I asked him. Momma said I could if I had to. He took a couple of days to think it over because he would have been helpful in setting up the logistics. He's in IT," she added, looking away.

I could tell she was somewhere else, but I found that I didn't mind. I wanted to hear more about the ex, see if he really was a douche.

Olivia sighed. "He came back and said that he thought it wouldn't be the best idea, all of us working together, that it would be too much family too close, and I accepted that. He told me later that he wasn't sure we'd last, or that Momma and I would be successful. He was having doubts even then when we were already engaged!" Her voice rose a little.

Then she took a breath. "It was so kind of him, you know, to come to me later, and tell me he was ready to be involved. When I asked him why now, he was kind enough to share his earlier concerns." She snorted. "He was so surprised when I told him no, thank you, that Momma and I were just fine." She looked out the window, and then back at me. "I wonder if that's where the first crack happened." Her face looked sad, and for a moment, I could see what she would have looked like as a kid, vulnerable and worried.

Which made me want to beat the douche's face in. Yeah, he was a douche. Even if she was a little off, his actions were that of a self-absorbed asshole. I knew one of those when I ran into them.

"The first crack happened when he didn't believe in you at the beginning," I said firmly. "Don't blame yourself, Olivia," I finished.

"Livvie," she said.

"What?"

"My friends call me Livvie. I think you qualify as a friend," she smiled shyly at me.

"Well thank you, Ms. Livvie," I said, squeezing her hand. "So now that that's out of the way, what can we do in San Fran?"

5

---

*O*livia

I felt like I'd run some kind of sprint. That bit of
conversation felt a bit like an interrogation, but it
was to be expected. If Momma had been here, she'd have
put him through worse. So I suppose it wasn't that bad.

"Food," I said. "I've heard that there are a lot of really
great places to eat, so definitely food. Do you have favorite
places?"

He laughed. "Do I? Yes, I do. So we'll eat. You want to
see a show or something?"

"You mean outside of your show?"

To my surprise, his cheeks reddened slightly. "You want
to see it?"

"Sure. You already know I'm a fan."

"Well, OK."

"Unless you'd rather I not," I said. He didn't seem
overly enthused.

"No, I want you to. It's just I don't normally have people with me during these trips," he said. "Don't worry about it. I'm just being a weirdo."

"I already knew that," I teased. "Listen, if you'd rather I didn't come with you, I'm fine with that."

He looked at me then. "Really? You wouldn't get all bent out of shape?"

I shook my head. "No. I understand needing to work, and I knew this was a work trip for you."

"That's really awesome of you to say," Xavier said. "But it's not like this is a super private event. Of course, you're welcome."

While he smiled when he said that, I got the impression it wasn't entirely the truth. That bothered me, but…I mentally shrugged my shoulders. This wasn't my issue to manage. I'd been honest with him all the way from the moment we'd met, and if he couldn't be entirely honest, as long as he didn't hurt me, I wasn't going to carry his water.

I'd been doing that for long enough. I wouldn't do it again, even for a guy like Xavier, who seemed fantastic.

Of course, that could be my hormones talking, too. I felt a level of desire for him that shocked me in its intensity. I'd been all but celibate with Royce for some time, what with one thing and another. Mostly with a thing named Suzan, I thought snidely. Well, he was her problem now. Careful what you wish for, I thought, the snark taking over again. She may think he's a great guy, but he's mad, and when he's mad, that makes him mean, and he lashes out. I'd feel sorry for her, but as she obviously had no problem with sleeping with my husband, I figured she earned whatever grief she'd brought on herself through that choice.

Back to Xavier. He was so…hot. So incredibly, amazingly hot. I wanted to just put my entire upbringing aside, and tear his clothes from him, and have hot and very sweaty sex, but I couldn't.

Put my upbringing and morals aside, I mean. Although I really, really wanted to.

I also needed to be careful because I was not far out of the shock of getting divorce papers. While I didn't have a slew of relationships behind me, I knew that people often rebounded into something unsuitable in times like this.

Would that be so bad?

I considered that. Would it really? If I was careful, what was the worst thing that could happen? I mean, getting over my mother's shocked intake of breath I could hear in my head, what was the worst thing that could happen?

I could have really hot sex. I could laugh a lot with a guy who thought I was hot, and who was fun.

Someone like me wasn't the type who would ever end up with someone like Xavier, XTC, Mr. I'm-all-that rapper. It just didn't happen.

Not outside of a Hallmark movie of the week, anyway.

So why not just enjoy myself? Let whatever happened, happen. Not sweat it, and enjoy that someone as fun as Xavier wanted to hang out and spend time together. Not every relationship had to be a forever thing.

With those thoughts, I felt as though a weight had lifted off me. It helped to dispel the feeling of awkwardness that settled over us after we'd nearly attacked one another before the coffee came in.

With that resolution in mind, I leaned over so I could look into Xavier's eyes. "Hey," I said. "We'll do whatever. I don't have an agenda. I wanted to come with you because this sounded like a lot of fun. You sound like a lot of fun. That's it, Xavier. Nothing more. Let's just have fun." I raised my eyebrows in a question.

I watched his expression and something I couldn't read crossed his face. Then he smiled, and the whatever I'd just seen fell away.

"That sounds like a plan, Ms. Livvie. Let me show you the places I like to go, and then you decide, OK?" He let go of my hand as he pulled out his phone.

*X*avier

I couldn't decide how I felt at her words. Happy? Disappointed? I didn't know. But wasn't I just the one who was sitting here pissing and moaning internally with what if questions? Her words should make me happy, relieved. It showed she didn't expect anything from me.

So why didn't I feel happy and relieved?

I wasn't going to focus on it. I studied my phone as we talked about where to go. Did I want her to come to the benefit? It made sense that she thought she would —it's why I invited her, after all.

I didn't have to decide until the day after tomorrow. We had the entire day to do whatever tomorrow.

"Oh, let's do that!" She took the phone from me to widen something she'd seen on Google. "Doesn't this look like fun?"

I peered at the phone. "The Exploratorium? What is it?"

"It's a science museum," she looked up, her face alight.

I wasn't a horrible student in school, but school wasn't a fun time for me. Mostly because of non-school related things, but still. I didn't have fond memories or anything.

"If you say so. But you'll have to hold my hand, " I said with a smile.

"Deal," she said.

———

*I*t turned out that Olivia—Livvie—was right. The Exploratorium had been a lot of fun. Everything yesterday was a lot of fun. We'd walked all over the piers, and stopped and eaten when we felt like it, being the basic tourists.

I'd contacted one of my PR people and gotten us tickets on the night tour to Alcatraz for tonight. The benefit was during the day, so we'd be free at night.

I loved how comfortable I felt with her, how she treated me like a normal person, not really making any references or allowances to the other side of my life. No fawning, but no studied indifference, either. I'd seen both in women I was interested in.

With every passing moment, I wanted her more and more. I could almost feel an ache in my bones—and not just the one in my groin—with how much I wanted her.

The trouble was, I couldn't tell if she and I were on the same page with that. We hadn't kissed again like we'd done on the plane. When we'd gotten back last night, she'd taken the other room. She'd kissed me before she walked through the connecting door, and it had been hot as hell. But she hadn't hesitated when she walked away, or when she'd shut the door behind her.

Was that good or bad? I realized I had no idea. The women I normally dated were ready to be naked about twelve seconds into our dates, so they weren't a good comparison.

I stretched, walking out into the dining area of the

suite. I'd gotten up and ordered breakfast right away. I found that I was starving, in spite of all that I'd eaten yesterday when we walked miles together.

A light knock on the door sent me to the door quickly. Livvie wasn't up yet, and I didn't want to wake her. The attendant brought in the cart and headed for the table on the balcony. It was sunny out, with mist on the other side of the bay. A nice day for San Francisco, and it was too gorgeous to stay in.

I loved New York, but I always enjoyed being out here. There was something about this city that drew you in, and wrapped itself around you, without you even being aware of it.

After the room service guy left, I sat and leaned back in the chair, enjoying the peace of the moment. The coffee was hot—what was that coffee Livvie had asked about? Community coffee? I'd have to get some, see why she liked it so much.

Then I wondered why I was so interested.

My train of thought was halted when Livvie appeared, looking delectable in pajamas. They were striped, and crisp looking like cotton PJs look, and she was adorable. She rubbed her eyes, and then stretched her arms out.

"Were you really going to sit out here with this deli-cious-smelling coffee and not get me up?" She asked as she walked around to sit down across from me.

I poured her a cup by way of an apology. "I didn't want to wake you. We walked a marathon yesterday."

Livvie laughed. "It feels like it, doesn't it?" She added cream to the coffee and took a sip, looking out at the view. "This is lovely, Xavier. Thank you for asking me to come with you." She turned back to me, smiling over the rim of her cup.

The flush that raced through me was unfamiliar, but I liked it.

As I was about to speak, the phone rang with Tibby's ring.

"I'm sorry, I have to take this," I said.

She nodded, still drinking her coffee.

"Hey," I said into the phone. "How was the honeymoon? You back at work already? I have problems, if so. If not, feel free to ignore me."

"Bryant told me you were firing Preston," Tibby said. She had her business voice on.

"Already did it."

"Where are you?"

"In San Francisco?"

"Why?"

There was a time when Tibby knew my schedule as well as I did, and I felt a pang for what we used to have, when it was just the two of us.

But that wasn't fair of me. She and I would never be a couple, and she deserved a great guy like Seth. Plus, I got Seth and Bryant as a family because they were her family. So I really had no room to bitch. There was something to be said for not feeling it was you against the whole world.

Tibby had helped me, and herself, to feel otherwise.

"Y benefit."

"Make sure you get all the records—"

"—to the accountant," I finished for her. "Yeah, yeah, I always do, Mom. How was the honeymoon?"

"It was amazing. I can only hope that you can finally find some woman to put up with you and your shit so that you can have this kind of happiness. You're a pain in my ass, but you deserve it."

"Tib, you are getting soft."

"I am, but since it benefits you, shut up. Why'd you fire Preston?"

"He wouldn't stop nagging. It was worse than my mom, Tib."

"That bad?"

She knew I didn't bring up my mom often. She also knew my mom, so she knew what the comparison meant.

"Yes. And he was convinced that I was ruined with going out the other night, and just harped on the whole gay club aspect to the point that I wanted to punch him."

"Oh?" Tibby's voice changed. "You think he was carrying his own baggage there?"

"For sure. I won't put up with that shit."

"Well, good decision on your part, but it means that you don't have anyone on site for you. "

"You could—"

"No. That's a big ol' nope from me, X. You know that. You need someone who can devote a lot of time to you and all the things that come along with managing your life. It's not me. Nice statement, by the way. I think you might have made Bryant cry."

When Tibby had first started, she'd had more time, and she was so annoyed with my casual attitude that she told me she didn't want to see me robbed blind so she'd look over my stuff.

She was still my main attorney, but I had entertainment lawyers who managed my contracts. They'd been picked by her.

"Well, damn," I said. I wasn't sure what to say to that.

"Don't say anything. He'll be pissed I'm tattling. It was a good thing. So, X?"

"Yeah?"

"Anything out of the ordinary happen while I was away?"

Tib had that tone in her voice she'd had at her wedding when she told me to go with anything that popped up. I sat up straighter.

"You gonna tell me what this is about?"

"I'll tell you when I see you again," she said.

I laughed. "That's just a bribe, and you know it!"

"Maybe, but it's nothing I want to talk about now."

"Well, I'm here in San Fran with a lovely lady I met on a plane."

"That is not out of the ordinary. You meet women everywhere."

"Then I guess I have nothing to report, oh taskmaster," I laughed again.

"You're so stupid sometimes," I could hear the huff of breath and knew she was rolling her eyes. "Please be careful, OK?"

"You saying that as my lawyer or my friend?"

"Both. Let me know when you get back."

She hung up.

Laughing a little, I hung up the phone.

"I'm surprised you told her about me, even indirectly," Olivia said.

"I tell Tib everything. But no worries, because she was too busy giving me hell over everything else she's missed by being away," I laughed again. "She's so funny. Sometimes I feel like she can't figure out what to give me grief over first."

"Do you really take that much management?"

"I'm pretty good with my own business stuff, but Tib is a lawyer, so she sees everything in terms of minimizing risk, and she is aware that being famous and having money brings a lot of risks." I shrugged my shoulders. "I know it too, and I think she wants me to be more aware of it. I can't help who I am, or that I've been successful, so I live with it. She's too suspicious for me."

"She sounds fearsome," Olivia said.

"No, just a best friend and good at what she does."

"Does she work with other entertainers? I know a lot of entertainment attorneys, and I don't know any named Tibby."

"Her full name is Tabitha, and she actually specializes in shipping law, so no, she doesn't have anyone else like me on her plate. It's a good thing too. She doesn't have the patience for a lot of people like me."

"You're lucky to have her," Olivia said.

"Don't I know it." I looked up. I'd felt something hit my head, but there wasn't anything above us, outside of the roof of the balcony. No birds, nothing floating in the air. I brushed at my head.

"It feels like she's been with me forever. I thought about having her do some web and IT work for me, but she looked at me like I'd grown another head," I added. I always wanted to ask her website questions for the longest time, and I had no idea as to why. She'd been an attorney from the moment she was accepted to law school. But the idea persisted, like a lost memory, or a dream.

"I imagine you've got a good team in place," Olivia said.

"Thanks to Tib, again," I said. "So you coming with me to this benefit thing?"

"You want me to?" Again with the gaze over the coffee cup. It was intoxicating.

"I do. I'd like to be discreet, though." I hoped I wouldn't offend her.

She laughed out loud. "Then perhaps you need to keep your hands to yourself, Mr. XTC!"

I stared. Was she complaining? Then I saw her expression. "Well, it's hard when I am with such a fine woman like you, Ms. Livvie, but I suppose I can try."

"I'm not the one who'll have fans crying," she was laughing harder. "Sitting in mourning, even," her laugh increased, and she set down her coffee cup.

"Are you making fun of me?" I mock-growled.

"No, no," she waved a hand at me, still laughing. "I wouldn't dare."

"Good thing," I said. "I am a big deal, I'll have you know."

"Oh, I know! I am well aware of my good fortune!" She laughed, even more, when I threw a strawberry at her. She caught it and popped it into her mouth.

The sight of her lips as she ate the strawberry drove all other thoughts from my head. I stood up and pulled her from the chair, snuggling her close to me so I could lean down and kiss her.

She tasted of the bitter and sweet taste of fresh strawberries, and it drove me wild. I swept her into my arms and walked through the balcony door sideways, holding her close to my chest. Her arms came up around my neck, and she pulled me close to kiss me.

With her clutched to me, I could feel her heartbeat, and it was as fast as mine, thundering like a drum. I devoured her mouth, wanting to get lost in the sensation of sweet fruit and sunshine.

Whatever I'd been planning to do this morning, or not do, or whatever reservations I had—they were gone. I headed to my bedroom. I didn't expect this, but since she was here, in my arms, and kissing me as enthusiastically as I kissed her, I wasn't going to look a gift horse in the mouth.

No way.

As I walked into the bedroom, I laid her on the bed

carefully. She sat up, keeping one arm around my neck, and kissed me as though her life depended on it.

Shit. Shit shit shit.

"Hang on, babe," I said. I went to the bathroom and dug through my bag. Thank God I'd brought them with me. I'd hesitated when I'd packed. They were a staple in my toiletry bag, but I'd been unsure about Olivia.

I came back and placed the small silver packet on the nightstand as I slid myself onto the bed and into her waiting arms.

"Missed you," she murmured into my lips, and then she didn't say anything else because I kissed her as though my life depended on it.

I ran my hands down her body, and she felt so warm, so good. Her hip curved sweetly into my hand, and I reached around and felt her ass. That felt even better. I'd watched her as she walked away once we'd gotten to the airport the first time we'd met, and the slight sway of her ass hypnotized me. To feel it in my hand, with only the striped PJs between us made me even harder.

She put a hand on my chest and pushed me away gently.

I was slightly dazed, and just about to ask her what the hell, when she pulled her top over her head and tossed it to the floor.

She was wearing nothing underneath, and her breasts rose and fell as she pulled me back to her with a greater ferocity than she'd done before. I reached up and cupped them, and as I felt her nipples, she moaned into my mouth.

I had to take a moment because that sound with the feel of her nipples hardening in my hand nearly made me come.

How had this quiet woman sent me to the edge like this? I'd never felt this before in my life.

I slid my hands down to the waist of her PJ bottoms, but she stopped me.

"No," she whispered, looking at me like she could see into my soul. "I want to see you," as she pulled my shirt up.

I leaned back and took it off, letting it fall wherever. I let my head fall back as she sat up and kissed my chest, little small nipping kisses, taking the time to run her tongue over my nipples, scraping with her teeth.

I nearly saw stars.

"Oh my God, Ms. Livvie," I muttered. I pushed her back so I could offer the same attention to her.

She let her head fall back, and as I glanced up at her, I could see the expression on her face. The idea that I was the one who put it there inflamed me and spurred me on.

Her eyes still closed, her hands drifted to my pants and tugged on them. I didn't need another hint. I moved away from her, which made her open her eyes.

So she watched as I undid my pants and let them fall from me. Like her, I wore nothing underneath.

"Oh, my," she breathed. "You're good enough to eat," she finished.

"If you insist," I crawled back onto the bed, stopping before I fell on top of her and devoured her. "But I think you are still wearing too many clothes, miss."

Without taking her eyes off me, she slid her PJ bottoms down, and my breath caught.

Olivia's skin, flush with what we were doing, practically glowed. I'd never seen a more beautiful woman in my life.

And she was mine.

Where had that come from?

Shut up, I told myself. Not the time.

I crawled up her body and settled myself on top of her.

She fit, she felt right. I could feel my tenuous control beginning to slip.

"Hate to admit it, but you're driving me wild, woman. I don't know how much teasing I can take," I said. It was true. She strained all my normal levels of control.

Olivia moved underneath me, causing my cock to get even harder as it moved along her body. Not sure how that was possible, but that's what it felt like. I could feel a lightness in my head.

"Well, you're not alone. Why don't you put that thing on," her hand waved in the direction of the nightstand, "And we'll stop teasing each other?"

Never had any words been sexier or more enticing. I reached over and leaned on an elbow to rip open the packet. I put it on the head of my cock, and her warm hand covered mine as she rolled it down.

Her hand on me made me tremble. I slid a hand between us and felt her. She was as excited about things as I was, which made me feel amazing.

"I don't know if I can—" I said in a rush. I wanted this to be good for her, and she was making me so crazy that—

"I don't want you to," she answered me, kissing me and stopping any further words.

None were needed. We both knew what we wanted. What I'd wanted since I'd met Olivia on the plane, her strength and her weakness on full display.

I moved my hand, and she put her arms around my neck, bringing me closer to her.

Carefully, sweating, I eased into her. Her legs opened further, and her hands went down my back to my ass, bringing me into her even more.

"Ohhhh…" she moaned, breaking off our kiss.

"More of that, all you want," I ground out, starting to move.

What I wanted was to pound into her until she screamed my name, until we both came a hundred times over, and collapsed, unable to move.

I wasn't sure I'd make it that long, but I concentrated on trying.

As I moved, she gripped my ass harder, her nails digging into me a little. I liked it, liked it even more as she wrapped her legs around my waist.

My hands went back to her breasts, and I played with her nipples as I kissed her. I wanted her to feel that everything I could touch was getting everything I could give. I wanted her to feel fulfilled.

Complete.

Just as I did.

livia

I was going to die. Xavier moved carefully, almost slowly, allowing me to feel every inch of him, every bit, as he went in and out of me. It was the most amazing, delicious thing I'd ever felt. Never, ever with anyone else had sex felt like this.

Certainly not the first time, either.

His hands palmed my breasts, taking the time to pinch and twist to the point where even the slightest breath sent me nearly into convulsions, and his mouth moved in harmony with his hands and his lower bits.

Lower bits…I would have laughed at myself if I weren't dying of pleasure.

His dick. His cock. I could see why his exes all got bitter. Who would want to give this up?

He increased the tempo, and I clutched him harder to me.

Jesus, could it get better?

It could.

It did.

Slowly, the bastard, he went faster, but at his pace, ignoring the fact that I was dying over here.

Finally, he placed his hands on either side of me, and lifted himself up, looking into my eyes. Then he moved, and this time, he went faster and faster, not bothering to take his time. His thrusts were hard, and each one seemed to drive me further into the bedding.

I wanted it. I never wanted him to stop.

I wanted to look away, to close my eyes, to close out the naked feeling I could see in him, but I was locked into his gaze. I knew that my own joy at this shone out of my eyes, and I didn't care.

I wanted him to see it. To give him back what he was giving me.

My hands let go of his ass, which was kind of a shame, because it was marvelous, and reached up to his arms, straining under his efforts. I held his wrists, letting my fingers curl around each one. I could feel the muscles and every hair on them.

He stopped for a moment and deliberately lifted up one hand and then the other, taking my hands under his. Leaned down, and kissed me. The slight motion drove me crazy, and I moved, wanting to be closer to him.

Without warning, he started to move again, even faster than before. I felt like I was on the back of a wild stallion, hanging on for dear life.

I was on a stallion, all right. I didn't even have the breath to giggle.

His thrusts were even more intense, and I could see a

sheen of sweat on his forehead. My palms were sweaty as we held hands and he took us to the edge.

As we fell over it together, he never took his eyes from mine.

"Olivia…" he whispered.

I couldn't speak. He lowered himself onto me, and I wrapped my arms around his back, keeping my legs twined around him.

I didn't want to let him go.

avier

$\mathcal{I}$ watched as Olivia chatted with someone at another table. We'd come to the benefit together, but she sat at the head table as my plus one, and there had been a lot of whispering—or maybe I'd just noticed it more.

Once she'd told people what she did, I could see the assumptions being made—that we were there for business. And Olivia knew how to do business. She was pleasant to me, but nothing like she'd been the past two days. No touching, no kissing, nothing.

Which was what I wanted, right?

I turned my attention back to the guy in front of me. He was on the board of directors of the Y, and I liked him. I just had no patience for anything normal right now.

Anything that had to do with something other than Olivia and whatever this thing between us was.

We'd gotten up, and she'd poured herself more coffee, and then shortly went back to bed. All the plans for the morning were gone. Since the benefit was early afternoon, it had been time to leave before I was ready to...but that was what I was here for. Raise money.

Focus, X.

Focus.

I hadn't been able to get the song together. I'd been writing about her before I flew out, so I did some of my less explicit work, ending with *Trying Again*. It was a crowd favorite, especially with this crowd. For all the money and polish here, I knew that a lot of the people had come from pasts like mine, and the Y had saved them.

A lot hadn't, but since they donated their money, I didn't judge.

Olivia drifted over to me, and I marveled again that such a beautiful, grown-up, non-groupie wanted to be with me.

Maybe I should be marveling that I wanted to be with her? She wasn't my usual type.

Before I could get into that more, she'd joined us.

"Hey," she said to me.

"Hey. Olivia, this is Paul Catterton. He's on the board of the Y."

She held out her hand to shake his. "Olivia Meroux. It's a pleasure. This is really a wonderful event, and I understand it raises a lot for the organization," she ended with a smile.

Paul smiled back. "It does, but honestly, we can't take a lot of credit for that. Having Xavier here every year has something to do with it. People love to see him, and hear his story."

I shrugged as they both turned to me. "I don't know why. It's not that different from anyone else's," I said.

"Oh, I don't agree with that," Olivia shook her head. "You've overcome a lot, it's true. But you turned it into something pretty tremendous, don't you think?"

"Well, I do, but I don't expect anyone else to," I said with a laugh.

"Give yourself more credit," Paul said.

I liked him. He was a kind man, and he backed it up with both the things he did, as well as where he threw money. I noticed that kind of thing. So many people in the entertainment world said one thing and did something entirely different.

"How did you get involved with the Y, Paul?" Olivia asked.

"My family has vineyards, and we employ a lot of temporary workers. I grew up working with them, and I noticed that people brought their kids with them, and the kids had nowhere to go. So when I got to be an adult who wasn't told to sit down and shut up," he grinned at us both, and it made him look a lot younger, "I asked my dad why we didn't have anything for them to do. We opened a Y in our town and arranged for our workers to be shuttled there. The rest is history," he shrugged.

Olivia beamed at him, and I saw his shoulders straighten a little. It made me want to pull her to me and show him that she was mine, but I stopped myself.

Casual, I'd said. I had to stand by what I'd asked for.

"That's a fantastic story," she said. "What a great thing you did."

"Are you involved in the Y in any way?" He asked. He'd made the switch from a guy telling a story to a guy on the board.

I could also tell that he didn't want to brag about himself.

"No, I have to confess I haven't. In my company, we

work with the local university and bring in interns, but I haven't done anything more. Which makes me feel bad," she confessed.

"So how did you end up coming to this?" Paul asked.

"I asked her to," I said. "Looking to lure more people in."

Paul laughed. "Good thinking. Well, Olivia, if you need any help, you can contact the local Y, and if you'd like," he fished into his pocket, "You can contact me for ideas on how to work with them. I'm outstanding at putting people to work for my favorite charity."

Olivia laughed as she took the card and tucked it into her purse. "Thank you. I might end up calling you. I honestly am not sure, even after talking to people here, how I could help, but I would like to."

I could tell that she was sincere, and I felt proud of her.

"Then my work here is done," Paul said.

A woman came up to him, putting a hand on his shoulder. "Darling? Could I possibly steal you away, since I seem to have arrived at the right moment?" She smiled at first Olivia and then me.

"Of course," he sighed with a lot of exaggeration. "Duty calls."

They both smiled at us, and the woman led him away.

"You don't have to volunteer for anything," I said. I didn't want her to feel that she had to cave to pressure. It was pretty intense at these sort of things.

"I know. But I'm really impressed with a number of the people I've spoken with. You're not the only success story," she said.

"I'm the best one," I said, leaning down to whisper in her ear. "At least, the best one you need to be concerned about."

As I stood up, I could see the blush race across her cheeks. I loved it.

"Well, yes, that's entirely true. But it's really inspiring, and I'd like to be part of it if I can."

"Oh, you will be, the minute you make the first call. They won't let you go. But—" I held up a hand, "It's actually a good place to put some time in."

"Yeah, you don't seem much like the kind of person that would give them time or effort otherwise," she said.

"Nope. I don't have enough time for all the things I want to do as it is."

"Like what?"

"Well," I leaned down again, "Like right now, I'd like to be doing what we were doing before we came here."

The blush deepened.

"Hey, I'm following your lead, Mr. Big Shot."

I rolled my eyes. "Yeah, yeah, I know. I'm good like that. Shoot myself in the foot every time."

"Well, what do you want to do about it?"

"We can't leave yet," I groaned quietly. "But you can bet we'll take a long way home when we do."

livia

I smiled, making the polite goodbyes expected of me as I walked out of the hotel with Xavier. Even though he'd been whispering naughty things to me at what seemed like every moment, we'd maintained our casual stance.

Unless you counted the permanent blush on my face. I'd gone to the restroom, and when I looked in the mirror,

I was shocked at myself. My cheeks bloomed, and my eyes were bright. Almost unnaturally so.

"It's just fun, no strings," I muttered to myself. "Just fun. Fun. Remember that." I had no idea what this was, but I'd told myself to let go and enjoy it, and I would, even if I had to keep reminding myself. I couldn't weigh this—and myself—down with expectations that had no place here.

In spite of the misgivings the normal, everyday Olivia was having, the me that was present right here right now was completely occupied with what would happen next.

Tonight had been hard. I'd done as Xavier requested, and put on my business face, keeping things casual between us. But even though it had been his wish, he'd regretted it, and spent a great deal of the evening making me regret it also.

It also made me absolutely wild with desire for him. I just wanted to be with him, naked, skin-to-skin, and never get up.

I couldn't remember the last time I'd had such a hunger for another person. Which was a whole other kettle of fish, but one I chose to let lie for the time being. I didn't need to be stirring it up. I wanted to enjoy the week and not get lost in my own fussing.

As we got closer to the car, Xavier took my hand.

"That was probably the longest event I've ever gone to," he said. "All I could think about was getting out of there, and being with you."

"This is all your fault," I started.

"Yeah, yeah. It is. But I plan on making up for my mistake. Into the car, Ms. Livvie," he grinned at me as the car came up.

How he could tell it was ours, I had no idea, but then, I'd not been paying attention as we'd left the hotel lobby.

As Xavier opened the door for me, not waiting for the driver, his grin turned feral. It made my skin shiver in anticipation of what was to come.

What I hoped was to come.

Besides me, I mean.

What was he doing to me? I never thought like this!

Once we were in, Xavier raised the divider, so we had a little privacy and then held his arms out to me. "Join me?" He asked.

I loved that he asked. Just like he had gotten two rooms for us. If you looked at his work persona, you'd never guess he was like this. Even though we'd spent the entire morning in bed.

I scooted over, and once I was close, he wrapped his arms around me and pulled me to him. He leaned into my hair and inhaled.

"I didn't realize what torture it would be to keep my hands off you."

"Hey, you're the one who said it was all business!" I laughed at his scowl.

"Yeah, well, you hadn't let me see you like you did this morning." He kissed me to punctuate his thoughts on the matter.

I felt like my breath was sucked away from me by being so near him, kissing him. It was like a drug. At the same time, I felt my entire body flare into life, even more than I had been trying to not look like a sex-crazed fan at the event. He took my breath away and then gave it back to me in the next moment, even sweeter than when it was originally mine.

"How long is this ride?" I asked when I'd gotten a little bit of my breath back.

"Too damn long," he growled.

Inspired, I pushed myself off him, using my hands on

his chest. "Then you can sit there and experience what you put me through, buster," I said, laughing at the expression on his face.

He wasn't pleased.

"And what was that?"

"Oh, that I wanted to do this every time I saw your profile," I whispered, running the tips of my fingers down his face, from his forehead to his chin. When I moved to touch his lips, he opened his mouth and took two of them between his teeth, biting gently.

I thought my thighs might just melt into the seat of the car.

"Ah ah ah," I said, trying not to melt. "No biting… yet," I added, fluttering my lashes at him.

I let my fingers run down his neck, reaching the collar of his shirt. I tugged it to the side and leaned in to kiss his collarbone. He let his head fall back and moaned. I saw the skin on his chest ripple into goosebumps. The sight of them made me smile. To know that I was doing this to him —to XTC—made me feel powerful and strong.

I licked the dimple at the base of his throat, loving how warm his skin felt. He radiated heat normally, and he was hotter now. Hotter in every way, I thought, resisting the urge to giggle.

"You're killing me," he said, not looking up.

"No, you're not going to die. You're not allowed—you have to live up to all those naughty," I bit one corner of his lip, "naughty things you were teasing me about today."

"Woman, you won't know what happened to you…" he stopped and kissed me, cutting off any further conversation.

I curled into him, enjoying the feel of his lips on mine, the little nips of his teeth when they came into contact with mine. He didn't hold back, didn't hesitate. He was all in.

So was I.

We both stopped when the divider dropped a little.

"Sir, we're here," the driver's voice came through.

"Finally," Xavier muttered. He opened the door and pulled me out behind him, not letting go of my hand.

That was comforting. I felt a little bereft at being so far away from him, even for just a moment. *Easy, Liv,* I told myself. *Easy.*

Xavier said something to the driver, but I didn't hear it. He didn't stop walking as he spoke, and before I knew it, we were in the hotel.

Everything went by in a blur, lights and flashing, nothing coming into focus for me. I knew we were heading for the elevator, but I felt so dazed...so...something. Not entirely connected to anything other than Xavier's hand tethering me to here and now.

I was glad he was leading. We made it to the elevator, and he hit a button, snugging me next to him as he did so.

His other hand came down and cupped my face, smoothing my hair back.

"You look beautiful tonight," he breathed.

I could smell the whiskey he'd had during dinner. It smelled marvelous. Made him smell marvelous.

Then he kissed me again, slower this time, and let the hand holding my waist slide down to my backside, cupping me and pulling me next to him so that I could feel him.

Oh, my dear and happy lord, I couldn't wait to feel him next to me, no clothing in sight...he rubbed himself against me, and I let out a sigh of my own.

"That has to be the best thing I've heard all night, Livvie," he whispered in my mouth.

"Even better than that guy we heard singing tonight?" I laughed a little, amazed I was able to speak coherently. I felt like I was in some kind of daze like I used to be at the end of a long night out with my girlfriends in college. But this time it wasn't Sex on the Beach shooters that were making me woozy.

It was sex. Sex and Xavier.

Sex and X, I thought. And the thought made me laugh.

"What's so funny?"

"Ask me later," I reached up and pulled his head down, wanting to kiss him again. The door chimed.

"We are finally here," he said.

Keeping his arm around me, we walked to the suite. He opened the door, and as he walked in, turned to look at me over his shoulder.

"You ready?"

I pushed him inside all the way with one hand, the other on my zipper. "I might could have been naked already, but you're too busy talking." I let my drawl get real deep.

The door slammed as he yanked me forward, spinning me around and pulling apart the back of my dress so that the zipper had no choice but to part. I held the top of my dress to me, and spun around.

Then, facing him, I dropped it.

"Time to make good on all that trash talk, Mr. All That," I grinned.

He scooped me up and carried me into the room I'd been sleeping in, the one we'd spent all morning in earlier today.

The dress was on the floor before my butt bounced on the bed.

At this point, I doubted even Momma's favorite tailor could save it.

I didn't care.

*X*avier

I woke, stretching my arms up over my head. The sunlight came into the room through a gap in the curtains, and for a moment, I forgot where I was.

Then I looked over.

She was still here, curled onto her side, back to me. Her naked, pink, rosy back, the back that I'd kissed from top to bottom more than once last night. The curve of it fascinated me, and I ran my hand softly down her spine, thrilled that I could.

I'd never woken with another woman like this before. Not ever.

Usually, I was looking for my ride, or a ride for her, or some kind of way out. Now? I didn't even want her to wake up. I wanted to look at her, and wonder what the hell I'd done to get so lucky as to meet up with her.

Lucky…I was supposed to meet her. Wasn't I? Something lingered on the edge of my brain, thought, something I was supposed to remember…something about Olivia?

I hated it when I couldn't catch the thought I wanted. It didn't happen often, but when it did, it was usually something like this. Something big.

I stopped my fingers at the base of her spine, loving the little dip I could feel. She stirred, and I didn't move. I wanted a little more time to think about this, about her. I was missing something, there was something just out of reach of conscious thought.

This was big. I was always an all-in kind of guy. When I got involved with someone, I was involved. It was why when I was done, I was really done. I'd never gone halfway with my relationships.

And even with that, this thing with Olivia was even bigger, more. If I didn't watch out, I could fall in love with this woman. She was funny and witty. That had come through in all the time we spent texting. She was strong, and she wasn't looking for me to be a knight and rescue her, not in any way. She had her own business, her own life.

But would she fit into mine? Would I fit into hers? Would her mom like me? The woman sounded scary as hell. Would Tibby like Olivia?

Yes.

I knew that without even having to think about it. Olivia was a lot like Tibby, although thankfully I didn't think about her like a sister like I did with Tib.

Olivia stirred, and from the floor, I heard my cell ringing. I wanted to ignore it, but when I did that, people got nervous. I sighed, and got up, hoping I would just miss the call.

No such luck. It was Tibby, and she'd just call me again

until I answered. I hit the green button, and walked out into the living room, closing the door behind me.

"Hey," I said.

"Where are you?"

She was at work. She had that voice on.

"Still in San Francisco. What's up?"

"What the hell did you say to your manager?"

"My ex-manager? Well," I sat down, thinking about it. "That he was not my mother, thank God, and that giving me hell for hanging out with my friends was not his business, particularly as the people I was with were family, not friends. And why the hell did he have a problem with me being in a gay bar? His answers were kind of fucked, Tib. He's a serious homophobe. Probably a gay basher in his free time." That wasn't entirely fair, but his ranting had started to give me the creeps, and it was why I told him to take his bullshit and piss off, and that my attorney would be in touch. "Why'd you call him?"

"He called me."

"Oh, well, hell. Guess he's pissed?"

"Yes. He's carrying on about you breaking contact, and all sorts of shit that is going to be nothing more than a giant pain in my ass," Tibby sighed dramatically.

Making sure I knew what a pain in the ass I was for making her deal with this.

I looked up to see Olivia come out, wearing only her PJ top, and I grinned at her. She smiled back, still sleepy, and I felt a rush of—I didn't even know what it was—happiness? Come over me.

She made me happy. When was the last time that had happened?

She headed for the bar, bending over to give me a fantastic view while she looked in the fridge for a drink. As she pulled out a bottle of water, she shot a flirty look over her shoulder.

It made me hard instantly. As I wasn't wearing anything, it was pretty noticeable. Olivia's cat-like smile turned into a big grin, and she waltzed over to stand behind the couch and lean down to the ear not attached to the phone.

"Come back in when you're done," she said, swiping the cool bottle across my chest.

And without a backward glance, she walked back into her room, and partially shut the door.

Holy.

Shit.

"What?" I said, aware that Tibby's voice had risen in my ear.

"You're not even listening, are you?"

Great. Tibby was pissed, and all I could do was think about the fact that I thought my dick might get up and walk away, so badly did I want to follow Olivia.

"I got…uh…distracted for a minute. Keep your hair on. Tell me again, and I am listening."

She was so used to me she didn't even keep up the yelling.

"How do you want to handle him when he files a breach of contract suit?"

"Tell him that I have our conversation on tape, and while I know I can't legally use it, I can let everyone know the way he talked about the gay community, which will certainly hit him in his professional side. And that me letting his bigot ass go quietly is a fucking favor, and should he not wish to see it that way, and keep bitching, I'll do a nice interview with HuffPo or something like that, to let them know how disappointed I am in my former manager."

Silence on the other end, and then Tibby burst out laughing. "I love you, X. You're a bigger bitch than I am."

"You know it, sister," I said, grinning at her through the phone. "Anything else?"

"What, you have a hot date or something?"

"Something like that."

"And you took my call? Hang up and stop being a jerk."

"Later, Tib." I hit the red button and dropped the phone. There was no one else I needed to talk to just this instant so they could leave a message.

I hurried to the room door and kicked it open. "You better be…" my voice trailed away.

Olivia lay on the bed, the top unbuttoned so that I could see the valley between her breasts, and only one button done where the bottom of the shirt hit her thighs. That was inched up so I could also see the shadow of her legs together, and she was kind of curled on the bed the way women do when they are feeling sexy.

Holy shit did it work on her. She wasn't the usual "type" of woman I always seemed to go for – she was petite and dark-haired, but she was without a doubt the sexiest woman I had ever seen. Ever.

She was drinking from the water bottle as my eyes met hers. Then after she swallowed, which made my heart beat in my ears, she moved the bottle away from her lips and dribbled the water down her chest.

"Oops," she said. "I think I spilled on myself. You'd better come over here and help me clean it up."

livia

I'm not sure whether or not his feet touched the ground in the millisecond it took for him to join me on the bed. He snatched the bottle out of my hand and pulled me lower on the bed. Then he straddled me, holding the water bottle over me.

Then he sat there, letting me see him in all his glory, and took a long drink of water himself.

"Well, now, Ms, Livvie, I can't drink this all, now can I?"

"Can you?"

"Nope. Because I need to take care of this," he leaned forward and moved the top so that my breasts were exposed. Then he tilted the bottle and poured water on them.

The cold water made them hard, and damn it, made me jump.

Two could play this game.

I rubbed my hand across my breasts, tweaking the nipples as I did so, not taking my eyes from him. Using both hands, I placed mine on his chest, and let them drag down, small drops of water racing towards his waist.

I only stopped once my hands reached his Mr. Happy, and then, I slowly dragged my wet fingers from the base to the tip.

Xavier groaned.

I have never heard such a sexy sound in my entire life.

"That's it. No more Mr. Nice Guy," he said, leaning down to kiss me.

I wrapped my arms around him, falling into him the way I wanted to, ignoring everything but him.

He leans over and reaches off the bed and then before I have time to complain that the water still on me is getting cold, he's on top of me again, warming me, enveloping me.

When we're done, when we've both fallen over that incredible cliff again, and together, he leans his forehead against mine.

"You are one amazing woman, you know that?"

I smile, and kiss him, gently, no teeth this time.

"You're pretty amazing yourself."

He doesn't answer, but I'm not just doing that parrot thing that people seem to do when they're first getting to know each other. He really is amazing. He's been nothing but kind to me, nothing but decent—which you might not expect, given who he is, what he does. It's not the image he puts out.

But with me—and I find that I'm on the lookout for— what? Insult? Assumptions? He's nothing but the kind of guy you want to bring home to your mom.

As Xavier moves off of me and goes into the bath- room, I lay still, stunned.

Am I really considering taking him home to Momma? Like, maybe after I'm divorced? Because I am technically still married.

And can I trust him? He's doing great now, but just like the parrot thing, people are usually on their best behavior when they first get together. I don't have a lot of experi- ence with that, as I married my college boyfriend, but that's what I notice with some of my friends. And all the romance books I read.

Probably not the best place to be taking advice from, I laugh a little at my own silliness.

Xavier returns from the bathroom, and crawls back into the bed, pulling the blankets up and snuggling next to me.

"I think you're trying to kill me, Livvie."

I wrap my arm around him, wanting to feel him close to me. "Oh, quit whining. There are worse ways to go."

He laughs next to my chest, and I can feel it reverberate through me. Dear lord. He's everywhere. Normally, this would make me feel claustrophobic, but with Xavier, it just feels…good.

A little later, he stirs and looks up at me. "You want to go out and eat? We're going to need to do that sometime."

"Can we order food and just stay in?" I find that I don't want to go out, because that would mean I needed to be on, be his date, or friend, or whatever. And probably put on clothes, which I don't have any desire to do either.

"Perfect answer."

I sit up. "I'll get the menu." I find that while I wasn't thinking about it before, the mention of food makes me feel like I'm starving.

*X*avier

I watch her get out of bed and pad to the other room in search of the menu. I like watching her walk. I like watching her do almost anything. Well, everything so far. She seems really comfortable with me in spite of the fact we just met, and neither of us has any clothes.

This is all new to me.

I know that sounds insane, given all the relationships that are littered throughout my past, but they all follow a certain pattern if you will. She's a fan, I like her, we hook up, I'm sort of comfortable, she loves being on my arm, then we're in love, and then it ends.

The whole reason I married Marcia was that she and I

could actually have fun together. Generally, I have a distance in my relationships. I don't really like that idea now that I'm looking at it, but it's the truth.

Olivia is both awesome and scary because I've never been with someone like her, someone so normal. *Someone who is not a groupie*, I hear Tibby's voice in my head.

Another sad truth.

Although there's nothing wrong with fans, even if they get a bit excited. I wouldn't be shit without my fans. I know that, and I never forget it.

But maybe I shouldn't consider them the dating pool?

If I do this right, if I don't mess it up—even thinking about that is weird. I never worry about this kind of shit.

But if I don't, maybe I won't need to look at my fans for a dating pool. This feels real.

Really real. It's why I took so long to call her.

Now we're having sex.

That's not completely out of the ordinary for me, but I know it is for her.

And she's dealing with divorce. I haven't even thought about that, and maybe I should.

Olivia returns reading the menu and then slides back onto the bed next to me.

"I wasn't hungry before, but I am now."

I grin. "That's a good thing. Burning off a lot of energy. You'd better eat well. I think you're going to need more energy."

She laughs. "I hope so. Stop so that I can focus, and let's get some food going."

We order the food, laughing at each other as we do so.

When it comes, we sit in bed, still naked—which I really like—and alternate between watching TV and feeding one another bits of food.

It's the most erotic thing I've ever done.

It scares the hell out of me.

What if I mess this up?

What if she's not really this amazing?

What if she doesn't feel the same?

But after we eat, and the trays are moved out into the other room, we fall back into one another's arms, and have sex all throughout the night.

I fall asleep with her, and then we wake up reaching for one another again.

Too soon, it's morning.

The worries of the night fade as the sun comes up, although I know they're still there.

But now it's time to go home.

livia

*O*n the plane, we're both quiet. We hold hands and talk a little. I noticed that we didn't really talk about a lot of the things you're supposed in the first date area—religion, do you want kids, who's your pick for president, that kind of thing.

He'd told me a little about his childhood, and since I could see it was painful, I didn't push. I told him a little about Royce, and thankfully, he didn't really push either.

Which is why, as I stared out the window, I thought it was weird that I liked him so much. I didn't really know him. He didn't know me. Not really. I'd spent ten years with someone, and that was—I stopped myself.

I'd thought I'd known Royce, thought I understood him. Even though I could predict how he'd react. I'd been wrong. So wrong, the hurt of it still bled within. So what did I know, really?

Because everything I thought I knew was wrong. I shook my head to clear the thoughts that were creeping up and getting ready to pounce. I had enjoyed this trip with Xavier, but I found that right now, I really wanted to get home and talk with Momma. I didn't know which way was up anymore, and she would ground me in a heartbeat.

"You okay?"

Xavier was looking over at me with concern on his face.

"Yeah, I'm just thinking about the to-do list waiting for me. You know," I smiled, not wanting to get into my thoughts.

He smiled back, squeezing my hand as he did so. "I hear you. I have a list a mile long at all times, and I have to get ready for my tour."

Oh, no. If Xavier was going to be touring a lot soon, that would make anything else between us tougher. "When does it start?"

"Not for another four months or so. But I like to get my song lists organized, and I have to go over all the plans for each stop."

"Don't you have someone who does that?"

He laughed. "I have a lot of someones, but I just fired the guy who manages them. I have to find a new manager, and since that may take a while, I'll get started on the managing myself. I've done it before. What's on your list?" He changed the subject.

"Oh, get my momma off the warpath—she and clients are not meant to be. I handle them. With me being gone a couple of weeks ago, and then this week, there's been a lot more interaction with her, and she doesn't have my…well, diplomatic touch."

"I don't know that I could see you being mean."

"I can be stern, but there's no need to ever be mean to

a client unless they are just horrible. Most of the people who come to me are referred, and like I told you, they want my help. I don't generally see horrible people."

"When can I see you again?"

I thought about it. I was delighted that he'd asked, but I was nervous about making a commitment before I got home and saw how things were.

"I don't know. I need to see—"

Xavier held up a hand. "I know, I probably do too. Can we still text like we have been?"

I opened my mouth to answer when I looked up at him. He looked nervous, looked almost unsure. How was that possible? One of the most famous guys in the world. One of the, in my opinion, most good-looking men I'd ever seen. He was nervous about whether or not I wanted to see him? Talk with him?

It just didn't seem real. Even though the tired feeling I had from not getting enough sleep and the way my body felt after what was essentially two days of smoking hot sex was very real.

"You'd better," I said playfully.

He lifted up my hand and kissed it. "Wouldn't miss it."

I thought he might say something else, but at that moment, the steward came in, and Xavier turned to me, beaming.

"Community coffee café au lait, just for you!"

He'd remembered. I'd forgotten all about it, but he'd remembered.

I take the cup, my hands trembling. I could feel the tears welling at the corners of my eyes, and I didn't want Xavier or the steward to see them.

"Let's see what's so special about this stuff," Xavier took a cup for himself.

No one would believe that I was sitting here trying not to cry over a cup of coffee.

avier

*a*s the plane landed, I felt a weight settle in the pit of my stomach. Our little vacation was over, and it was back to real life. I couldn't believe how much I liked this woman, how much I wanted with her, from her.

I'd never worried about rejection, and now…I was like a teenaged boy asking the Homecoming Queen to prom. Worry all over the place. Like a rash.

Once we'd taxied to a stop, we stepped off the plane together, and the car was waiting.

"Hey hot momma, can I give you a lift?"

She put her arm around my waist. "I'd like that."

She'd been quiet since we'd had coffee. I don't know why, but it made me uneasy. I could see why she liked the stuff—and she'd said she loved that I remembered—but I still felt less-than-perfect at the moment.

If there was anything constant about my life, I avoided that not perfect moment. I hadn't been kidding when I'd told Olivia that you throw enough money and/or lawyers at a problem, and it goes away. Even my mom went away, sort of. The lawyers stepped in when the money itself wouldn't be enough.

But the coffee was a good thing, right?

Maybe this was why I didn't have relationships with normal women. I didn't get them, and after a while, I stopped trying.

I found that I didn't want to give up on this one. Not yet.

"I'm going to miss you," I told her as we settled into the car.

"I am going to miss you too, which is strange as we only just met."

"Hey, when you know something is right…" I stopped, looking out the window. Where had I heard that? Why did it feel like that was supposed to mean a lot more than just a cliché to me?

"Yes, it has been very right," Olivia turned my face back to her and kissed me. "I haven't enjoyed myself so much in a long time. Thank you for taking me with you."

"No, thank you for coming with me," I said quickly. "I always have fun doing these gigs, but this has been the best one."

We both grinned, and I knew she was thinking about the sex. Just like I was.

All too soon, we were at her front door.

"I'm not trying to be rude, but I think I should skip walking you to your door. Unless you're ready to out us," I said.

I couldn't say why my heartbeat sped up when I said that.

"What? Your perfect gentleman score just dropped a little!"

"I have a score?" I asked.

"Oh, yes indeed."

"And how is my score, Ms. Livvie?" I kissed her, holding her tightly to me.

"Oh…well," she said after a moment, "Pretty good."

I loved that she sounded all breathless. Like I'd just kissed her senseless.

It was better than any drug.

"I'll talk to you tonight?" I asked.

"Yes." She looked like she wanted to say more, but the door opened that moment, and I could see the driver standing with his hand out and her bag on the curb behind him.

I blew her a kiss, and she slid out of the car. I watched the driver walk her up to the door. As he came back toward the car, she looked over her shoulder and blew me a little kiss, and then was inside before I could respond.

I couldn't wait to see her again.

livia

Once the door closed, I leaned against it, taking deep breaths. I could breathe again, but I wasn't sure I was happy about it.

That had been the most amazing time of my life, and that included the honeymoon for my now nearly dead marriage.

Never had I been with a man who was so easily accepting. That was it—that was what was so different about Xavier. He accepted me. He didn't care about all the things I'd been worried about with Royce—things I knew that Royce would complain about.

He didn't worry about anything. Or if he did, because everyone had some worry, he kept it to himself and didn't make it my burden.

My eyes, drooping until now, flew open. That was it. Everything up until now had been my burden. I had accepted it and spent the last ten years trying to make Royce happy by taking on the things that irritated him. As well as the things that irritated me. And the house, and my business.

While he fucked another woman.

I couldn't carry anyone, not anymore. Not even Xavier. And I was pretty inspired about him.

The door wasn't the best place to rest, but all these revelations coupled with the past several days left me feeling exhausted.

All while there was still a call to Margarite Meroux to be made. I sighed. No sense in waiting. Pushing myself off the door, I headed for my room and flopped down on the bed before pulling out my phone.

Xavier had already texted me.

'I miss you already, super southern lady. Can't wait to see you again. Thanks for coming with me. ;)'

He was so earthy in his humor. I liked it, although I found it took me back a little. I guess my momma rubbed off on me more than I thought.

'Thanks for inviting me. It was the best weekend I've had in ages. I can't wait to see you either.'

He replied faster than I thought he would.

'Let's plan on this weekend, k?'

'Sat? Sun?'

'Both'

'Greedy'

'You know it. Let me get back and see what shit I have to take care of and then I'll call k?'

'OK. A call? You sure you want to get all serious like that?'

I couldn't help teasing him.

'It's a risk, but I guess I can take it. If you're too much, I can hang up and hide.'

I burst out laughing.

'Right. I don't think you hide from anything.'

'Not much. Get some rest. I want you ready for anything this weekend.'

'Sounds enticing.'

'It's meant to. Night.'

'Night, Xavier.'

I almost added a kiss, but then I hesitated. Then I got mad at myself. Why was I hesitating? Because I didn't trust myself anymore.

But a kissy text certainly wasn't going to go further than I already had this week. To hell with it.

'XOXOXO'

He didn't respond immediately, and I felt my stomach drop out and land on the floor. I set my phone down and closed my eyes. After what seemed like an eternity, it buzzed next to me.

'Tease. I expect all those and more when I see you.'

'Deal.'

Another pause and then he responded.

'X's and O's to U 2.'

Could he be any sweeter? I had to pinch myself, he seemed so unreal in his sheer awesomeness sometimes.

But there was no time to sit and swoon. I had to call Momma.

Dialing her number, I braced myself for the interrogation.

She answered on the first ring. "Sugar bean, I'm so glad to hear from you! I was beginning to get worried, but I called the Ritz this morning, and they put me through to your room. Did you get my message?"

"Why didn't you call my cell, Momma?"

"Because I wanted to see if you were still in the hotel, or if your mystery man had carried you off somewhere."

Sometimes, it didn't pay to ask questions.

"I told you he was not like that!"

"Yes, darlin', but you're not in the best place to judge. And I looked up your Mr. Xavier Reede. Really, Olivia?" Her voice dropped.

"What does that mean?" I immediately felt like I had to put up the defenses.

"A rapper? And one from a troubled background? That ex-wife of his? All those girlfriends? I'm not sure any of them owned an entire outfit that covered the basic body parts."

"Well, there's a reason she's an ex, and that all those other women are also exes, Momma. I am not one of them, and he seems just fine with that."

"Did you sleep with him?"

"Is that any of your business?" I was pissed now.

"Yes, darlin', it is. You're barely separated, and your whole life has been turned on its ass. All the things you thought were good and right are neither, and while Royce is a grade A bastard, I know this hurts. When have you ever been interested in this sort of man?"

"I have been a fan of his since college, Momma."

Silence, and then, "You listened to his music in my home?"

"Yes, Momma, and somehow, I managed to not be a devil-worshipping slut!"

"There is no need for such language, or that tone, missy," she began.

"No, Momma, you are absolutely right. I cannot believe you're making assumptions about me, about Xavier, and you haven't asked me one thing that might be based on fact versus something that you can read in some tabloid rag! As if we don't deal with that sort of nonsense regularly from our clients! You know how much lies and trash are put out there as truth! I can't believe you'd assume it of me, even though you don't know Xavier! I'll talk to you later, Momma."

I hit End on the phone. My anger chased away the earlier feelings of exhaustion. I got up and collected my bag, muttering to myself as I emptied it and sorted laundry.

Then I went around the house, cleaning up and making sure that things were in place for me to start back to my regular life.

Damn her. I'd have to see Momma at work tomorrow. She'd be fuming, and ready for a fight because I sure wasn't talking to her again today. I'd left my phone in my room. She could leave another message since she was so fond of them.

I threw myself on the couch and turned on the TV. This was going to be a day of camping out and watching all my favorite chick flicks.

To hell with the world right now. Well, at least the world that had Marguerite Meroux in it.

avier

$\mathcal{I}$ thought about her all the way back to the plane, and then all the way back to New York.

For the first time, I wondered if I should introduce her to Tibby. I'd never bothered before, not in making time to set it up or anything.

But Olivia was different.

And she'd texted me kisses and hugs. I wondered if she got the meaning of my X's and O's comment. When I'd been working on the song about her last week, I kept hearing a refrain of X, X, X—X's and O's in my head. Part of the chorus. But along the way, X's and O's had become the title of the song. I liked it. The more I thought about it, the more I felt it was right.

Like her.

The thought startled me.

I knew this had been moving differently than anything else I could remember, but I hadn't moved past that.

Until now. Was this really something that I could say, *This is it?* This is the one for me?

Did it happen like that? Because as far as I knew, it didn't. Even Tib, who had the best marriage I'd ever seen, had gone through hell with dumb ass guys.

Like I hadn't?

As the plane took off, I couldn't sit still. I got up, walking back and forth in the small cabin. Byrne came in.

"Can I get you something, sir?"

I held up a hand. "No—wait, yeah. How about some of that fancy coffee?"

He smiled, and I grinned. I wasn't a coffee person in that I went to the local shop and engaged in a dissertation to get a cup of coffee. Regular, cream, sugar. That was me. But I found that I really liked Olivia's coffee. What was it? Community?

"What's so special about that coffee, Byrne?" If anyone would know, he would. And I could ask him without feeling like a turnip that just fell off the truck. He was a foodie, and ever on the alert to enlighten and share with the rest of us. It's why all four of us kept him as the steward no matter which one of us had the plane.

"Community is made in New Orleans, and this flavor has chicory in it. Chicory is a root that the French first used to make their coffee last longer. Café du Monde, which is a famous café in New Orleans, makes their café au lait with chicory, and it's delicious. This would be better with beignets, but it stands on its own."

"Do I want to know why there is something other than coffee in coffee?"

"We have some time before we land," he said with a small laugh.

"No, no, I'll just have some coffee, and consider myself as educated as I need to be for the time being," I said.

"Of course." He turned toward the galley.

Normally, I enjoyed talking with him. I grew up on Hamburger Helper, so it was nice to have someone I could ask about food that didn't come out of a box. Not that there was anything wrong with Hamburger Helper—it was just that I didn't realize, until Tibby started inviting me over for dinner, that there were dinners that could be cooked from scratch.

Speaking of which, I wanted to call her. I needed her advice. I hoped she wasn't too mad at me over the whole manager mess.

Since it was the middle of the day, she ought to be in her office. She answered on the second ring.

"What?"

"You don't sound like someone who just had a blissfully naked honeymoon."

"Stay away from my nakedness," she snapped.

"Seriously, Tib, is this a bad time? I can call back."

She was silent for a moment. "What's wrong?"

"What do you mean?"

"Who are you and what did you do to my friend X?"

"What the hell?"

"That's more like it. Since when do you care about my mood enough to change the subject?"

"Are you saying I'm kind of a dick?"

"Oh, just with me. So what's wrong?"

"You first. You okay?"

"I need to get together with you sometime, but other than that, I'm good. Great, in fact."

"Married life good?"

"It's fan-fucking-tastic, X," she said, and her voice lightened. "I didn't realize I could be this happy."

"I am really happy for you, Tib. I mean that."

"Since I'm all sorted over here, what's up, X?"

"Uh…" I found that I wasn't sure where to start.

"I already know this is somehow involving a woman. So let's start there."

"How did you know?" I hadn't said much to her.

"Because it's always a woman with you, and you had even worse examples of how to have a relationship than I did," she sighed.

I'd never thought of it like that, but she was right. While Tibby and her family literally saved me, Tibby hadn't had it much easier. Her parents drank too, but they were able to function, and they didn't beat the hell out of their kids. So it was a big step up for me.

But their relationship wasn't what anyone who was remotely sane would call healthy.

"Stop stewing," she said. "What's up? What's going on? You didn't get married again, did you?"

"Hell no," I said reflexively.

Her sigh of relief was audible.

"I met someone last week."

"Where?"

"Will you let me talk?"

"Oh, please, do." Her sarcasm dripped through the phone.

"I met her when I was flying back from firing Preston."

"We need to talk about that, too. I have news, but not right now. Carry on," she interjected.

"I asked her out, and then I wussed out, and didn't call her until she'd left New York. She wasn't happy, but she didn't tell me to fuck off, so we started chatting. Just texting, nothing big. But she's funny, and there's something about her—so, well, I invited her to San Francisco."

"You took her to the benefit?"

I could hear the surprise. Tibby knew that I kept my involvement in the Y low key. I'm not exactly the best role model for kids. I know that, and I'm cool. It's another reason I don't advertise the things I do with them.

"I did, and I asked her to be casual. She was, and she was brilliant."

"What does she do?"

"Some kind of consulting for… I don't know. People who are trying to get ahead? She was kind of vague. She said she works with people in the Grand Old Opry."

"Where's she from?"

"Nashville. Anyway, we had a great time, and I just dropped her off at her place."

"And you're calling me because?"

"I don't know! She's not like anyone else I've ever dated—"

"You're dating her? And you just met her?"

Was I? "I would like to date her, but I don't know if she wants that yet."

"It's good that one of you has sense," Tibby said.

"She's got her own business, and she's in the middle of a divorce—"

"Oh dear baby Jesus, please do not get involved in that! If she's still legally married, you can be named in some states!"

"Well, it would certainly toss a big monkey wrench into the rumors I'm just hiding out in the closet, refusing to come out, wouldn't it?" I grinned.

"Or make them worse. That doesn't matter, X. You do not need to be in the middle of someone else's marriage issues."

"I know. But it's not the middle of anything. He cheated, he bounced, he has a new piece, and he's trying to take Livvie for everything he can."

Silence again, and then, "So she's the one with the money?"

I could practically hear her brain working.

"It sounds like it. She dresses nice. When I met her, she was on her way to a week at the…" what the hell was that place called? "The Red House spa? In New York? Elizabeth something or other?"

Tibby laughed. "You've spent enough money there, although you don't realize it. The Red Door. It's a nice place. A little old lady for her, but a nice place."

"She's not old. She's younger than us, thirty-one."

"X! I'm impressed. She's not right out of college, and she has her own business! You sure the pod people didn't come and take you away?"

"Shut up," I said with no heat.

"So you like her. She sounds the divorce aside, like a nice woman. What's the problem?"

"She's not like anyone else I've met, that's obvious. She is nice, Tibby. I actually thought about asking her if she wanted to go to DC so you could meet her. What if…what if she doesn't want to be part of the circus that's my life?"

I'd said it. Not only did I just commit myself to wanting something more than sex with Olivia, but I also went ahead and said what it was I was afraid of. Out loud.

"If she is as nice as you say, and she doesn't see you, the real you, for who you are, then as nice as she is, she's not the best person for you," Tibby's voice broke into my thoughts.

"Yeah, I'm such a catch."

"You totally are, in spite of being an ass sometimes. Everyone is an ass sometimes. I've been an ass. So has Seth. And Bryant, regularly!" Her voice rose to almost a shout.

Bryant must be nearby. Listening to the two of them in

their office was hilarious. They yelled at each other from their offices. I'd been sitting in the waiting area, and I could hear them, and their staff laughed quietly when it was happening.

"So if she can't see that, then let her go, and move on," Tibby finished.

"Not so easy," I muttered.

"I know, but I know you, and you deserve nothing but the best."

I smiled. 'Thanks, Tibby."

"Don't bring her here, not yet."

"Why?"

"Because if you're still getting to know her, don't drag her to your family for inspection. Let her get more comfortable with the XTC circus."

"That makes sense."

"Now go work. Oh, and I heard from your ex-manager again. I happened to mention your recording, and after some thought, he's decided he'll make a basic statement that you two have decided to part ways and wish each other nothing but the best."

"Yeah, that's what I thought. He was an asshole when I needed him to be cool."

"You over your freak out?"

"Enough. I still need a manager."

"I am working on it," she said, and the business-like tone was back. "Don't nag. I'm cleaning up your mess for free, even though it meant that I had to get out of bed and haul your drunk asses home."

"Come on. You laughed your ass off almost as much as we did."

"No, I did not."

"Liar," I said.

"Whatever. Love you. Go away."

"Love you, too."

She hung up on me.

I felt better.

Best friends did that for you.

 livia

I woke early, probably because I went to sleep early after refusing to get up last night other than for the delivery guy. I'd ignored my phone until I went to bed. A couple of missed calls and texts, but even though I wanted to talk to Xavier, I thought I needed the time alone.

So when I rolled over to turn off my alarm, I picked up the phone. Three calls from Momma, and one from Xavier, along with texts.

'Hey figured u r busy but call me if u want to talk.'

'I miss you even more.'

'Night Ms. Livvie'

Now I felt bad. It wasn't his fault that I was in a foul temper. That honor belonged solely to my mother.

'Sorry that I didn't reply last night. Life got in the way.'

I figured that he didn't need to know that Momma was hating on him.

'Life does that. Everything ok?'

'You know how it is. Life always looks harder after a great vaca.'

'IKR? My list of to do is friggin insane. Talk tonight?'

'Definitely!!'

'Have a great day, Liv XO.'

I loved that he wasn't afraid to show affection even in text. I was glad that I'd taken the chance yesterday—God, was it only yesterday? It felt like a lifetime.

'You too. XO'

There was no getting around it. I needed to get up and face the battle. Since I hadn't called her back, Momma would be on the warpath.

Unlike our normal patterns, I would be armed and waiting for her.

I didn't stop to think about why I was willing to fight her so hard on this.

---

*W*hen I got into the office, it was still early. I'd gotten ready so fast I'd surprised even myself. But I wanted to be waiting for when Momma came in. Hopefully, she was mad enough to haul ass in here too so we could fight before the rest of the staff got in.

I'd made a cup of coffee and was at my desk when I heard the door slam open.

Momma.

"In here," I yelled. Might as well get it over with.

She came in, and boy, she was like a train, huffing, and puffing. I could practically see the steam coming from her.

"Why didn't you call me back?"

"Because I didn't want to talk to you."

Her mouth opened and closed. I forced myself not to laugh, looking down at my coffee. That would only make things worse.

"I did not raise my daughter to talk to me this way."

"I didn't think my mother would be so disrespectful

toward me. I've always done the right thing, always thought of others. Now I am thinking of me, and doing something for me, and I'm not hurting anyone else, and you call me names—"

"I did not call you anything at all!"

"Momma, you insinuated, and girl, please, your insinuations are as good as taking out a billboard."

She glared, and then sat down in the chair across from my desk. When she looked up, she had a rueful smile on her face. "Well, I am good at it, aren't I?"

Oh, no. I knew this sneaky side attack routine. "Yes, you are. And you basically said I was a tramp who wasn't thinking straight or at all." I crossed my arms and glared.

She looked down again, and I knew that I'd won that small round. My mother was very skilled at conversational warfare. It's what made her such a fierce advocate for clients. But I wasn't a client.

When she looked up, the warrior was gone, and she was just Momma. "I did, and I'm sorry, Livvie. I love you. I admit I looked up your…friend. There are a lot of less than…" she stopped, obviously debating what sort of adjective she could choose that would keep the fight tamped down, "Savory tales about him online."

It was my turn to look down now because only Momma could say 'savory tales' and not sound silly.

This was why we didn't fight often, and when we did, it was short-lived.

I looked up to see her studying me.

"I am gonna ask you, and I want you to answer me truthfully, Olivia Anne. Did you sleep with that man?"

I hesitated for a moment, and then said, "Yes. More than once. It was absolutely sinfully amazing. In fact, I can't wait to do it again."

It wasn't often I stunned her, but I did. She opened her

mouth, closed it, and then crossed her fingers together in her lap and looked away.

The urge to laugh got stronger as I thought I heard her take a few deep breaths.

"Sweet baby Jesus, please give me the strength," she muttered.

I gave in and laughed.

"Don't you laugh at me, Olivia Anne! That is no way to start a relationship!" She shook her finger in my direction.

"Momma, I'm not sure there is a relationship. It's too soon," I said, as my brain yelled, *Liar!*

"But you've already slept with him!"

"Momma, I am so glad that I did. So glad. Not just because the sex was amazing but because it was a revelation to be with someone who wasn't a selfish prick."

Which was true. The difference between Xavier and Royce in the bedroom was like being on two different planets. Only the name of what we were doing was the same.

I felt the sting that I'd tolerated such shit for so long, but I shoved it aside and focused on what was in front of me. Time for regrets later.

Her lips pursed, and then she relaxed. "All right. We've got time. Tell me how you met him and how this…whatever happened."

"Shut the door, Momma. That way, we won't have anyone hearing anything that might add to the pearl-clutching already happening in here."

"You hush, girl," she said as she got up and closed my office door. "Now spill."

Lord help me, I spilled. It felt good—delicious, even—to talk about him. I knew that I couldn't say anything to anyone else, because I wasn't sure where this was going, and I didn't want to accidentally say something that would make it into the public arena. Most people aren't jerks, but want to talk to seem important, or have some kind of dish.

Or money. I'd seen that enough with my clients.

So Momma was it. Thank goodness this fight ended easily.

"In spite of everything that is written about him, he sounds like a nice young man."

"He is."

"I am impressed he gives so much to the Y. That's an honorable charity."

"He says they were one of the things that saved him."

"Saved him from what?"

"You didn't read anything about his mother when you were busily snooping?"

She sniffed. "Wait until you have children, Olivia Anne. You'll do things without a second thought where they are concerned."

"You didn't answer the question, Momma."

She glared. "No, not really. I was reading more about his dealings with women."

I burst out laughing. "Yeah, they don't look so hot. But I don't base my thoughts on a person on how they look— look at Royce. You know darn well he's painted me as the bad guy in this whole thing."

Momma rolled her eyes. "That man is trash, as are his people, and always has been."

"That makes no difference at all. He'll make me out to be a ball-busting bitch, who is unnaturally bossy and robs a man of his God-given right to whatever."

"Well, you're not far off, sugar bean."

I knew then that our fight was done. 'Sugar bean' was her name for me. "What do you mean?"

"Well, I've heard some talk."

"From?"

"There's been a bit here."

"Who?" I nearly came out of my chair in outrage.

"Jessie, one of the assistants, is apparently still friends with that hussy."

"Really?" I leaned back. "And Jessie is foolish enough to talk about that *here*? There's a lot more stupid going around than I thought. Well, let's make sure if she starts to dish, we find out. I'll leave that to you, Momma. Just don't do anything illegal."

"I am on it, Livvie. Did Royce call you?"

"He did indeed. Fairly angry, too." I shrugged.

"His attorney is ready to die of shame, I'm thinking. Doesn't stop her from trying to screw you, but she's not proud of her client."

"She said that?"

"No, but we understand one another."

"Even he deserves an attorney, Momma."

"He could have picked one less competent," she grumbled.

"He's not a complete moron," I said. "So what's the latest?"

"Well, he is carrying on like the stuck pig he is over Lloyd's response, but he's having a hard time proving that he was somehow "instrumental" in you and I setting up the business," she used her fingers to assign the air quotes. "Still wants alimony, and now he's saying because you'll inherit a lot from me, he deserves to be supported by you now."

"How can he face himself? It's so smarmy," I said.

"It's who he is, sugar. Smarmy. That's a wonderful word."

"I never thought he was," I said, and I noticed that my voice was small.

It was hitting me again like it had before. I was about

to be divorced, and the man I'd given ten years to—twelve if you count the years we dated—was doing his level best to rob me blind.

When had he begun to hate me? The bigger question was, why hadn't I seen it? I'd been considering asking him to go to counseling right before he dropped the paperwork on me.

In all that was going on, my part in this was the worst. I should have seen this coming. I should have known my intern was screwing my husband. I should have known my life was about to be turned upside down.

But I hadn't.

What did that say about me?

avier

fter talking with Tibby, I felt better. This might
end up ending, but this thing with Olivia had legs.
It had a lot of potential. I needed to not be my normal self
—hell, I hadn't been my normal self! I needed to be a part
of moving things forward.

It had been a long time since I'd been willing to put
forth as much effort, but just from the short time I'd spent
with her, she was worth it. If I was an asshole, it was a
good return on my time investment. I felt better than I had
in ages, and I was excited about being with and doing
things for and with someone else.

With these good thoughts in mind, I got up early and
headed down to the studio. Marcus was there when I
came in.

"How was San Fran?"

"Good," I grinned.

"Good to see you back," he grinned back. "'Cus I need to ask for a favor."

"Sure." Marcus hadn't, in all the time I'd been working for him, asked me for anything. It was amazing how many people did—how many people felt that because you had a lot, you were fair game for handing some of it out. "What can I do?"

"You know my girl? Kristine?"

"Yeah," I'd met her a few times. She was tall and quiet and beautiful. They'd been together for a long time.

"I want to pop the question—"

"Wait! What? You're gonna get married? What? When did this happen, man?"

He laughed. "It's been coming for a while. We've been together six years, and it's time. That's where the favor comes in. There's this booze cruise thing out in LA—the singer Kristine loves, Jazmine Sullivan, is going to be there. It goes out and sails around, and she performs, and there's dinner and whatever. I want to ask her there, at sunset, before Jazmine comes out to sing."

"Okay?" I didn't understand.

"It's invite only."

I understood immediately. "You want me to get you tickets?"

"I think you're going to have to be there. We'll be your plus ones. I can pay you for it," he held up his hands, "So don't think I'm asking for your time and money, man!"

"Shut the hell up," I said. "I don't want your money. I'm happy to. She's a lucky lady."

"No, man, I'm the lucky one. But you think you can do it?"

"Yeah, let me see who I need to talk to." I headed into my office and went through my contacts to see who would know how to get them on the boat. I supposed I would have to go, too.

"Hey," I yelled out of the office. "When is this thing?"

"This weekend," he yelled back.

"Kinda close, isn't it?"

"She just told me about it. She was reading something and saw it. She didn't think we could go or anything but just mentioned it. I kept thinking about it, and thought I'd see if you could help at all."

"You got a ring?"

"Sure do. I got it last month, but the right moment keeps not happening."

"Why didn't you say anything?" We'd been working hard on the album. "I'd have given you at least a day off."

He laughed. "Yeah, but then I would be here trying to set up something way better than a picnic in the park."

"True. Okay, get the hell away, and let me see what I can do."

"Thanks, man," he said, and I could tell how much this meant to him.

What I really wanted was for him to get out so I could call Olivia and see if she was free.

As he left, I pulled her up on my phone and called.

"Hey," her voice sounded surprised.

But not annoyed, or anything negative. Which was good. I got a little squirrelly when she didn't respond last night.

"I know you're working, but I wanted to ask you if you're free Friday night. To go to LA," I added, so she'd be ready for the time needed to travel.

"Um…"

I could hear the click of computer keys.

"No, I'm not. I have some client meetings late that

night so I won't be free until Saturday," she said. "Damn it."

"It's okay. I wanted to know if you could play hooky with me for the night, but we can get together Saturday," I said.

"Go ahead, tell me what fabulous thing I'm missing out on."

"My sound guy, he's been with me forever, he wants to get on this booze cruise thing, he's asking his girlfriend to marry him, and it's—it doesn't matter. I said I'd help him, and I need to be there so he can go."

"Oh, so it's a rich and famous thing?"

"Are you laughing at me?"

"I might be. But not too much—you get to go out on a cruise at night in LA—it will probably be gorgeous."

"No, it will be a bunch of people I may or may not know, talking about other people we know," I grumbled. It didn't look as fun now that she couldn't come with me. "You would have made it gorgeous. So what are we going to do Saturday?"

"Do you," she hesitated, "Want to come here?"

"Yeah?" I was thrilled she was asking me to come to her home. Remembering her comments about her mother, maybe I should be scared.

"Yes, although I don't have any solid plans. But I'd love to see you," her voice softened.

"I want to see you, too. It's a date. I'll do the boat thing Friday night, and fly out to you Saturday morning. Maybe not coffee time, but right after. Sound good?"

"Yes, it does."

"Okay, let's talk tonight then?"

"Call me."

"Count on it."

I hung up, feeling good. So I wouldn't have Olivia as a date, but I got her for the weekend. It was a fair trade.

A few more calls and I'd managed to get three invitations to the cruise, and then I called around to see who might need the plane this weekend. If this kept up, I might need my own. Luckily, no one was using it, so I was able, within the hour, to set up my whole weekend. I booked the plan to come back on Sunday night. It was a little presumptuous, but I wanted to spend that time with her.

Maybe I'd see where she thought we were headed.

Maybe.

I went back into the studio. "Hey, man, we're on, so tell your girl to pack up for a surprise."

His face lit up like I'd just given him Christmas. "Seriously? Man, that is fantastic! Can I have an hour or two? I'll get back to this, but I have to make reservations—"

I cut him off. "I already booked the plane. Don't worry about it," I held up a hand to forestall his protests. "I have to travel a little, so I'll have it back for you in time to come home whenever you want to."

He looked at me strangely for a moment and then his face cleared. "All right, whatever you want. It's your ride, and thanks for letting me hitch a seat."

"Anything, man, you know that." I meant it. Marcus had been with me a long time, and he never traded on our relationship. This was small.

And I'd get to see Olivia. The thought of spending the entire weekend with her, naked at least part of the time, made my heart race.

"I'm going to go work on some new stuff unless you're ready now," I said. Enough with the touchy-feely at work.

"I'm nearly done. It'll be ready for you to listen to later today."

I nodded and went back to my office, where I could stretch out on the couch and work.

livia

With Xavier to look forward to this weekend, I was fairly easygoing at work. We had a couple of new clients that we were getting to know, and even the promise of drama from one didn't faze me.

"I don't know why you're smiling," Momma groused. "That was exhausting."

"Yeah, she is, but we'll make her fee commiserate with the level of effort required."

She laughed, not looking at me. "I like your style, sugar bean."

"I love you, Momma."

She picked her head up off the back of the couch where she'd collapsed. "You okay, darlin'?"

"I'm fine. I just wanted to let you know that."

I'd been talking back and forth with Xavier at night. It was nice that he realized I really didn't have time during the day for a lot of the personal. That was yet another thing Royce hadn't respected. For many years, it had been "your little business," and once my little concern started paying the bills, he didn't refer to it at all, just expected me to take care of things.

Thank goodness we'd never had kids.

But back to Xavier—a lot of who he was, how he'd grown up, had come through in our conversations. It wasn't that we got all deep or philosophical. I could tell that we'd had vastly different childhoods in the way we looked at the world. He was both more cynical and giving than I was. I found the mix interesting. Who was I kidding?

I found everything about him fascinating.

Work and long talks with him at night had so far allowed me to avoid the conversation I was about to have.

"What are you doing this weekend, Momma?"

"Why?" She was still looking at me intently.

I thought about how Xavier was so honest, and just cut to the chase. Nice ladies like Momma and I weren't brought up that way, but I found that I liked the directness, and I decided I'd take the plunge now. If she didn't like my decision, it wouldn't matter how I said it. "I want you to meet Xavier."

"Why?"

"Because he's coming here this weekend, and while he and I really are excited to spend time together—"

"Rolling around like a couple of cats," she muttered.

"Well, yes, thank you for pointing that out," I said, although I wasn't offended. Teasing Momma was fun. "But I think this is going to become something, although I don't know what, and you are the most important person in my life, you and Lloyd, so I would like you both to meet him."

I think I saw tears in her eyes. I couldn't be sure, and I squinted, wanting to see if I was just imaging things.

She sniffed. "When will he be here?"

"He's going out to Los Angeles tonight and then flying here tomorrow morning. He'll be up early, so we have most of the day to spend together," I said, unable to hide my pleasure at the thought.

It wasn't even that I wanted to roll around like a couple of cats, as my mother so eloquently put it. Just being around him was intoxicating.

"Would you like to have dinner tomorrow night? That

way, it won't be too long, and everyone will behave," she said.

"What, you're worried about Lloyd? Really, Momma?"

"He's rather fierce in his protective instincts. Just because you don't see it doesn't mean it's not there."

"I love that about you both."

"And I promise I will keep my less than ladylike comments to myself," she added.

I burst out laughing. "As long as you're not mean, I think it will be fine. I've already told Xavier you're a shark in good jewelry."

Momma looked pleased. "That is a truly lovely thing to say, darlin'."

Right there, that's why she and I are such good friends. Because she knows she's a shark, and she appreciates it when others recognize it. Sharks have a bad rep when in reality, they're just doing their thing.

Just like my momma.

"What does he eat?"

"Whatever. I introduced him to Community chicory, and he was sold on it, or at least I think he was. Whatever we decide to have is fine."

"You tell him he's having dinner with us?"

"Not yet. He'll be fine with that, too."

"You seem awfully sure for not knowing this man all that well."

"Well, you're right, but in this, I can tell you he'll be fine. Now, can we get out of here?"

"You gotta go wash your hair?" She asked as we got ourselves out the door.

"No, I need to go sleep."

Momma laughed, a deep throaty laugh that was understanding. She kissed me when we got to our cars. "Call me tomorrow when you're on the way over. Love you, girl."

"Love you, too."

When I got in my car, I checked the phone. I made it a policy not to look at my phone when I was with clients and had gotten into the habit of not checking it until after work. It felt more professional to me.

Xavier had texted.

'Getting on the plane. I know you're slaving away at the whim of some drama llama, but I wanted you to know I was thinking of you. XO'

'We're here. I wish you were too. Gorgeous sunset would be better with gorgeous you. I'll text you later—there's a phone ban since there's a lot of the rich and famous here.'

He ended that one with an eye roll emoji.

'Almost forgot. XO'

That was a couple of hours ago, and he hadn't texted again. I'd never heard of a cell phone ban, but it made sense. No one wanted to go and party and have someone recording it. I didn't know if I could live the life that Xavier did. Thankfully, we hadn't gotten to any talk about that. I didn't want to.

Not yet, anyway. Maybe later.

It was better that he was busy. I needed to make sure my house was presentable, and more importantly, make sure that there was no trace of Royce. I'd thrown away a lot of stuff that he had left, but I'd already planned to go through again. Just to be sure.

I hummed along with the radio all the way home. Once I got there, I pulled up a playlist on my phone, and a speaker, and sang as I cleaned.

When I went to bed, all I could think about was seeing him again. I couldn't wait.

I woke up before my alarm. I stared at the ceiling for a few moments, and then tossed the blankets off. I needed to get everything in shape. Xavier was coming today, and I wanted him to see my world, see how I lived.

I'd been nervous last night, but today, I was nothing but excited. I'd given myself plenty of time to get ready, and I forced myself to eat, and then tidy up once more. I went through the house, one more time.

Time to go. The nerves were getting the better of me. I had a nice house and a nice life, but it wasn't the life Xavier had. I didn't want him to be disappointed.

For a rebound, I had a lot invested in this. I didn't want to think about what would happen if this fizzed out. I'd been doing a lot of reading about what happened after people divorced. Everyone seemed to rebound. Then they moved on to a real relationship.

This felt real, though. How could you tell?

I thought about it on the way to the airport. Xavier had told me where to go to meet his plane. It was separate from the larger airport.

When I got to the gate, I told the guard I was meeting a private plane, and he directed me to an office. He also informed me that if I wandered around, I would potentially be arrested.

Sheesh. I didn't think I looked dangerous.

When I got to the office, I went in.

A young man looked up as I closed the door behind me.

"Can I help you?"

"I'm meeting a plane. I am not sure where I'm supposed to go, and the guard at the gate sent me here."

Xavier hadn't been sure as he'd not been here before, but he'd told me that these people would help me out. He said every airport had a section for the private planes, and keeping track of them was their job.

The young man, who wore a nametag that said Dave, smiled. "I can help you with that. When is the plane expected?"

"I was told it was planning on landing at nine a.m."

He checked a sheaf of paperwork on the desk in front of him. "Where was it leaving from?"

"Los Angeles."

I could see his eyes moving down the list.

"Oh, yeah, here it is. That flight was canceled." He looked up. "I'm sorry."

"What do you mean? I don't understand."

"The pilot filed a cancellation as his passenger didn't show up. The plane never left. You can't leave without the person who charters the flight."

My head spun. "What does that mean, the passenger didn't show up?"

For a moment, there was pity on Dave's face. "I'm sorry, ma'am. I only know what's in the notes, here." He gestured at the paperwork. "It's all the information I have."

"Well…" I didn't know what to do. "Okay. Thank you for your help. I'll just wait to hear from…the passenger."

I turned and walked to my car. What had happened? I spoke to him yesterday before work. Then he texted. He'd given me no hint that he wouldn't be here, wouldn't be getting on the plane.

Was he hurt? Should I call someone? His manager? Oh, that's right. He didn't have one. He'd fired his manager the day we met. Xavier hadn't replaced him yet.

I sat in my car, trying not to cry.

Either he was hurt, or he'd changed his mind.

Don't jump to conclusions, don't jump to conclusions, I

told myself. You don't know anything, nothing good, and nothing bad. There's nothing to assume.

Inhaling deeply, I found some tissues in my bag and wiped my eyes. Okay. What did I need to do? I needed to make sure that he wasn't hurt. How to determine that?

The cruise. Check the cruise. It was a no phone cruise, but maybe there was some publicity about it anyway.

I searched for the singer that he'd told me about—the one his friend's girlfriend liked. I found it, listed on one of the entertainment magazine sites. It had pictures of her walking on board, and then I read the little blurb.

This power cruise will certainly be rocking as they set sail for a weekend of fun in Los Cabos! Stay tuned for pics!

Where the hell was Los Cabos?

I pulled up maps and searched. It was in Mexico, at the tip of the Baja peninsula. I looked at the distance from Los Angeles to Los Cabos. There was no way—wait. I looked back at the blurb.

The words blurred.

…a weekend of fun in Los Cabos!

He'd lied to me.

11

*O*livia

I was crying. Not nice little rivers of tears artfully dropping from my eyes, either.

Big, huge sobs.

I drove out of the airport, and once I turned onto the road in front of it, the tears started, and I couldn't stop them.

There was no way I could get on the highway like this. I could barely see, much less drive.

My nose was also running, which was all kinds of gross.

When I finally looked at my watch, I'd been sitting there for twenty minutes. I couldn't just sit here, and I couldn't get in touch with Xavier. He wouldn't have his phone on him.

Maybe he'd just told me that, so that I wouldn't call. Oh, God. Was I being dumped already? I didn't know what to do.

I pulled out my phone and called Momma.

"Sugar bean, I didn't expect to hear from you until tonight."

Feeling a huge sense of déjà vu, I burst into tears at the sound of her voice.

I tried talking, but the words came out as unintelligible hiccups.

She didn't say anything until my crying calmed a little.

"Olivia Anne, are you all right? Are you physically hurt?"

"No."

"All right, can you drive?"

"I think so."

"Drive slow, and come to my house, darlin'," she said.

"O-okay," I sniffled.

"Put down the phone, take your time, and I'll see you in a little bit."

She hung up. I set down the phone and applied the tissue again. I kept some of it out again in case I lost it on the way over.

Why did this hurt so damn bad?

Focus. Just get to Momma's. Maybe this is a mistake, and it can all be sorted. She'll help me look at this without being a sobby mess.

That was it, it had to be a mistake. He'll be calling me soon.

With that thought, I sat up and headed for Momma's. This sucked, but it would be okay.

If anything, I was taken aback by the strength of my reaction. When I had come to care for him like this?

The phone rang, and I grabbed it, hoping it was Xavier telling me he was fine so I could yell. Get this all out.

"Hello?"

"You are such a bitch."

You know when a balloon has a tiny hole, and all the air leaks out rapidly? That was me. I gripped the steering wheel, so I didn't drive off the road.

"Royce."

"Why are you making this difficult?"

"Hold on for a moment, Royce," I moved the phone to my handset, and hit speaker.

"…you're just doing this because you're pissed! Grow up and get over yourself, Li—Olivia."

"Okay, first, Royce, I asked you to contact my attorney because I am not discussing the specifics with you. Second—"

He said, "I don't—"

"Second!" I yelled, my worry and frustration coming out. "I have every right to be pissed. You screwed another woman, and then had the hellish nerve to show up, drop papers on me demanding a piece of everything that I built, with no help from you, and in fact, built into success despite you. So I can and will feel any damn way I want. And THIRD, I told you I am not discussing anything with you. We're almost divorced. I don't have to listen every time you have a temper tantrum because you've shit your own pants and are wanting someone else to wipe your ass! Do NOT call me again!" I punched End on the phone.

I stared out the window, listening to the silence inside my car. I couldn't believe I'd just talked to him like that. I didn't talk to anyone that way.

Although if anyone deserved it, it was Royce. Asshole. I couldn't believe he was still calling me. Probably—

Oh, God. Because he thought he'd get farther bullying me.

How long had I just accepted this?

The realization that this was just the chickens coming home to roost in a situation I'd allowed made me start to cry again.

I grabbed the tissues I'd left in a handy spot, and swiped my face. It wasn't much further, which meant I could get out of the car and cry on my momma's shoulder.

I knew she'd ask what I was crying about. Apparently, I'd need to go down a numbered list. There was more than just one thing.

Which made me laugh. In that crazy, slightly unhinged way.

As I pulled into her driveway, I wondered if I was having a breakdown. JC on burnt toast, I couldn't get myself in a straight line.

Momma was out the door before I even got out of the car.

"What is going on?"

"I am having either the worst day of my life or a nervous breakdown. I don't know which one."

"Where's Xavier?"

I inhaled. Please don't let her say it.

"His plane never took off. So he wasn't there when I went to pick him up."

Momma looked at me. Her nostrils flared, but all she said was, "Come in and let's talk."

I followed her in and found Lloyd sitting in the front room.

"Hey, Lloyd—hey, did you do something else with the divorce that I don't know about?"

He looked at Momma, and they both *snickered*.

"Yes, dear, we did."

They looked gleeful, which distracted me from my

crisis for a moment. "Okay, what? I got a call from Royce, and before I screamed at him and hung up, I got the impression he had a new burr under his ass to bitch about."

This made them both laugh even more.

"What did you two do? I don't need your mean girl stuff making it tougher for me."

That sobered Momma immediately. "As if we would do anything to jeopardize you legally. No, my suspicious daughter, the only thing we did was enforce the law."

"How?"

Lloyd sat back down. "It wasn't even deliberate. I've had my PI following Royce and the young lady—Suzan? And he called me two nights ago letting me know that I might want to check the arrest records the next morning. Apparently, Suzan was out with friends, drank too much, and then got in the car to drive home. He said she was really drunk, and he didn't feel he had any options other than to call the cops. So now, not only does Royce find his legal position is shaky, his lady love is facing DUI charges, and…did you tell her yet?" He looked at Momma.

"No, I haven't had the chance." She grinned. "Remember that I told you that Jessie was still friends with Suzan? Well, Lloyd reminded me that any and all emails sent from one of our web addresses are our property, and suggested that we take a look. And honey did we hit gold!"

"What did you find?"

"After Suzan left, and the news came out about you and Royce," her mouth twisted, "Jessie emailed and asked her if the rumors were true, and not only did the bimbo admit it, she also said that Royce was going to get our agency for her to run! Can you believe the nerve of that girl?"

I nodded. "I can. I also reported her actions to the university. If she's going to intern, she really shouldn't be sleeping with the boss's husband."

"I can't believe she thought she'd just toss you out," Momma was indignant.

"I can't believe she believed Royce," I said. "But she's young. I was fooled, too. So how much of this does Royce know? What is it he's blaming me for?"

Momma shrugged. "No one but us knows about the emails. But the DUI—well, since he's shacked up with her, he has to know about that. Maybe he blames you? Who knows? That man has never taken responsibility for anything other than good things and other people's efforts."

Exactly the sort of thing I'd screamed at Royce.

"Enough of him. What is going on, Olivia? You scared me when you called."

"Like I told you, I was supposed to meet the plane this morning. It didn't show up because it never left Los Angeles. The pilot notes said the passenger never showed up." I could feel tears welling up. I ignored them and went on.

"Xavier told me it was something going on Friday night. But I read an online gossip piece that it was all weekend. He also told me it was a no cell party—that everyone had to hand over their cell phones, so no bad pictures get out, apparently. I can't even call him."

"Call him now," said Momma.

I pulled out my phone and texted. I didn't want to try and talk when I was such a mess.

'Hey, you okay? The plane didn't leave, so it obviously didn't get here. I'm worried.'

Then I stared at it, willing an answer to come back fast like he usually did.

Nothing.

"So that's it? He didn't show up?" Lloyd asked.

"Being stood up is nothing to scoff at," Momma rounded on him, hands on hips. "C'mon, honey, let's go have some coffee. He'll get back to you."

"What if he's hurt?"

"You think that wouldn't be in the news?" She towed me into the kitchen, where a pot of coffee was already brewed. "Someone like him?"

She had a point. I sat down, feeling even more like the deflated balloon.

Waiting sucked.

---

*L*ater that day, I gave up and went home. Xavier didn't text. I hadn't found anything online, despite being a stalker and searching several times. Momma finally took the phone from me and sat on it while we watched a movie.

What could have happened? My mind went to all sorts of things but kept coming back to the simplest, easiest answer.

He didn't want to see me anymore, and this was his way of telling me. Part of me not only wasn't surprised but didn't blame him.

I wasn't anything special, couldn't even manage to keep a jerk content. Why did I think I could be good enough for someone as amazing as Xavier?

Well, he'd be amazing if he wasn't ghosting me.

I hoped he wasn't. I'd rather him just tell me.

When I finally flopped onto my bed, I plugged the phone in and put it on my bedside table. I didn't want to miss his call. If he called. I was still hanging on to some sort of hope.

No matter what he said, I had to hear it from him. Even if 'it' would break my heart.

The sunlight hurt my eyes. I looked over at the clock and saw that it was morning, and somehow I'd slept through the night.

Feeling like an addict, I went for my phone—nothing. No call, no text.

Nothing.

Just like an addict about to hit rock bottom and taking the hit anyway, I searched the site where I'd initially seen the news about this thing being all weekend and not just one night.

There were pictures. I hit the slideshow button, cursing my phone for taking too damn long.

Scrolling through, there were pictures of the guy that I guessed was his friend proposing to the girlfriend, her crying, the ring—and then I saw it.

Xavier.

With a woman wearing what I supposed was called a bikini lounging on his lap. With her hand on his face.

I studied his face. I couldn't tell what he was thinking. It looked like a lot of his pictures that were public.

But he wasn't pushing the perfect looking nearly naked woman off his lap, was he?

Or brushing her hand away from his face. The face I'd only been touching a few days ago.

The face, I admitted to myself, that I was starting to think of as mine.

Studying the picture, as much as I wanted to, I couldn't find any major faults in the woman. She was gorgeous. And she was with my date this weekend.

Was this why he hadn't gotten on the plane?

Or even called to cancel?

It's not like I wouldn't understand. I've been in a state of shock on one level ever since I met him. I'm not part of his world. *She* is.

Setting the phone down ensures that it doesn't get thrown across the room. I get up, leaving the phone on my bed, and head for the kitchen. I need coffee.

As I start to make it, I see the label, and the tears burst forth like a dam breaking.

It's Community chicory coffee.

---

*X*avier

"*W*hat the hell do you mean, it's all weekend?"

I stare at Marcus, lost for words for once. This can't be happening. I have plans. I have a plane waiting for me.

Olivia is going to kill me. Well, I don't know that. But if I were her, I would kill me. I'm gonna look like a dick because I already stood her up once.

I can explain, I know that. But it will be another hurdle to this budding whatever, and I don't think it needs that kind of hit.

Damn it all to hell.

"I have plans this weekend, man!" I said, unable to keep the frustration from spilling over into my voice. "Plans I cannot change, Marcus."

He held up his hands. "Hey, hang on, man. Kristine," he said to his girlfriend, "Give us a minute, okay?"

She looked from him to me, and then back at him. He

nodded, and with a half-smile, she left, tossing one last nervous look over her shoulder.

"Okay, look, we'll just talk to the captain, or whoever it is that's driving this thing, and see if we can get you off here, okay?" He looked at me earnestly, not wanting me to pull the plug. Jazmine hadn't sung yet. She was on for during and after dinner, and Marcus had already arranged for a couple of minutes to pop the question.

"Listen, no, you do your thing," I said. This was his time to set his life up for the future. "I just wish I'd known this was all weekend." I would have insisted that Olivia come with me.

"You sure, man?"

"No, but I'll work it out." I cursed the fact that I hadn't told anyone about her so that they would know how important she and our time was.

Damn it.

I threaded my way through the crowd of people as Marcus left to find Kristine. Nodding and muttering as I did so—I didn't need to offend everyone this weekend, even though this kind of thing had never been my scene.

I found the bridge, and a guy who looked too young to be driving this thing ignored all the noise around him, focused on the space in front of him.

"Excuse me?"

He turned. "How can I help you, sir?"

"When are we getting back to land? Where are we docking next?"

"Los Cabos, sir." He gave me a smile. "We have great weather all the way down."

"I'm sorry," I shook my head a little. "Did you say Los Cabos? How long is this cruise?"

"We'll be down there tomorrow, and there's another show with Jazmine and fireworks, and we head back right after that. We'll be back in LA by Sunday evening. Earlier rather than later." Another perfect grin.

"I really, really need to get off this boat before then."

The grin fell away like ice in hell. "I'm sorry, sir, but we're not scheduled to stop anywhere. It's basically one long ride."

"Oh, shit. Is there any way I can use a phone?"

"I'm sorry," he really did look sorry. "But this trip was designated no phones, no cells, no cameras. All of the guests agreed to it."

I waved a hand and turned and walked from the bridge. "You have got to be fucking kidding me," I muttered. "It's like the digital dark ages here."

Who was in charge of this thing? I had the guy's name…on my phone. That was in a bucket, locked in the ship's safe.

It had been a big deal when they walked the bucket downstairs. I looked around. I knew, if I didn't want to get the hell out of here, that I would enjoy the chance to be out on the water with people who wouldn't be after something from me—there were mostly other people in the entertainment business here—and no pictures. While this was basically an industry thing, I'd seen plenty of young, scantily dressed men and women that suggested there was full-service entertainment as well.

And again, with no cameras.

A treat most of us didn't get very often outside of our homes and private compounds.

But a complete pain my ass at the moment.

I took a drink off a waiter passing by with champagne, needing something to hold onto. How was I going to get out of this?

Maybe there was somewhere on the boat where a

computer was open or something. Anything. It couldn't be a complete communication blackout.

I prowled around the main deck, and then slipped down the stairs on a stairway I found almost hidden away at the back of the cabin. There had to be a computer somewhere.

An hour later, I had to give up. I'd snooped everywhere I could, including all the cabins. There was one with my name on it, I'd noticed. How had this happened without me realizing it? How did I not even clue into the fact this was a weekend gig? I hadn't packed a thing, but curiosity led me to check out 'my' room, and there was everything I would need. Marcus and Kristine had one, too.

Damn it to hell.

"Okay," I said to myself, "This is not the end of the world. She'll understand when I explain to her. It was just a mistake, and I'll make it up to her."

But I hated that she would worry. That's what normal people did when someone didn't show up. They worried. And I couldn't find any way to get word to her. When they'd said no communication, the planners obviously took this shit seriously.

I didn't get that—why try and be famous if this was what you wanted to do? Much better to party like a crazed person at your own place. I could tell, just by the atmosphere on deck that this was going to get crazy.

I'd have to make sure to keep myself out of it.

As I came back on deck, I found the bar. "A sparkling water with lime," I said. I wanted to stay sober, so I didn't do anything stupid.

She handed it over with a beaming smile. "Here you are, Mr. XTC."

I turned away. That smile came loaded with all kinds of offers, none of which I was interested in. But I didn't want to be rude or ruffle any feathers. I just wanted to get through this damn thing.

---

*S*unday morning, I was one of the first people awake. Last night had been insane, and I'd had to run and hide in my cabin. Someone of the feminine persuasion had banged on my door in the middle of the night, but I pulled the pillow over my head and ignored them.

I'd had to run and hide. Before I'd finally fled, I'd been sitting on the deck, minding my own business, making small talk with, of all people, Jazmine Sullivan, who'd gotten me into this mess by being awesome, and a gaggle of the young women I'd seen moving around had stopped.

"You're XTC," one of them giggled.

She was a little slurred in her speech, but I made nice. When you made nice, people would usually move along.

"I am. And I can see you're having a good time, so don't let me stop you."

"Oh, no," she took a few steps forward, and then turned and fell into my lap, causing Jazmine to scoot away with a look of annoyance on her face. So much for making nice getting her to move on.

The girl threw her arms around my neck and planted a sloppy kiss on the face. It would have been on my lips had I not seen it coming.

"I've been looking for you all day," she whispered loudly. "I'm your biggest, hugest, best fan."

"Christ," I muttered, glancing over at Jazmine. She snickered and got up.

"Traitor!" I yelled at her back.

"Wha?" The girl in my lap said.

"I need you to please get up," I said. "I am delighted you're such a great fan, but I'm heading off for the night."

"Oh, I can head off with you," she tightened her arms around my neck and pulled me close to her.

I could hear people talking behind her friends, and without warning, the girl was moved from my lap. Two men in white uniforms pulled her away. She was protesting, but I couldn't understand what she was saying, and I didn't care.

I got the hell out.

So now that it was Sunday, I was restless, waiting to get back into LA and a phone and Olivia. I'd been pissed as hell that I'd been trapped in this, but Friday night, I'd decided that there was no getting around this, as it had been planned so well.

So I talked with other singers, got a couple of recommendations for managers, shot the shit and didn't drink. Me and the sparkling water got real cozy.

I also saw how out of control some of my fellow entertainer types got, and I wondered when I drank and partied like normal, if I was that bad. That much of an asshole. Normally, I wouldn't have been all that bothered by lap girl. Regardless of my relationship status.

But now—it all seemed hard and desperate.

Maybe it was just this thing and my irritation at being trapped here.

I headed for the bridge. A different guy, older this time, was in what I guessed was the driver's seat.

"Can you tell me when we'll get our phones back?" I tried really hard to keep the irritation from my words.

"We're about three hours out, sir, so about an hour before we dock."

"You can't—"

"No, sir, I'm sorry. That was part of the contract." He looked forward again.

Clearly, this conversation was over.

I went back on deck to find a safe spot to wait it out. We were almost back. Then I could get on with the business of repairing the mess of my weekend.

12

Olivia

stared at the picture. I'd made coffee, done my laundry, and everything I could to stop myself from going back to add salt to my wound.

But here I was.

Xavier had a drink in his hand, and the woman—girl—was pulling him close to her, looking like she was about to kiss him.

Son of a bitch.

Momma was right to be worried. I remembered that I'd asked him if he cheated, and he'd said no. Better to just end things.

Was this what he meant? While I felt a lot more than I wanted to let on for knowing him such a short time, I wasn't sure I'd call this a relationship, either.

But it sure as hell felt like one, and damn it, he'd treated it like one. So had I.

The tabloid site I'd been reading—okay, obsessing—said the cruise ended today. When? Would he call me?

It was only 11:30 in the morning. How would I manage for the rest of the day?

Why would he do this to me?

Was he really this bad?

Why was I so insane?

All these things went through my head, swirling the like tornadoes you saw storm chasers filming. Every little tidbit, every piece of trash—it all went into that tornado and became part of the oncoming storm.

He was a hell of a con man.

He just didn't want to be with me.

I was stupid, and I'd been taken in.

The tears came again, and I dashed angrily at my face. I was tired of crying over lying, faithless men. Royce had taken ten years from me and tossed it back, making sure to tell me how everything I'd done wasn't good enough. From the time we got engaged, I was always told that I needed to try harder, try more, do better, give more.

It was never enough.

I'd know Xavier maybe a month? And he'd taken what I freely gave, said things that implied promise, implied future, and then at the first chance, jets off and starts canoodling women my momma would call a hussy on a good day.

Okay, maybe that wasn't fair to the girl I'd seen. She probably didn't know that Xavier was dipping his toe—and other things—into something with another woman. I'm sure he didn't tell her.

You know, in the interest of keeping things 'casual'.

I was working myself into a snit of royal proportions. I knew it, knew it wouldn't do me any good, but I couldn't stop it. I didn't want to.

Fuck this.

I thought it, and those were words I usually didn't use.

I tried it aloud. "Fuck this."

It sounded harsh and angry in the silence of my home. The home I'd worked to build, design, and make my own. For what I thought was my future. And then when I found it wasn't, I'd invited someone in who might have a place in that future.

But he'd spurned me.

"Fuck this," I said again. I took a deep breath, and screamed at the top of my lungs, "FUCK! THIS!"

The words seemed to echo round and round the empty, lifeless house like the growing, growling tornado in my head.

From my bedroom, I heard my phone ringing. Probably Momma checking in, but it would be worse if I ignored her.

I padded to my room, and when I turned it over and looked at the caller ID, my heart leaped up into my throat right before it plummeted to the floor.

It was Xavier.

I almost hit the green button, but my finger hesitated. I debated, the tornado raging, and then the ringing stopped.

I'd missed him.

But hadn't I wanted to?

While I pondered this, the phone rang again. It was him again.

Did I want to talk to him? I couldn't even think straight. And did I care what he had to say? What was that saying? 'A picture is worth a thousand words'? That picture had been. What could he say to counter the thousand words I'd already heard in my head?

Thanks to the tornado, those words were now on repeat status.

Because I wasn't enough.

I'd never been enough.

There was no room in his life for someone like me, and there would always be women like that, women with more, younger, better in ways I couldn't even compete with.

I let the phone ring again.

When the ringer stopped, I turned it down and set the phone down on my bedside table.

I would go and work on something—anything. Anything to take my mind off this, off this rebound gone so wrong.

That's what I would do. I'd Google *How to survive your rebound*, and I would work on healing myself.

Alone. With no man.

Because fuck this.

avier

She wasn't answering. She was pissed. I didn't blame her. I didn't leave a message because if she was pissed, I needed to see her.

"We're going to Nashville," I told the pilot. He'd been worried, leaving several messages on my phone. He'd laughed when I told him what happened.

If he only knew.

"We can leave right away," he said.

"Do it."

I strode into the cabin and tossed myself into my chair. I felt gross. I needed a shower. I'd had a change of clothing on the boat, but I'd changed back into my own things before I left. I wanted nothing to do with the cruise.

Marcus wasn't with me. Apparently, he and Kristine had gotten married early this morning at sunrise. The captain had performed the wedding. He told me later and asked if I could do without him for a week or so. I told him to take two.

He beamed with such happiness that he'd not even asked me anything about myself. That was fine. It wasn't always all about me, which I needed reminding of from time to time. I did tell him to call when they were ready to come back, and I'd send the plane. It wasn't his fault I was in this shit fest.

It was my own for not reading details. Much as I wanted to blame him. To blame anyone else.

But the guy was deep in the love thing, and whether it was I was getting old, or soft, or both, I couldn't fault him for it.

I sat in the seat and closed my eyes. For the first time since I'd stepped foot on the damn boat, I could relax. At least here, I knew that no one would bother me.

The only good thing about the damn boat was that there were no pictures, no media. There'd been a few paparazzi hanging around when we docked, but I'd called my car service before we got back and I hustled my ass to the car with glasses on and head down.

I'd also managed to escape the roving herd of younger women.

Thank God. The paps would have gone nuts over pics of that.

A little sleep would be a good thing. I needed it. Something told me that this was going to be a tough reunion.

Byrne woke me with a gentle touch on the shoulder. He knew that I didn't like to be startled awake. Long years of waking up to shit made my fists fly first, with questions later. So I warned the people who might have to wake me to be low key.

"We're almost there, Xavier. You might want to…er… tidy yourself up."

"I showered this morning," I protested, stretching.

"Well, you look a little worse for wear."

"It's because I'm stressed," I groused. "Damn it." But I went to the restroom and did what I could. I looked like someone who was worried and hadn't slept well for a couple of days.

Which is exactly what I was.

When I came out, Byrne said, "I arranged for a car. It's waiting for you now."

"Good. Thanks, man. You're the best, as always."

He smiled. "I hope it goes well today."

He didn't know what was up, but he'd been working for me long enough to know that something was.

"You and me both."

In the car, I gave the address to the driver and sat tensely tapping my fingers on my leg as we drove to Olivia's house. What was I going to say? Big apologies weren't my style. Particularly when it wasn't my fault—no. I stopped myself. If there was a fault, it was mine for not paying fucking attention. I needed to own my shit.

As the car stopped outside her house, I didn't wait for the driver but flung the door open and bounded up to the door.

Ringing the doorbell, I send up a prayer—to who or what, I didn't know—that I would say the right thing. Just not fuck it up more.

She opened the door.

"Olivia, can I come in?"

She looked me up and down, and I looked at her as she did so.

She looked terrible. I could tell that she'd been crying.

It was like a knife in the heart.

When was the last time I'd seen a woman cry over me? Despite what people thought, I was honest about my casual involvement. Like I'd told Olivia, it made for some bitchy episodes at times, but there weren't usually tears.

There'd been tears here, and she was plainly still angry.

Finally, she spoke. Her voice sounded lower than normal, and a little hoarse. "Come in."

Without waiting for an answer, she turned, expecting me to follow.

Which I did, shutting the door.

"In here," she said, stopping and gesturing to a room.

"Thanks," I said. "I missed you."

Her eyebrow—just one—went up, and she crossed her arms.

"Really?"

"Yes. Can I tell you what happened? I'm sorry to seem like a dick. Unlike before, this was not through me being a dumbass."

She walked past me and sat down in a chair. She didn't offer me anything or invite me in further, but I sat down across from her.

"Please tell me what happened. I was worried about you."

Her face looked pissed in spite of her words. But I'd been right. She was worried.

"When I made arrangements to do this cruise, I thought it was a one-night thing. No biggie, go sail around and come back in after dinner and a show. But I was wrong. I didn't bother reading all the details, and missed the fact that it was a weekend thing entirely."

"And you couldn't call?"

"No, they took all our phones. I tried. I asked the

captain, and the crew, and went through the whole boat. It was on lockdown."

"So no pictures or anything?"

Why did her voice sound so weird?

"No. Marcus asked Kristine to marry him, and they got married this morning, though. That's positive."

"So what did you do all weekend?"

"Drank sparkling water and tried to stay low key. I got a couple of recommendations for a new manager, talked to some old friends, nothing big."

"Nothing else?"

Why did I feel like this was an interrogation?

"Other than miss you and feel like I was counting the minutes until the fucking thing was over? No."

"Oh."

"Why are you asking me all this shit, and talking like this? I haven't done anything wrong, Olivia. I fucked up in not knowing what was going on, but I did what I could to try and get out of the situation, and when I couldn't, I made the best of it."

Whatever I'd said made her shoot out of the chair, and head over to the desk that had an open laptop on it. She bent over it, looking for something.

"Made the best of it, did you? You mean like this?"

She turned it around, and I saw a full-screen picture of the drunken girl on my lap pulling my face towards her ample cleavage.

Oh, hell.

"There weren't supposed to be any pictures!" I said. This was frustrating as fuck.

Then I saw Olivia's face.

Oh, fuck.

livia

*D*id he really just say that? Nothing about how this was all a bunch of trash—no, it was about there weren't supposed to be pictures.

I turned around, trying to stay calm. It was Royce all over again, although this felt as though it had more bite. The viciousness of the bite was upfront, whereas Royce ate a little at a time until he brought me down to the bone.

Bastards, both of them.

Facing him, I was determined not to go all banshee. "What is it you're more upset about? That there were pictures, or that I saw them?"

His answer was immediate. "Both, because they make it look like there was something to this, and it didn't mean shit!"

I raised an eyebrow.

"Look, I understand how this looks. I also get that part of this is my fault, because I was a weasel initially, and I didn't do what I said I would. Will you let me show you that this isn't a big deal? Just give me ten minutes."

I wanted to believe him, wanted to trust him.

What the hell? He was already here, and it was only ten minutes.

"You have ten minutes."

"Will you sit down with me?"

I sat across from him and waited.

He scrolled through his phone. Then he hit a number and put the phone on speaker.

"X! Hey, where'd you run off to? I was going to ask

you to lunch to talk a little more shop," a woman's cheerful voice answered.

"Hey, Jazmine, I'm sorry. I had some things that couldn't wait. Let's make a date the next time I'm out there, or you're in NYC."

"It's on. You have some interesting ideas. So why the call?"

"I just saw some pics from the boat."

"What? There weren't supposed to be any!" Now she sounded mad.

"No shit. They had one of me when you abandoned me Saturday night," he looked at me as he spoke.

She laughed. "I only abandoned you to find security. I'm sorry though if they have a photo of you with that chick. She was drunk and silly. She didn't bother you again, did she?"

"No, I hid in my cabin after that."

"Smart move. You see any of me?"

"Only from you working Friday night, but you might want to keep an eye out. It looks like whoever took these are looking for a money shot—they're all couples."

"Oh, well no worries. I didn't even have the accidental meeting you did," Jazmine chuckled. "I'm going to hold you to that date! Thanks for the heads up."

"You're welcome. Let me know when you're in town."

He hit the end button. Then he looked at me again. "I was sitting on that couch, talking with Jazmine. Then the girl plopped herself in my lap, and I didn't want to shove her away from me. I was trying to figure out how to get rid of her nicely when Jaz came back with a couple of crew who took her away."

"Why was it you couldn't just push her off your lap?" I couldn't get over this part. He was a poor victim?

"Because I shove someone, and they fall on their ass

because they are drunk, and I get sued for assault. That's how it goes. This girl was young, drunk, and I didn't want to be an asshole, plus I don't need any legal troubles. It meant nothing, Olivia! I've done nothing wrong other than not read. I made a mistake, and I am so sorry if I hurt your feelings in the process. I want to make this right, but I'm not sure what it is you are looking for here."

I filed away that he got as mad as I did, but was willing to talk it out, even if it meant an argument.

We stared at one another for a few minutes. Then I sighed and sagged back into my chair.

"You're right. I'm sorry. I am making a mountain out of a molehill. I'm sorry, Xavier. Thank you for putting up with my questions."

He waited, and then got up and pulled me into his embrace. "I get it. I really do. You don't know me really well, and this shit is fair game for questions. But thank you for letting me explain." He tipped my chin up so that he could look into my eyes. "I'm really sorry. I knew you'd be worried, and I felt bad enough about that. I felt bad because I'd already stood you up once."

"You did, but I think you've made up that first time."

"Only the first time?" Now he smiled.

"Well, this does seem to become a pattern. And I had plans for this weekend for us," I added. I was so relieved, and at the same time, I was…I didn't know. Off balance? Definitely.

"Really? What would those be?"

"You were going to get to meet my mother."

"What?" His jaw dropped.

"Yes."

"And you didn't warn me?"

"There's no warning that will you help you with Momma."

He opened his mouth, then stopped, thinking. "So she knows I stood you up again?"

I nodded.

"Oh, shit. She hates me now?"

I hesitated, not sure how to put it nicely.

"What's your mom doing today?"

"Um, I don't know? Why?"

"Call her and ask her to meet you for dinner."

"What? When? This really won't be enough time for her, and I need some time to get ready."

"Nope. Call her and tell her you'd like her to meet us at Monell's."

I stopped, caught by the fact that he knew one of our restaurants. "You've been to Monell's?"

"No, but two different people mentioned it to me this weekend as worth going to, so I figure it's a good call."

"They do family dining there. We'll end up sitting next to strangers."

"That's fine. Less chance your mom will brain me."

I just stared. He was in earnest. I shrugged. "Okay. Your funeral."

But secretly, I was delighted he was willing to take on my mom.

"Momma?"

"How are you, honey?"

"I'm good. Xavier is here. He—"

"Did he come back with flowers and an overly extravagant present?" She shot at me.

"No, but—"

"There are no buts here, Olivia Anne. A man needs to apologize when he makes a mistake."

"He did."

"Satisfactorily?"

"Well, you can see for yourself."

"What does that mean?"

"He wants you—and Lloyd—to join us at Monell's."

I could hear the wheels turning. "Fine. When?"

"Say an hour and a half? I'm not dressed."

"Well, don't delay. Who knows how long we'll have to wait."

"Okay, bye Momma."

She hung up without a word.

"Did you hear any of that?"

"Yeah," he grimaced. "Your mom is a hardass, isn't she?"

"In the best way," I said.

"No reservations at this place?"

"No. They are first come, first serve. You'll love it if you love southern food."

"Well, okay. What do we do now?"

"I need to get ready."

He looked me up and down. "You look good."

"Trust me on this, this is one of the things I just need to do. I don't just roll out when I'm with my mother."

Xavier held up his hands. "Peace. I don't want to even think about arguing anymore. Tell me the truth, Olivia. Are we okay?"

I stepped closer to him and put my arms around him, enjoying that my head felt right against his chest. His heart beat softly in my ear.

"We are," I said.

He sighed. "Thank God."

avier

I held her, wrapped my arms around her, and enjoyed the feel of hers around me—willingly, which was a big step from where she was when she let me in.

It was a good thing that she'd let me explain. So many of my exes would have been throwing shit and demanding things. Usually from a store that started with Harry and ended with Winston. Olivia didn't do that.

Again, this must be what it was like to be normal. To be with someone who didn't live in the sideways world that I did.

I loved it.

Olivia let go of me. "I really do need to go shower," she said, and she reached up and kissed me. "Make yourself at home. There's coffee and stuff in the fridge."

She left. I'd had a moment where I thought about asking her to let me join her, but I didn't want to upset things. I couldn't tell why I thought it might, but something warned me to take it slow right now.

Although thinking about her worry over meeting with her mother, maybe I needed to clean up a little.

I headed for where I heard water running. She was already in the shower. I walked into her room, enjoying the smell that was uniquely hers. I'd seen her spray some kind of body spray on herself when we were in San Francisco. This must be it because it was all over this room.

The bathroom door was open, and I poked my head in, determined not to look at the shower where I knew she stood naked, and probably soapy and…stop it!

"Olivia?"

She yelped. "Holy hell, Xavier, you scared the life off of me!"

"I'm sorry," I said to the back wall, still ignoring the

shower. "I just wondered if you had anything I could use to clean up a little. I got a look at myself, and I'm a little rough.

The shower door opened and Olivia's head appeared. "If you look on that vanity over there—" she pointed at the one furthest from me—"There's still some of Royce's stuff. I know it's not ideal, but it's here, and it probably won't have his stupid cooties."

I burst out laughing, not only because I couldn't believe she'd just used the word 'cooties' but because I was so relieved. I hadn't realized how stressed I was until I talked to her. Until I felt we were back on normal ground.

We wouldn't be that, in my head, until we were together again, and alone. Until we were able to speak the physical language that we spoke—there were no lies when you were naked with another person. I'd learned that the hard way, both with my own lack of telling the truth and with some of the woman I'd dated.

The lack of transparency always showed.

Part of me wondered if I was putting too much on this brand new thing via sex, but sex was important, and it was so good with Olivia, for both of us, that I didn't think so.

I heard the water stop, and I left the bathroom. I could get cleaned up, but I didn't want to crowd her.

"I'll wait until you're done in here," I said, ducking back out.

The living room seemed the safest place at the moment.

Twenty minutes later, Olivia came out, her hair still wet. "You can come in if you like. I'm going to be a bit longer, but you can have a little privacy."

I followed her in. She sat at a little vanity that was in the room. I slowly walked back to the bathroom, watching her brush her hair.

It wasn't long, but I loved watching her hands move back and forth as she did whatever it was women did when doing their hair.

I'd always just washed mine and tossed some gel in it and called it a day.

Olivia smiled at me in the mirror. "I'm moving it along, I promise. Go on, it's all yours." The brush in her hand waved at the bathroom.

When I'd finished, I looked in the mirror. "Good as it's gonna get, son. Drop the swears and don't be a dick tonight."

Then I went to join Olivia.

When we got to the restaurant, I looked around. This was nice, and the fish in the koi pond were great.

I'd always thought that only really well-off people had koi ponds. A leftover from my assumptions as a kid. But I loved them and loved watching the fish. If I didn't travel so much or live in an apartment building, I'd love to have a koi pond.

"We're here first," Olivia scanned the place. "I'll go and put our names on the list."

I waited as she ran lightly up the steps to the door.

"It's a little while," she said when she came back. "You want to sit down while we wait?"

"No, I've been sitting too much today," I said. "I love koi ponds." The fish were huge and colorful, and they were hovering around where we stood.

"Olivia," a voice said behind us.

"Hey, Momma," Olivia answered, smiling, as she gave the woman, who was small, well-dressed and glaring a hug.

13

Olivia

 hugged Momma hard, whispering in her ear, "Be nice. He wanted to meet you, even after he knew you were mad, so be nice."

Then I pulled back from her and gave her the stink eye. She pursed her lips, and then a smile slid across her face as she focused on Xavier.

"So you're Xavier. I am Marguerite Mereoux, Olivia's mother. This is Lloyd Basterson, my friend."

Xavier shook both their hands.

"You get us on the list, Liv?" Lloyd asked.

I nodded. "It won't be that long."

"Have you been here before, Xavier?" Momma asked.

"No. I've never been anywhere in Nashville other than the airport. I have some friends who recommended this place, though. Although I think they went to a late night breakfast or something."

"That's on Saturday nights. It's great," I said.

"Yeah, they were raving about it. And they're both foodies, so I figured that was a good thing."

"It's very good here. But let's get the elephant out of the middle of the room, Xavier," Momma said.

"What are you doing?" I whispered to her.

"Shush, Olivia. I'm your momma. And this young man knew what was coming. No sense in letting the elephant sit there. Don't you agree, Xavier?"

To my surprise, Xavier was smiling. "I do, Ms. Marguerite. You leave them just sitting there, they shit in the middle of the room."

A very heavy, very long moment of silence, and then Lloyd burst into laughter. Big, loud, belly laughs, to the point that he only laughed harder as Momma and I stared at him, and he put his hand on her shoulder, leaning over.

"Don't go gettin' your gussie up, Ri," he got out. "Let the boy talk. You're all ready for a fight, but that gun might be half-cocked."

"Could you fit any more good ole boy in that?" I asked. He must have had a cocktail before they met up with us. Normally, he kept the southern side kind of quiet.

"Don't you sass me, Lloyd!" Momma fumed at him.

"Momma, ease up," I said. "Xavier agreed with you. I know it derailed you a little but don't let it stop you."

I'd been horrified when she'd started in on Xavier, but he handled himself perfectly. I wasn't worried at all. It was also nice to see someone else get under Momma's skin.

Lloyd was still chuckling, and I couldn't stop my smile. Xavier, wisely, had kept an outright grin off his face, but I could tell it was an effort.

As awkward as this all was, it was lightening my heart.

"As I was saying, and you agreed, before we were so rudely interrupted by…this," she gestured at Lloyd, "I like to get things out in the open. Especially when it concerns my daughter."

"Did you stick up for her with Royce?" Xavier asked.

Oh, sweet baby Jesus on a pogo stick.

He did not. But as I looked at him, he didn't look smug, or anything, just curious.

Momma also was staring at him, and she sighed. "I did as much as I could. I encouraged him to let us try our hand at our little idea, and when he said he was better suited for something else, I acted sad."

"Momma! You never told me that!" I gasped.

"Well, you loved him," she said with a shrug. "Sometimes a woman can't be out in the open. You have to work with what you got. Anyway, and now that the bastard has hightailed it out to more…," she glanced at Lloyd and grinned, earlier anger forgotten, "Drunken pastures, I am going to make sure that Livvie gets everything that is hers and that man can never bother her again.

"Drunken pastures?" Xavier asked.

"We'll tell you that over dinner. Quit misdirecting, young man. You're handsome enough, but I am too old to be bothered by that. Why was my daughter crying this weekend?"

Xavier looked at me, and put an arm around my waist, drawing me close and kissing the top of my head. He must have balls of steel, I thought. No fear or sense whatsoever, and he was in enemy territory.

"Because she's having a tough time in general, and although she and I are something positive, there was a miscommunication between us. It's been explained, and I even have evidence. Isn't that what you lawyers love, evidence?"

No sense at all. None. You didn't just tease my mother.

"When it's on your side," Lloyd said.

Xavier laughed. "You sound like my best friend."

"What, he's an attorney?" Momma asked.

"She is. She works in DC, does shipping related stuff. Tib's widely feared for her negotiating. I make her do mine when I can get on her schedule. She scares the shit out of the person on the other side."

"That's a good talent to have, in a woman," Momma said. "It's always so unexpected. But you will not hurt my daughter again? Because as you said, she's having a tough time in general."

"I can't promise that. People who are in a relationship do hurt each other sometimes. I can be a thoughtless jerk. I'm sure Olivia has faults, although I haven't come across them yet. So I'll promise you that I'll do my best."

I loved that he was so honest, but I didn't really know how Momma would take it. Lloyd liked him. I could tell. If Momma decided she didn't, she'd make my life hell.

Not that it was her business, but…this was the way it was.

I realized that Xavier had figured that out earlier. He knew he had to make things right with not only me but my family.

"Well, that's honest, and that's the best anyone can do. So you make sure you try, and enough with the rough language," Momma added.

Holy shit. He'd actually scored points with Momma. I don't think even Royce had ever gotten this far with her.

Probably because he was Royce, I thought with a snicker.

"Yes, ma'am," he said, his grin widening.

At that moment, with perfect timing, the hostess called my name. As we walked in, Xavier whispered in my ear, "No problem at all, darlin'," he added, putting a terrible approximation of a drawl on the last word.

"You have no idea what you have avoided," I whispered back.

"Oh, I do," he said. "But I like her. She's what a mom is supposed to be."

I didn't have an answer for that. I remembered what he'd told me about his mom, and all that I'd ever read.

So I squeezed his hand as we went into dinner.

*X*avier

*A*fter dinner was over, I felt pretty good. Olivia hadn't been kidding. Her mother was intimidating. But I remembered that Olivia appreciated honesty over everything else I'd done, or not done. She didn't want bullshit.

I figured her mother would be the same way.

What I did, although I would never admit it to anyone else, was picture Tibby as an old lady, defending her daughter. Tibby had defended me, on more than one occasion. She was ferocious.

This was a lady who loved her kid so much that she went into business with her, and then went all out to protect her after her divorce.

Olivia said her mother was her best friend. So it wasn't hard to figure out I'd be facing a hard ass.

She was quiet as we drove back to her place.

"Can I stay?" I asked. I didn't want to assume, although it made sense to me.

Olivia glanced over at me, and said, "Yes, please."

Nothing more.

Well, shit. That would suggest things weren't settled in Ms. Olivia's mind.

When we got into her house, her phone went off, and it was like a siren in the quiet of the place. She looked at it, made a noise that indicated great disgust, and ignored it.

When she made eye contact, I raised my eyebrows in question.

"The ass," she said.

"Oh, well, fuck him," I answered cheerfully. "Let's talk about something else."

"I can't believe how you talked to my mother." She smiled as she said that.

"Your mom is your BFF, and I got the impression she doesn't put up with shit. So I thought it better to meet her on her terms. Plus, I like her. I like that she fights for you." I wasn't lying. I would have loved a mom who fought for me like Olivia's did for her.

"She liked you, I could tell," Olivia looked kind of shy.

"I'm glad. I want her to." I went to her and wrapped my arms around her the way I wanted to wrap myself around her.

"Are we okay?" I asked.

I heard her sigh. When she didn't answer right away, I wanted to sigh myself. I was right. All was not well. Better to get it out on the table now.

"I feel like an ass," she confessed. "I assumed all sorts of terrible things, assumptions you didn't deserve because you're not...well, you're you, and no one else."

Damn it. I knew she was thinking about her ex. But I just nodded, and let her keep talking.

"I had all kinds of crazy talk in my head, and I figured you were lying to me because I wasn't enough, didn't belong to the world you live in...all that sort of thing."

I let go of her, moving her away so that I could see her. "Olivia, if I didn't want to be with you, I'd just tell you."

She threw up her hands and walked to the other end of the kitchen. "I know! That's what makes sense, and that's what you'd think normal, rational adults do, but I'm in the middle of a divorce that's about to get mean because he couldn't just tell me and leave. It's always easier to say these kinds of things!"

Olivia turned back toward me, and I could see the intensity in her over what she was saying. I held out my hands.

"Listen, I get it. If I were you, I'd be pretty low on trust. I'm not the most trusting person myself. But I don't lie, and if I don't want to be with you, I will tell you. You have to believe me on that. What can I do to prove this to you?"

Normally, I would say fuck it and move along. But this wasn't normal, and Olivia was worth the effort.

"It's why I called Jazmine and let you listen in. I wanted you to know there was nothing for you to worry about."

"This is your life, Xavier! This kind of thing happens a lot, doesn't it?"

I thought about it for a minute before I answered. Did it?

"Yeah, it does. I don't even think about it anymore. It's just…there."

Olivia looked miserable. "I know that. I know it, and it still hurts me like hell. I don't have any real claim on you—"

I strode to her and kissed her. "Oh, I think you do."

Her cheeks pinked. "Well, okay, there's a claim, but we're still getting to know each other, and I have to understand this is part of your life, but I am really struggling with it."

I gathered her close again. "None of that matters. You are the one I want to be with. It's you I choose to be with. Yeah, there's always some chick who has other ideas, but I don't. You are the only one I want to be with. Can you believe that? Can you trust that if that changes, I will tell you? I'll be upfront, and I won't be a dick?"

She stared at me, and it felt like she was looking to stare down my soul. Honestly, it was unnerving. But I knew, I just knew, that if I didn't give it my all with her, I would, as I told her before, be kicking my own ass.

"I can try," she said. "I won't lie to you either. I'm struggling."

"I get it. I know that I'm not the easiest person to deal with. My life is a pain in the ass for just about anybody else. It's a pain in the ass for me, and I love it. It's okay for you to take some time to figure out how to manage the shit that comes along with me." I felt bad. I did have a lot of shit.

She looked sad. "No, this isn't your fault. You don't deserve this from me. You haven't done anything to have me get all bananas."

"I didn't call you when I said I would."

"Well, that's first date kind of stuff. Not the end of the world. And you made up for it pretty well," she smiled.

Which made me happy. It was the first genuine smile I'd seen from her since we'd left Monell's.

I smiled and kissed her.

"Okay, I know I'm totally a pig, but could you indulge me? Is it possible we could get naked together?"

Her laugh was the best thing I'd heard all weekend. "You are honest, aren't you?"

"Yes, I am. I know you're mad—well, you were mad as

hell at me, and this is not really ideal, but I've been thinking about being with you all weekend, and it's making me crazy. You smell good enough to eat," I finished.

She ran her fingers through my hair. I felt a chill go through my whole body. She was that intoxicating. Even a little touch like this made me insane.

"Okay. I think it's a good idea. Even though I've been mad as hell, I was thinking about you naked, too."

"Well, hot damn tamale, Charlie."

"I'm a tamale now?"

"Yeah. Habanero hot."

We both laughed.

"Olivia, I know this isn't easy. This isn't your life. But I will make this as easy as I can, and you have to trust me, okay?"

When her eyes came up to mine, I could see the smile in them.

"Okay. But I reserve the right to get you a floozy swatter."

We were both laughing again as I carried her into her bedroom.

14

Olivia

I stretched on Monday morning, feeling rested and sated. Makeup sex really is the best.

Beside me, Xavier was still asleep. His breath was soft, but I could tell that he wasn't even near waking.

Which was kind of nice. I wanted to lay here, to think about this weekend.

Not even Momma knew the depth of my crazy.

I felt like I was going insane. I couldn't get all the thoughts out of my head. Not only thoughts that Xavier was lying to me, but that once again, I was wrong, wrong, wrong, and I couldn't be trusted to tie my shoes, much less be in a relationship.

That I had been wrong about Royce, and he was still trying to screw me. What if I was wrong about Xavier? Or, worse, what if I wasn't good enough for him? He needed someone strong, someone who could handle all the aspects of his life.

Given this weekend, I wasn't sure that could ever be me.

But he'd asked me to try. And he'd said that he would make sure he did whatever he could to make it easier for me.

When had a man ever gone out of his way for me?

Royce certainly hadn't.

Part of me felt reassured, and part of me was uneasy. This was new territory, and I wasn't sure I could be comfortable.

My musing was interrupted when Xavier reached out and pulled me close to him.

"You're so warm," I said, wrapping my arms over the top of his.

"Mmmhmmm….you're not warm enough," he muttered.

"I do have to go to work," I said, as he scooted closer.

"Right this minute?"

"Well, no."

"It's good to be the boss, isn't it?"

I faced him, and he traced the line of my body from my cheek down to my thigh. "You are so lovely."

"Even now?" I teased.

"Especially now."

I kissed him and felt myself go up in flames. Every time I got close like this, any sort of rational anything went right out the window. It was probably naked, too.

"Why don't you stay here with me this morning?"

"I can't keep…taking…vacation," I said, kissing him between words.

"Why not?"

"I'm not an artist who is expected to be all higgledy-piggledy with my schedule like you. I have to show up in the office. Or things start to get dicey."

"Higgledy-piggledy? What the hell does that mean?" He started to laugh.

It felt so nice to hear someone laugh with me in this house. Not at me, or with someone on the phone, but with me.

"Crazy, all willy-nilly, cattywampus," I said.

"I love the way you talk," he nuzzled my neck. "And I have my own schedule to keep, Ms. Bossy Britches. I just work a lot, so that when I want to take time off, I can. Do you ever take a vacation?"

I opened my mouth to say, *Yes, of course*, when I realized it had been three years since I'd taken a vacation. Royce had…well, it didn't matter what Royce did. As with most thing I was seeing, it was clear that Royce hadn't been on my team for quite some time, a lot longer than I'd realized.

Would I ever get past the point where a new betrayal didn't insert itself into my life on a regular basis? This seemed to be a daily thing.

"Uh, huh. That's what I thought. You have to think about it. That means you haven't taken enough. Take one with me."

"Right now?"

"No, I have a lot to do, in spite of what you might think. I got to get this tour organized, and I have some new stuff I'm playing with…I don't know, it might not be anything, but I need to work through with it. Let's go away right before the tour. Then we can both have a break, and you can devote yourself to me because for the next four months, I won't be able to see you much. Unless," he stopped, thinking.

"Unless what?"

"Unless you come on tour with me?"

"The whole time?"

"Well, no. You can't leave your business, can you? I'd have you the whole time, but I'm realistic, and know you can't just toss life aside and indulge in my greedy bastard wants." He grinned widely.

"How do you not have morning breath?" I blurted out. All I could smell was how warm and inviting he smelled. I figured mine was awful, but I couldn't do anything about it. But his breath didn't smell bad at all.

"Because I'm sweet through and through," he came back swiftly. "One more reason for you to be with me."

"The magical morning breath?" I started to giggle.

"You know it," he kissed me fiercely.

I gave up at that point. I could be late to work.

*X*avier

*T*he smell from the bathroom filled the room. Whatever Olivia used in the shower, the smell came out and spread out across the bedroom with the steam. It was light and fruity. I liked it. I liked being here in her place, feeling her in every part of this room.

I knew that she had lived here with her ex, but he didn't seem to be present. I mean, why would he? He'd moved out. But this place didn't even have the memory of his flavor. The flavor of shit, I snickered.

I knew she struggled. I knew that it was going to be hard. But nothing—nothing—I'd seen so far had shown me that this was a waste of time.

It made me think about Tibby and Seth. How she said

they just knew, and things went from zero to one hundred miles an hour in an instant. That's how this was.

I knew. This was the right one.

Thinking about today, I decided I'd take her to lunch, and then I had to get back. I'd already been gone longer than I planned, originally thinking I would be home Sunday night.

I had to get shit done so that I could start planning where she and I would spend the week before I went on tour. Hopefully, she'd consider coming on tour with me on some stops. That would be fun. I'd miss her all the time she wasn't with me, and I wasn't kidding when I said I wouldn't see her much. We scheduled the shit out of me when I went on tour because I went out every couple of years. I couldn't get anything else done if I toured yearly.

The pilot answered on the second ring. "Hi, Xavier. You okay?"

"I am. Can we get back to New York today?"

"What time?"

"Say two p.m.? I have a lunch I need to go to, and then I'll be ready to go," I said. Well, I wouldn't be ready to leave, but I did have to go.

"Yeah, that works. Brent called, and he needs us tomorrow, so that will give us time to run through things before his flight."

"No one else has been calling you, have they?" I hoped not. Normally I wasn't this schizophrenic with my travel. "And you have a pick-up in LA for Marcus and Kristine next week, right?"

"You're all good. No one else has been put out," Kirby, the pilot, knew what I was talking about. "And I have that flight scheduled."

"Good. Make sure you get some good champagne for

the flight, too. They just got married. Put it on my bill specifically."

"Got it. See you this afternoon."

I hung up as Olivia came out of the bathroom, in a robe with her hair in a towel. She was pink and smelled amazing.

"What's up?"

"I am sadly arranging my ride home. I really do have to get back."

"Of course you do. I understand."

I held her face in my hands. "Do you? You're really okay? I need you to be honest with me."

She nodded. "I am. What time do you have to go?"

"My flight leaves at two."

"I'll take you to the airport," she started drying her hair with the towel.

I loved that she felt comfortable enough to get ready in front of me. Even if it was just this little bit. Most of the women I dated only came out once they were totally done. This felt…nice.

"No need. I'll get a car. You need to work, too, remember?" I teased. "But I am taking you to lunch. Where do you want to go?"

"I have a place if you like little local places."

"Love 'em."

"Well, go get ready, and I'll finish up. I'm hungry! It's all this strenuous exercise."

I laughed as I went into the bathroom and closed the door.

It smelled awesome in here, like Olivia.

Thank God I still had one clean change of clothes. I'd had a bag on the plane, planning to come and see her.

I stepped into the shower, enjoying the steam. This was an awesome shower, with two of those big square waterfall shower heads, and jets on the wall. It was extravagant, and I wondered if she'd designed it.

In spite of the amazing shower, I managed to get ready in a decent amount of time—it was hard to get out of the shower—and we headed out for lunch. Olivia drove.

"Where are we going?"

"It's this little place called Hattie B's. They do chicken, and their specialty is hot chicken."

"What makes the hot chicken special?" I wasn't sure if she was serious.

"You'll see. I love it. It's total comfort food."

"I am all for comfort food."

"I thought you might be," Olivia grinned. "There shouldn't be too bad of a line," she added.

"There's a line for lunch?"

"There can be. I always seem to go when there's a line, but I'm not rushing into work, and you have time before you have to leave."

"Good, because I want to plan something next weekend with you. Will you come up to New York?"

She considered. "I think I can. Can I get back to you? I want to double check at work."

Now it was my turn to grin. "And with your momma?"

"You know it, Yankee."

At that moment, I was hit, almost like being hit by a lightning bolt. Was this what it felt like to fall for someone?

I'd thought I'd loved other women, and I loved Tibby, and Bryant, and Seth—but this was different.

It was…amazing and scary all at once.

I'd known her all of three weeks.

She laughed, and I watched her, considering.

Yep. That's where this was heading.

Scary as it was, I was completely okay with it.

*O*livia

*H*e loved Hattie B's, as I knew he would. Even Momma did, and she was prim and proper at all times. Except when she cussed.

We laughed and talked as we ate with our fingers, sitting on the edge of a long picnic table. I could tell that other people recognized—or thought they did—him, but no one came over.

I did see a few cell phones come out, and people tried to be discreet, but I chose to ignore it. As he said, this was part of his life.

Because I was so engrossed in him, I didn't pay attention to the other diners after that.

Which is why I nearly jumped out of my seat when she came over.

"Oh my God," she breathed, flipping her long brown hair over her shoulder, her back to me.

I leaned away. I didn't need stray hair all over me.

She was wearing a skirt and a jacket, obviously here on a lunch break. "You're XTC!"

Xavier smiled and having seen his smiles, I could tell this was his public smile, although his manner was his normal Xavier way.

"I am."

"Can I get your autograph?" She breathed, fishing in her bag for paper and pen. Her eyes never left him.

I understood it. He was gorgeous. And he looked happy. He was good looking no matter what, but him looking happy was irresistible.

It gave me a small, shy surge of pride to think I was part of the reason he was happy. I hoped I was.

"Sure, and then I need to get back to my lunch," he met my eyes and smiled.

The girl didn't even turn around. "Here," she handed him a piece of paper and a pink pen.

It was hard not to roll my eyes. But I didn't want to come off bitchy, so I restrained myself.

She bent over, and for heaven's sakes, her ass was nearly in my lunch. I glared and reminded myself to be calm.

"Thank you!" She squealed as he handed her back the paper. "Are you visiting? I thought you lived in New York."

"I do, but I'm with my friend," Xavier gestured to me.

The girl looked over her shoulder at me, with a toss of her hair I noticed, and then promptly ignored me. "Well, I can give you a tour if you like. Nashville's a—"

"No, thank you," Xavier said firmly. "I'm all set in that department. Now if you'll excuse me," he looked over at me again and smiled, turning from her and letting her know the conversation was over.

She made a noise, but Xavier took my hand and ignored her even harder.

She flounced away, and I felt about ten feet tall.

"See? Not so bad. I can be polite, and put the pushy in their place."

"You did that nicely," I said. "But next time, since I assume there will be one, will you please put her in her place before she nearly sits in my lunch?"

He burst out laughing. I felt everyone, especially Autograph Girl and her friends, because of course, she had a group of friends with her, looking at us. I focused on Xavier holding my hand, and he kissed it.

"You're so funny. I'll keep that in mind with the get the fuck out of here nicely vibe I'm sending out."

It was my turn to laugh.

He looked around. "You heading into your office?"

"I was planning on it. Why?"

"Can I hitch a ride with you? I'll meet the car there, rather than here."

"Sure," I said.

As we left, he held my hand. I resisted the urge to wave to Autograph Girl.

avier

She was so easy to talk to. We went over what we were planning for the week during the ride to her office. I was glad she didn't mind me coming there with her. Although I wondered at myself. Why did I want to see all the places that Olivia went?

It felt kind of like a dog pissing all over the place, marking his territory. Was that what I was doing?

Maybe.

She pulled into a parking lot next to an older house. I'd been so deep in my own shit that I hadn't noticed we were in a neighborhood. Similar to the place we went to dinner last night.

I got out. "I like this."

Olivia beamed. "Yes, we got lucky. There was a house here, but it burned, and the city had it razed. I got in when they were considering what to do. I said if they let me put in a parking lot, I'd make sure I made the house totally in line with the historic look, and I'd pretty up the parking lot."

I looked around. "You did a nice job. The lot is almost hidden. It looks more like a garden from the street."

"That's the idea. Keep the city happy. I'm sure Momma helped that along, too. She knows everyone."

I circled my finger around my face, keeping a serious look. "This is my surprised face that your mom is all over the connections thing."

"You like her, don't you?" Olivia asked as we walked toward the porch.

"I do. She's probably not easy on you, but she's like a tiger, and she'll always be there for you. I love that. I like her boyfriend, too."

"Yeah, he's like my dad."

"Does he work here?"

"No. He's our guy in court," Olivia said with a laugh. "Come on in, you can wait here while you wait for your car."

"You don't want me hanging around like some kind of stalker on your front step?" I asked, chuckling.

"Not good for business. Come say hi to Momma."

She stopped at an office door. "Momma, I'm in, and Xavier is waiting for his ride."

I peered around Olivia. "Hey, Ms. Marguerite."

She watched us over the top of her reading glasses. "You two look guilty as sin. No!" She held up a hand as we both started to speak. "I don't want to hear it. Save it. I am too old to hear lies or confessions. When will we see you again, Xavier?"

It felt like some kind of queen was talking to me.

Olivia said, "Momma, I'm going to go check all the messages and whatever. Can Xavier wait here a minute?"

"Of course. Sit down, young man. And Olivia! The place runs without you, you know," Marguerite yelled as Olivia left. "As you might have noticed with your recent absences!"

She looked at me and smiled. "I wasn't kidding. You coming back?"

"I hope to. But Olivia's coming to New York next weekend."

"She does need to work," Marguerite said.

"So do I. I have a tour coming up, and I'm working on some new material," I said. Which wasn't entirely true. I was set with my playlist, but I was fooling around with 'X's and O's.' I wanted to get it done, get it ready—ready for what?

Didn't know, yet.

"Good to know you do work."

I barked out a laugh. "How do you think I make a living? Of course I work. It's funny though, you all seem to think I lay around and drink and party."

"Don't you?" She asked sternly, although a smile lurked at the corners of her mouth.

"Sure I party. After I work."

"Weren't you in Washington, D.C. recently?"

I laughed. "There were pics? Yeah, my best friend, Tibby, the one I told you about?"

She nodded.

"She got married, and her fiancé and other best friend and I went out. Bryant ended up taking us to a dance club. It's also predominantly gay men who go there, so of course, there were rumors, and all that shit," I waved a hand.

But I watched her. I wanted to see what she thought of that if she had any sort of intolerance I should know about.

"Yes, indeed there were. Your ex was rather voluble on the subject."

"Marcia?" I asked.

Marguerite nodded again. Interesting. She watched me as carefully as I watched her.

"She's such a pain. I wish she'd get remarried, or at least, date someone long term. She needs a hobby other than riding on being my ex coattails."

I wanted to cuss, but I'd already gotten the eyebrow of stink at my use of 'shit' a few seconds ago. Fucking Marcia. If there was a way to make things sound worse, that woman was right there with a comment. Why couldn't she let it go?

I sighed. Once news of Olivia and I got out, and I hadn't missed the pictures people were taking at lunch, I was guaranteed some kind of angry call. And the tabloids would get an 'exclusive.'

"Well, exes are like that."

I looked up. "Yeah, they do seem to be." My phone rang. I picked up, and the driver from the car service let me know he was nearly here.

"I am enjoying our chat immensely," I said, getting up, "But my ride's almost here. I want to say bye to Olivia. Where's her office?"

"End of the hall," Marguerite said, pointing off toward the back of the house.

On impulse, I stepped around the desk and kissed her cheek. "Thanks for giving me another chance," I said.

She opened her mouth, but I could tell that I'd surprised her. I stifled a laugh. Keeping people on their toes was a good thing.

"Have a good trip," she said as I walked out.

I hurried down the hall, ignoring the buzz of conversation I heard off to my right. Couldn't avoid that people were seeing me.

Olivia was glaring at her computer screen. She looked up as I came in.

"I gotta go. Car's here," I said. I closed the door behind me. "Give me a kiss. It's going to be a long week without you."

She was in my arms almost instantly. I loved it. She wrapped her arms around my neck and kissed me. Every time she did, I felt myself alternately go up in flames, and melt a little more toward her.

My phone buzzed.

"Car's here," I said. I didn't want to leave.

She sighed. "I wish we lived closer, but count on me this weekend."

"Yeah, I got permission from your jailer," I teased.

"Oh, go on. She likes you."

"I know. It's mutual. Walk me out?"

I opened the office door, and holding her hand, walked down the hall. I felt her stiffen as we got close to her mom's office, and as we kept walking, I saw a guy standing in the doorway. Everything on him screamed *angry*.

He opened his mouth as he spotted Olivia. Then his eyes went to our linked hands and flew back to hers in such a look of outrage, it was almost not real.

She held up a hand. "Wait with Momma, please. I'll be in in a minute."

He said something else, but I heard Marguerite drown him out, and the click as the door to her office closed. I caught a glimpse of Marguerite as she shut the door. She winked.

"The ex?" I asked.

She was trying not to laugh. "Yes. Did you see his face?

He looked as lost as last year's Easter egg!" She gave in and laughed.

I joined her. Sometimes these expressions were just too much.

"Hey," I said, stopping at the door, "Take care of you. I'll see you Friday night."

I leaned down and kissed her, soft, not crazy like I wanted to.

We were in public after all.

Then I hustled out the door, grabbing my bag from where I'd left it when we came in.

livia

*T*touched my lips where he'd kissed them, watching the door and seeing his silhouette bounce down the steps.

I had it bad.

Unfortunately, I couldn't just go and sit in my office and daydream. No, I had to deal with Royce the drip.

I sighed. He always did ruin a good time. Then I stopped. He did. He always was what Momma called a party pooper. When I would tell him this, he would cross his arms and tell me at least he was an adult, and that I was stuck in being an overgrown child.

Asshole.

What an asshole.

I squared my shoulders. He had no business here whatsoever. We were divorcing, his floozy wasn't here anymore, and this wasn't his office.

I slammed the door open, surprising both Royce and Momma.

"What do you want, Royce? There is no good reason on the Lord's green Earth for you to be here. Was I unclear in any fashion when we last spoke? Anything you need to say goes through my attorney. So while I politely asked what you want, I don't give a shit. Get out." I stood at the door, with my arm pointing out.

I knew the two assistants that were sitting in the open area were watching this open-mouthed, and that Jessie, Suzan's friend, and spy, would be letting her know about it, but I didn't care.

He was an asshole, and he needed to go.

"I want to talk to you—"

I crossed my arms. "Nope. That time is over. The time for talking was before you were sleeping with the intern—" I rolled my eyes for the benefit of the audience, "And before you both plotted to take over this business, which your girlfriend would kill even without your help dragging it down to the gutter, and before you dropped divorce papers on me. There is nothing for us to say, Royce."

"Royce," Momma drawled, standing up from her desk. "You're in a bit of a pickle. Except for one person here, we have all seen and heard Olivia ask you twice now to leave. Another time and it becomes harassment." She looked down at her desk, shaking her head. "Not really what your attorney wants to hear, Royce."

I kept my face stern, trying not to laugh. Royce looked between the two of us, first bewilderment, and then his standard emotion, anger, coming to the forefront.

"You're both such—"

"I wouldn't finish that, Royce, were I you. Course, were I you, I wouldn't have pinned all my hopes on a lush, now,"

Momma looked up and met his eyes with a wicked grin. "Oh, didn't you realize that arrest made the papers? We all saw it. Leave my daughter, and fall in with drunkards. Another unhappy call from your attorney, I would bet. I hope you're payin' him well." Momma stepped away from her desk, taking his arm as she did so. She ushered him out past me.

He glared like I'd run over his dog.

I glared like he'd stolen the dog from me first.

"He is earnin' every single penny," Momma muttered. "But that's good. Make those sharks work for it, right?"

I could hear her suppressed laughter. She was quoting some of his less kind remarks about lawyers. He'd actually said that to her and Lloyd.

That had taken a lot of apologies on my part to smooth over.

Why in God's name hadn't I seen all this before? I hated how much I'd been asking myself that recently.

Royce looked back at me, at the office, and then at Momma as she opened the door for him.

"Get ready for court, Olivia."

I'd never heard such an ugly tone from him. Surprisingly, I didn't care anymore. Royce—the man I married, the man I thought I knew—he was dead to me. I didn't know who this was.

Nor did I care.

The door slammed behind him. Asshole. He was trying to break the glass.

But it held.

Just like I would.

I smiled at Momma.

She peered intently at me. "You okay, darlin'?"

"Never better, Momma. Now 'scuse me," I said in the most obnoxiously cheerful manner I could find, "I have a plane to book."

"You can't have any more time off!" Momma yelled as I sauntered out of her office, not meeting the eyes of either of my assistants, but feeling so smug I could burst. "It had better be your personal time, on the weekend!"

I laughed out loud as I shut my office door behind me. I was out of here Friday night.

---

*T*he rest of the week went quickly. Lloyd got a few calls from Royce's attorney, but he made it clear that if Royce came near me again, in person or via phone, we would be bringing the police into it. I was angry, but it was a good, clean anger. It felt good to be angry at him.

I realized I'd been angry for a long time. I just hadn't felt I could express it.

Boy howdy was I expressing it now. I smiled to myself as I looked in the mirror. The plane was getting ready to land, and I wanted to check my face and make sure I looked all right.

A little face powder, and then I finished my water. Xavier told me he'd have a car waiting for me. He was annoyed I hadn't let him send his plane, but I'd insisted. I didn't mind paying my own way at times. While Xavier had a metric ton more money than I did, I wasn't hurting. In spite of Royce, I'd saved a lot. I could afford my own plane ticket when I wanted.

A driver holding a card with my name on it met me, and I followed him to the car, impatient to see Xavier. He told me that he'd be waiting in the car.

When we reached the car, the driver opened the door, and I hurried in to be enveloped by warm, strong arms. He smelled good and warm. I could tell he'd had whiskey when he kissed me, but I found I didn't mind.

Which reminded me—I'd need to check my bag and make sure it didn't break. I wanted to get Xavier something, but what do you get the guy who can get anything he wants?

I'd found something, and I was excited to share with him.

But first—I had to kiss him.

He beat me to it.

"I missed you," he murmured into my lips.

"I missed you, too," I closed my eyes and lost myself. He had the best lips.

The car pulled away from the curb, and I didn't even care if the driver could see us.

Okay, maybe I did. I pulled away from him and settled into the seat. He glanced forward and smiled back at me.

He already knew why it was I pulled back.

"I'm glad you came," he said.

"I couldn't wait to see you," I confessed.

Xavier laughed. "I'm glad I'm not the only one."

"Not even close."

He leaned against me, and I could smell his warm, spicy smell. It enveloped me. He smelled like a man.

Not that I was thinking about Royce all the time, but as I noticed and appreciated more about Xavier, I saw how much I hadn't been able to enjoy with Royce.

Xavier had problems like everyone else, although his problems were not mine, I thought, but he enjoyed life so much more.

"So what do you want to do this weekend? I'm yours to command, for the most part," he said.

I raised an eyebrow. "What does that mean? What are the limits?"

"I need to go out to a party tomorrow night, and I was really hoping you'd come with me."

"You have to?"

"Sometimes you have things you gotta do," Xavier shrugged. "This is business, and I can't weasel out, as much as I'd like to. So I might as well enjoy it and bring you with me," he ended with his wide smile.

Those lips. He had like, the best lips, ever.

"Sure, although you've put me in a clothing frenzy."

"Don't stress. We can shop tomorrow morning. As long as I can be your personal shopper." He leered at me.

I laughed. "I don't want to be arrested if we go shopping. We'll see. Are you obligated tonight, oh mighty one?"

"Only to you, Ms. Livvie."

"Well, good. We're going to stay and in catch up." I shot him a flirtatious look.

"Oh, I like the cut of your jib, Ms. Livvie."

"I thought you would."

I couldn't wait to get back to his place. I wanted to be next to him sans clothes and spend the whole night in bed with him.

We could deal with tomorrow, tomorrow.

*X*avier

I stretched carefully. Livvie was still sleeping. Honestly, I couldn't believe that I was awake at all. I wasn't usually a morning person, but having her here made me not want to miss a second with her, even if I woke up first and lay here watching her.

She was so gorgeous, so strong. We'd watched a movie last night, and ordered in, and it had been fantastic. I couldn't remember the last time I'd enjoyed hanging out with a woman with no destination.

Which was kind of a sorry comment on my own life.

But no matter. Olivia was here now, and if I had my way, she wouldn't be leaving.

She stirred. "Hey," she looked over her shoulder at me. "What's up?"

"Both of us, now apparently," I said, sliding my arm around her waist and pulling her close to me.

"Oh," she said. Then, "Ohhh."

I kissed her neck, loving the warm smell of her hair. I loved how it looked on my pillows, in my bed.

She made to turn to me, and I stopped her. "No." I ran my hand down her body, taking the time to squeeze her ass.

It was close to noon when we finally got out of my apartment.

Not that I was complaining.

J pulled my hoodie up over my hat. Olivia looked up at me, a faint smile curving her lips.

"Worried about being seen?"

"I want to spend the day with you, Liv. This helps. New York is better than most places, too. There's a lot of big fish here, so I'm a lot less special. I have a shot at having a relatively uninterrupted day with you."

"Relatively?" Her eyebrows rose.

I shrugged. "I am never totally optimistic about these sorts of things."

"Don't you have to shop for clothes?"

"I usually get them delivered. I'm not exactly high fashion," I said with a laugh.

"So what kind of party is this? What will other women be wearing?"

That made me nearly choke. "Well, uh…as little as possible, probably."

"That is a big ol' no, Xavier."

"I don't want you to look like that!" I held up the hand not holding hers. "I don't want other guys looking at you. So the less skin you're showing, the better."

She gave me a look but didn't say anything.

After we stopped for a sandwich in my favorite deli, I got us a cab down to some of the places I thought might suit her.

I was prepared, even with Olivia, to be bored out of my mind but having her try things on made me think about taking them off, or dancing with her, or just being the lucky bastard who got to be with her.

It was sexy as hell. Olivia had good taste, and with a little encouragement, chose a dress that made her look like a mermaid. I didn't say that out loud, though. It sounded so cheesy. But it was that sea-green you see in the ocean sometimes, and it made her skin look like it had a glow. The dress was high necked and sleeveless and almost form fitting. There were also little sparkles or some shit that I didn't really get, but in the light, she shimmered.

I couldn't believe this woman was with me.

Please don't let me fuck this up. It all felt fantastic, but there was a piece of me that felt it was almost too good to be true. Maybe I was cynical, but things were going too well.

Even in spite of the fact we'd fought. It had been resolved like grownups, and that was something I wasn't used to.

Said more about me, though, didn't it?

When we got back to my place, Olivia went to take a

shower. I could tell that she was nervous about stepping into my world. Until now, we'd been pretty low key. Even though the charity event had been a big deal, it wasn't part of my professional world like this thing tonight.

If I'd had my way, I would have skipped it. But back when I had a manager—Tibby really needed to get on that for me—he'd set this up, and all the people I worked with would be there, as well as some of the studio heads.

Even though I ran my own show, I had to make nice with the other people in my business. That was just how it was. It wasn't what you knew, but who you knew. Even for me.

I made a few calls making sure she was on the list with me, and checking in. I'd been a bit of slacker since I'd met her, and this made the nagging business side of me calm down a little.

I heard the shower end, and although it was tempting to go in and delay her further, I thought she might need the time.

Finally, she came out in a cloud of what I thought of as 'How Olivia smells' and she smiled hesitantly.

"How does it look?"

"How does it look? You mean, how hot do you look?"

She blushed. I loved that.

"You look fucking fantastic. Everyone there is going to be asking themselves what someone like you is doing with a bum like me."

"Oh? Now you're a bum?"

"In comparison, yes," I grinned, getting up and putting my arms around her waist. I leaned down and kissed her. "You look good enough to eat, or drag to bed, or both. But instead of either of those delightful ideas, I'm going to grab a shower, and we'll get out of here."

Another kiss and I went to try and make sure I looked as good as she did.

---

*W*e stopped and had some dinner before getting to the club. The booze would be on offer, and I wanted to eat. More importantly, I wanted her to eat.

After dinner, Olivia was fidgety.

"You okay?" I asked.

"Nervous," she replied.

"You're going to be great. Most of the people we'll see are my friends. Those who aren't..." I shrugged. "We'll blow by."

One side of her mouth lifted. "I'm not sure that's helping, Xavier."

I held her hand since I couldn't pull her close to me from the other side of the car. "I'm not going to leave you. Okay?"

"Promise?"

"Totally." The car slowed, and I could see a crowd waiting to get in and damn it, there were photographers. Paparazzi, actually.

Fuck.

They were often assholes.

But I smiled and gripped her hand a little tighter. "It's going to be fine."

This time, I waited for the driver to open the door, and I leaned down and held my hand out to help her out of the car.

"Look ahead, look over everyone's head, and smile," I whispered.

As she got out, I saw her exhale, and then she put a

smile on that made her look even more amazing than she normally did.

I'd forgotten that Olivia ran her own business, and handled her shit all the time without me.

"You are so fucking amazing," I whispered as we walked to the door.

The doormen didn't even hesitate, opening the door before we got close.

"The hostess will take you back," one said to me over the noise coming from the club.

"X!" The calls came from the people outside the door. "How about—"

I held up my hand as I ushered Olivia in with the other hand. I didn't want to expose her any more than she would be just by being with me.

The shouts of the paparazzi faded as the bass from the club enveloped us, and a small blond woman appeared with a huge smile. She said something, but I couldn't understand her. She gestured for us to follow her, so it must not have mattered that I totally missed what she said.

I could hear shouts as I walked by, and I held Olivia a little closer to me. The hostess stopped when she reached a set of four stairs that went up to a raised area, cordoned off with a rope.

"Right up here," she leaned in to say so I could hear her. "The hostess will get you whatever you need." The big, toothy smile nearly blinded me.

"We're here," I said to Olivia as she walked up in front of me.

I bounded up the stairs and stood right next to her, holding her hand. I knew what it was like to face all these people, and I didn't want anyone to give her any shit.

A few flashes from the back of the upper room made me blink.

"What the fuck?" I asked, looking around for someone I knew.

Marcus, of all people, came towards me, towing Kristine with him. "Hey, man, thanks for the invite!"

I'd invited my entire production crew to this. Although I really hoped that no one would be out to steal them from me. I thought I paid them well enough to work for me alone, but I never made my team promise to work for me only. That was a recipe for disaster.

"You're welcome. How was the honeymoon?" I grinned.

He smiled, and Kristine echoed it. The happiness spilled off them both.

"It was wonderful. Thank you for setting up the cruise," she said.

"Olivia, this is Marcus, who works with me, and his wife, Kristine. It's their fault I had to cancel that weekend. They kidnapped me," I said.

Olivia shook hands with both, offering her hand to Kristine first. I saw Kristine give her a fairly appraising look.

"It sounds like it was for a good cause," Olivia said.

"It was incredible," Kristine answered for the both of them. "I'm sorry if we messed up your plans," she directed that at Olivia.

"I made it up to her," I said, feeling smug.

Olivia hugged me with one arm around my waist. "He did, which was smart of him."

Marcus laughed. "I'm glad."

As we made small talk, a man approached me.

"X? How about a picture of the happy couples?"

"No, man, we're on personal time, if you don't mind," I said, moving to shield Olivia. Fuck. Why couldn't these assholes get it through their heads? We were in a private area—usually, these were off limits.

He opened his mouth to protest, but I turned further and led Olivia away from him. Kristine and Marcus followed. With one ear, I could hear the women talking, and it made me glad to know that Olivia could hold her own.

While I wasn't close to Kristine, Marcus had been with me for a long time, and it made sense that his gir—wife— would know a bit about me and that Marcus felt protective of me.

Finally, a hostess approached, and I ordered champagne and a glass of whiskey for Marcus and me.

People came and went, many remarking on my continued lack of a manager. Olivia did well, in spite of the fact that she must have been bored out of her skull.

"Hey, I'll be right back," I said. I really had to hit the restroom, and I thought I could leave her safely for a little bit.

Still...I leaned down to Marcus as I left. "Keep close to her."

I saw his nod, and I ran down the stairs to get to the restroom.

Heading down the hallway where they were, the smell of old beer and sweaty people increased. Along with some other shit I'd rather not think about.

"Oh, my God!" I heard a breathless feminine voice, and then I was knocked back into the wall by a very warm person. A woman, apparently, more than one.

The hallway was dark, and I put my hands out to steady myself.

"Sorry, ladies, but I need to—"

My words were cut off as someone kissed me.

Mother of holy hell. I pushed her away and didn't even

try to make an excuse. When I got to the men's, I shut the door behind me and leaned against the wall, which probably wasn't a good idea, but shit.

A guy washing his hands glanced over and saw my expression. Then I saw him recognize me. I smiled the XTC head/nod/smile move.

"Crazy night?" He asked.

"Yeah, be careful leaving. It's wild out there," I shook my head.

He laughed and left. I chose to go to a stall because being me and trying to use the urinals led to a lot of uncomfortable encounters. Much safer to just go to a stall. I'd actually seen pictures of me taking a leak at one point.

I peered out of the bathroom before I left, but the women who'd been there were gone, hopefully to drunkenly grope someone else.

We left a little later. Business social obligations met, and no real harm was done.

And I still got to unwrap Olivia in that mermaid dress. I wondered if she'd let me peel it off her in the shower.

'Cause you know, mermaids.

16

*O*livia

 woke up in the dark, not sure where I was for a moment.

Then it all came back to me. I was in New York, and in Xavier's apartment. We'd been out tonight, and he'd bought me the most incredible dress to go out in.

I hoped it would be good for a second wearing. When we'd gotten home, he'd asked if he could take me in the shower as he undressed me.

"Why?" I asked.

"Because you always make love to mermaids in water," he said.

Well.

When put like that, what woman would say no? I smiled to myself. I certainly couldn't. I glanced at the clock. It was only about two hours after we'd gone to bed, and I knew I would be sore tomorrow morning. These sexual encounters were more like marathon gymnastic sessions.

Not that I was complaining. The sex was incredible.

But now, oddly, I was wide awake.

Moving slowly so as not to wake Xavier, whose steady breathing made me feel good for some reason, I slid out of bed and grabbed his shirt from the pile of clothing around the bedroom.

I loved that about him. He lived in the moment, and didn't care about whether things were messy or involved at the time—he went with what was happening right now.

Feeling thirsty and restless, I headed for the kitchen. After getting a glass of water, I went for my messenger bag and pulled out my laptop.

While I didn't like to admit it, I'd seen all the photographers. I wondered if they'd gotten any pictures of us—I wanted to see how we looked together, and if my dress looked as wonderful as it felt.

As Xavier said it did.

The thought of what the dress had inspired made my cheeks warm.

Best sex ever didn't even cover it.

My eyes stopped as I scrolled through the Google headlines.

'XTC Out With New Lady Love? So Why The Backroom Orgy?'

What?

What the hell?

I clicked.

There were pictures of us coming into the club, walking through. Seeing these brought back all the noise and the light show that had been going on.

Then there was a picture of the two of us as we came

up the stairs into the private party area, and I noted how protective Xavier looked with me. He was really close.

In all of the pictures, he had a hand on me.

Then I saw what prompted the second half of the headline.

He was in a small hallway, and there were four women around him. One was practically glued to him, the tart, and he had his hands on her chest.

I looked at the caption. *'Attentive lover in public, all hands on the decks in the dark halls'*

What asshole had written such horrible copy?

I almost laughed at my business mind critiquing the presentation, and then I looked again.

His eyes were closed, and no one in that picture looked unhappy.

This was the club tonight.

When had he been away from me? He'd only left my side to—

The restroom.

To go to the restroom.

And, apparently, get his freak on.

Tears sprang to my eyes. We weren't freaky enough? He had to kiss and grope multiple women on the way to the bathroom?

Just a few hours ago, he'd made me feel like a princess.

This picture, this garbage—this wasn't him.

But this feeling, this sinking feeling, this nearly crippling insecurity—it was me.

This was his life. There would always be drunken women waiting for him in a dark hallway. He was too beautiful, too sexy, and to fabulous to always keep them at bay, even with trying.

There would always be some tart waiting to grab him

and her fifteen minutes—and I would need to live with that.

Could I?

After the mess of the previous weekend, where I'd suspected the worst of him—I didn't know.

But what I did know was seeing this was like a knife in my heart. Right in the middle of it, where it was so shocking, the hit so deep, that it took your breath away.

I looked at the picture again. The tears fell unchecked.

I couldn't.

He deserved better. His world was so not my world, and if I wanted to be in his world, I had to live with the things that came with it.

I couldn't.

The answer was staring me in the face, but I sat and cried, not wanting to acknowledge it.

Finally, I got up.

Quietly, I gathered my things, which seemed to have exploded all over Xavier's apartment. I packed my bag up and then called for a cab.

I could call the airline on the way to the airport.

But I couldn't stay.

At the door, I took a last look around the apartment.

"I'm sorry," I said to the quiet room. "I wanted to stay."

The door made no noise as it closed behind me.

*J*ust before boarding the plane, I sent a text to Xavier. It was a picture of what I'd seen, and then I sent another.

'You deserve better. I can't live like this, with

this, having to see it. I'm sorry. I'll always care about you.'

It seemed inadequate to cover why I was leaving, but he would know what upset me. I didn't want to send him a weeping text because that was even more pathetic.

It nearly killed me that I'd found a guy I could be with and thought I was falling for, and I had to leave.

He didn't leave me, he wasn't the asshole—it was me.

I couldn't trust. I couldn't handle the scrutiny. The rush to make problems where there were none on the part of the press. And the women.

I couldn't handle the women.

The kind of women that Xavier would have following him until he died. He was that sexy.

No.

It was better that I leave, and let him find someone who could manage it, and not fall apart, or need constant reassurance, or whatever it was I needed.

For Pete's sakes. I didn't even know what it was that I needed. But I couldn't take the knife in the heart on a regular basis, and it wasn't Xavier's problem to fix it for me.

Once the plane took off, I started to cry in earnest.

This was my fault.

For the first time, I couldn't get what I wanted, and it was all my fault.

avier

I felt the sun on my face, and I rolled over, reaching for Livvie.

The space next to me was empty and cold.

I sat up.

How had she gotten up so early? We'd had the most amazing sex I'd ever had. I'd nearly told her I loved her, but that was pretty high on the creeper factor. I'd kissed her instead, telling her with my body.

I smiled. Maybe we could do it again this morning, and then go out and have a long, lazy brunch. That sounded like a great fucking way to end this weekend.

Swinging my legs out of bed, I pulled on my sweats to go see what she thought of my fantastic plan.

But when I went out into the living room, it was quiet and still.

"Livvie?" I said.

No answer.

What the fuck?

"Livvie!" I shouted.

There was no one to respond.

Where was she?

I found my phone and saw that she'd texted me.

Oh, holy shit.

I looked at the picture she'd sent. And the text.

'You deserve better. I can't live like this, having to see it, with this. I'm sorry. I'll always care about you.'

Those fucking women in the hallway. Groping me, kissing me—where had the pap been? That asshole. I looked at the byline, and I recognized the name.

It was the guy who wanted a picture of Olivia and me with Marcus and Kristine. Guess this was his way of telling me to fuck off with my refusal.

A wave of anger rolled through me, feeling like a rising wave that would pull me under.

I punched a number. I needed to deal with this before I tried to talk to Olivia. I was so mad, and I didn't want to talk to her mad.

Plus, I felt guilty. I lived such a fucked up life, who could blame her? She didn't, but she was honest that this wasn't for her.

Which made sense when you looked at my exes. What kind of woman could handle this?

The sort I'd ended it with.

No, I would talk with Olivia, but not until after I took care of this asshole.

"Brandon, you fuck, you're going down," I muttered.

"What in the hell do you want?" Tibby's tired voice finally answered.

"I want you to file harassment charges for me," I said.

"What?" She was awake now.

"I was assaulted when I went out last night. I didn't make a fuss, because I knew no one would believe me. I want to file charges with the NYPD, and I have pictures to show it happened." I was so mad, I could feel my heart racing, and my hand not holding the phone clenched and unclenched without me even thinking about it.

Tibby could hear it.

"Okay, slow down, X. Tell me what happened."

"Go to your computer, Tib. I'll show you."

"Good night, Maggie," she muttered. "Hang on. I'm all naked and shit," she added.

My anger eased a little. Tibby could always make me laugh.

I could hear Seth in the background, and she said something in response, but she was trying to be quiet.

Then her voice came back, and she was All-Business Tibby.

"Okay, I'm at my desk. What is it I need to see?"

I directed her to the site.

"Oh, X, these pics of you are great! Is that Olivia? She's really gorgeous. Like, too gorgeous for you! What is so ba—oh."

She stopped.

"Yeah. Oh."

"Okay, that's a big downer for the night. How did this happen?"

I explained, starting with the Brandon asshole who wanted our pic, to the fact that he was the guy who had taken this one of the women with me, and how Olivia had found it.

"She left. She left, Tib. She told me that I deserved better because she couldn't handle this."

"She said that to you?"

"Well, she sent me a text."

"A text?" Her voice rose. "She broke up with you via a text message?"

"I understand why she did it," I defended her.

"I don't!"

"I do. You don't know the whole story," I said.

"Before I do anything, you need to tell me everything. Everything, X. I'm not going out on a limb to help you with someone who isn't worth your time."

So while it made me grit my teeth to not be on top of the asshole who took the pics, and the women who were probably planted to make the pics, I explained.

About Livvie, and where she was with her ex.

Her fears. Her hurt.

How we'd fought after I disappeared for a weekend.

The way we'd made up.

And how she'd agreed to trust me.

Finally, I told her how Olivia didn't blame me for this latest shitty mess, but herself.

"I get it," I finished. "My life isn't easy for someone who isn't all fame hungry or doesn't have an agenda. She's got an asshole ex, but her life is pretty normal."

"Then why do you want her back?" Tibby asked. Her voice was softer than normal.

"Because I've been looking at the people who want to be part of the world I work in, and they are insane. You know that. Do I need to remind you? Marcia?"

"Yeah, yeah, I know. She's a damn nut. Maybe this is just too far the other way?" Tibby didn't sound like she was going to be convinced.

"I want her, Tib. And I think she wants me."

"Have you talked to her?"

"Not yet. She's probably on a plane, for one, and two, I'm pissed. I don't want to say something I might regret."

"If someone loves you—"

"We haven't gotten that far yet," I interrupted.

"Then they understand that mistakes are made. And this one isn't even your fault."

"It sure looks like it, and I appreciate that she's being honest about whether or not she can handle it."

Tibby sighed in a loud, exaggerated fashion. "X, you make my point. If she knows she can't handle the shit that is part of your life, why do you want her?"

"Tib, you married Seth in what seemed like an awfully hasty amount of time."

"What does that have to do with anything?" She sounded annoyed.

"I didn't say anything, even when I hadn't met him, and I was worried. I figured after all this time, you'd learned who was good, and who wasn't, and I trusted you when you said to me that you loved him and were happy, and you knew this was right. I trusted you." I left that sitting there.

There was a silence, and Tibby sighed again. "You're right. You had no reason to believe anything. Listen, I'll help you, but can I come up and see you?"

"When?"

"Today."

"What the hell?"

"We are coming to see you. I need to talk to you, and then, if…well, then I'll work with you, and I'll help you get her back if that is what you want. Okay?"

"You are making no sense, and kind of scaring me. Are you pregnant?"

"Bite your damn tongue. No. Are you going to be around today or not?"

"Yes."

"All right. Here's what I want you to do, so you don't go off half-cocked and cost me more time than I'm already going to take off for you. Text Olivia, tell her you're sorry, and you'll give her some space, or whatever, and DO NOT," she emphasized, "I repeat, DO NOT, one, go out of your apartment. Two, do not so much as look at a reporter of any sort. Three, do not attempt to get in touch with this site. Do you understand?"

"What are you, my mom?"

"No, I'm your long-suffering attorney. Promise me, X."

"All right," I said after a moment. "I promise. I'll wait for you to get here."

"She's not going anywhere," Tibby said cheerfully. "You know where she lives, don't you?"

"Well, yeah."

"So keep your shit together, and I'll be there as soon as I can. Seth!" I heard her yell. "Get up! We gotta go! So hey," she was back talking to me, "Go easy on yourself, okay?"

"All right," I said again. I sounded like a grumpy twelve-year-old.

"I love you, X."

"Love you too, Tib."

"All right," she said, mocking my tone. "See you soon." She hung up.

What the hell was I going to do until they got here?

 livia

I got off the plane and headed for the taxi area. Silently, avoiding the eyes of others, avoiding my own thoughts as much as possible, I gave the driver my address.

Laying my head against the window, I closed my eyes and tried not to think.

But all I could see was his face.

When he'd come back to me, heart in hand, he'd been earnest. I knew he was telling me the truth. I kept seeing it, seeing the hurt in his eyes.

So why had I run?

Because I didn't want to get sucked back in, so that when the next picture came out, or the story, or whatever —I would be hurt all over again.

I didn't want to be hurt anymore.

Everyone got hurt in relationships. I knew that. But at some point, there has to be a place where you just say 'Stop.'

As much as I lov—liked Xavier, I couldn't go any

further. I'd given everything to Royce, and I was still trying to heal the open wound he'd put in my back.

These things with Xavier were like someone hitting me in that wound. It seeped, and bled, and couldn't heal.

This wasn't on him, and I couldn't change how I felt.

So…that meant I needed to be the one to stop things before they got too out of hand. Before I was perpetually angry. Before he was upset and resentful.

Seeing those women surrounding him, I felt anger that I hadn't ever experienced. The anger I felt towards Royce when I found out about his infidelity—that was close.

This hurt more.

I couldn't live in a world where I was so open, so vulnerable to hurt.

When I got home, I called Momma.

"Hello, sweetheart!" She trilled. "How was your weekend?"

"It was all right," I said.

Momma knew me well. "What is it?" Her voice changed.

"I ended it, Momma."

"What?" Her voice went up at least an octave. "Olivia Anne, you'd best explain yourself. Right this moment! Lloyd! She's gone round the bend!" She yelled.

"Momma, I am not round the bend. I'm unfortunately disturbingly practical. I didn't know that you liked him all that much anyway," I added.

"I liked him just fine, missy. He was good for you, and in spite of what I might have been led to believe prior, Xavier is a good man. So what the hell went wrong?"

Led to believe? I nearly laughed. Leave it to Momma to take no blame for her assumptions.

"I don't want to talk about it right now, Momma. Can I call you later? I just want to go to bed."

I was ignoring the fact that in the time since I'd left I'd heard nothing from Xavier.

Surely he'd noticed me gone. Gotten my text. Seen why I was gone.

Why hadn't he called?

Because you left him, again, my snide inner voice told me. Who wants to run after someone who always leaves?

I had to leave, I thought. I can't let myself go crazy.

Maybe you could just trust him, the inner voice responded.

"Oh, shut up," I muttered.

"Did you just tell me to shut up?" Momma sounded beyond indignant.

"No, Momma," I said, feeling the tears coming again. "I'm tired, and my head is all over the place. I'll talk to you later." I ended the call because I just couldn't take it.

Not right now.

The only thing I could take was a shower.

Leaving my bag on the floor, I stripped, letting my clothes fall where I dropped them. I turned the heat up as high as I could stand it, and stood in the shower, my tears mingling with the hot water.

When it got to the point I thought I might fall over, I got out, brushed my hair, pulled on a nightgown, and crawled into bed.

It was over.

avier

I paced. Tibby had texted when she and Seth landed. They'd be here shortly.

I was glad because being here with only my thoughts was enough to drive me crazy. I wanted to call Olivia, to text her. To let her know, we could get through this. To tell her not to give up on us.

To tell her I loved her.

That I'd never loved anyone like I loved her.

But as I listed, in my head, all the reasons I wanted her with me, I struggled with why she might want me with her. I was fan-fucking-tastic, but was that enough?

It was clear, to Olivia, and to me, too, that it wasn't.

The relief nearly knocked me over when I heard the buzz of the door down below.

"Yes?"

"Let me in. I'm tired," Tibby said.

I hit the buzzer, and within minutes, she was walking in my door.

"X, you look like shit," she said.

"I feel worse, so thanks."

"Hey, man," Seth held out his hand. "I'm sorry about all this."

"You didn't do anything," I said, surprised.

"Doesn't mean I don't feel for you." He smiled.

Once again, I found that I really liked the guy. Tibby had chosen well.

So had I. So why was she running, damn it?

"What do you have to drink?" Tibby dropped a bag and went to the kitchen.

"Whatever you want," I answered. Not even booze sounded good.

"Well, get something."

"Why?" I turned to look at her. Her tone sounded different.

"Because I have something—well, we—" she looked at Seth, and he nodded encouragingly, "Have something we want to share with you."

"Okay," I said slowly. I poured a glass of whiskey.

Tibby poured two, and then she went to the couch, handing one to Seth. "Sit," she said. "This may take a while."

"You're making me nervous," I said.

"X, what do you remember about our lives after college?"

"What the fuck are you talking about?" Whatever I'd been expecting, this was not it.

"Humor me, jerk. What do you remember?"

"You went to college, and then law school. You and Bryant opened a practice and then like ten minutes ago, you met Seth. Three minutes ago, you got married. You do my legal stuff. I don't know why you won't help me with all my website shit. I don't know why I keep asking," I shook my head, listening to myself.

Tibby wasn't looking at me, but at the couch where she sat. She ran her hand along it, and then looked at her hand closely. "Glitter," she said, showing her hand to Seth.

"What. The. Fuck?" This made no sense. And I was supposed to be the one who drank and ran around.

Even weirder than Tibby's actions, Seth raised his eyebrows at her and nodded. "It's him," he said.

"Tib, you need to tell me what drugs you're on," I interrupted.

"Let me tell you why you keep asking me to do web stuff. In another life, I handled all your online shit. I did web development and management. I went to college, but I dropped out of law school because I was fooling around with a partner where I interned, and his wife went apeshit on me. Bryant and I lost touch with each other, and I partied and drank too much, and lived like a hermit because I kept fucking up all my friendships, except yours."

"I'm calling the doc," I said, getting up.

"Where'd the glitter come from?" Seth asked.

"What do you mean?" I stopped.

"Why is there glitter all over your couch? Do you remember how it got there?"

"I thought it was just one of the cleaners with body glitter or something," I shrugged. "I planned to bitch about it, but forgot."

"You don't remember a guy? A guy who floated around, shedding glitter like a dog sheds hair?" Seth continued.

"No! I have no—" I stopped, sitting down. "No, I—" Something about what he said triggered a memory, the barest sliver of—something. "I can't remember!" I said angrily.

Looking over at Tibby and Seth, I could see both of them nodding, and a look of pity on Seth's face.

"I know where it came from. I don't know why you don't, but I do."

"Okay, wise-ass, where's it from?" I sat back.

"It's from a djinn—a genie," Tibby said, seeing my eyebrows go up. "His name is Dhameer, and he grants wishes. But only wishes he wants to grant—he's free. Doesn't live in a lamp, or anything. I think. Anyway," she waved her hand, as though talk of lamps wasn't important. "He gave me three wishes, a long time ago. But not normal wishes. He told me he could hear me regretting some of my past choices, and he offered me the chance to go back and make a different choice. I could choose three times in my life where I wished I'd done something different, and then I could see what door number two held." She smiled at Seth, and he lifted her hand up to his mouth and kissed it.

Then she looked back at me. "I went back, and I did things differently three times. The catch for agreeing to this, for letting Dhameer give this to me, was that he got to determine where I ended up. In the life he found me in, I was pathetic, and working for you. It's why I don't kill you with your nagging about the web shit."

"Hold it," I held up my hands. "Where does Seth come in, since he obviously knows all this nonsense and didn't commit you?"

"Seth was wish number two. I met him in college, and I didn't call him back. I should have."

"So how did you end up with him?"

"Because in wish number three, I ran into Seth again, and when he hinted that he remembered wish number two, Dhameer yanked me from the third wish. He ended up letting me stay there, and Seth and I worked through the things from wish number two."

"He knew about it?"

Seth nodded. "Dhameer came to me after I was divorced, and I was thinking about Tibby. He said I could go back, and see what happened. Then I woke up one day, and I was back in my own life. I was furious. He said I needed to be patient, to wait. It was over a year, but I met her again. And we've been together ever since."

They beamed at one another.

I nearly threw up.

But I was too confused to take the time to vomit.

"I'm missing something here."

Tibby waved. "It doesn't make sense, I know. The point is, I know that you've seen Dhameer at some point in time. I don't know why you don't remember. But he's been here," she looked at her hand. "Tell me how you met Olivia again.

I went through the plane meeting.

"That was totally him," Tibby said, looking at Seth. "Don't you think?"

"You think some glitter guy set me up?" I asked. I was having a hard time with this.

"Yep. Have you made any wishes, to yourself, lately?" Tibby asked. "Not stupid shit, but something big, something really important to you?"

I was about to say no when I remembered their wedding. "Ah, yeah. I did. I was at your wedding, and I wished that I had someone who looked at me like you guys looked at each other."

"I knew it," Seth said.

"Yep, the glitter." Tibby nodded.

"What the hell am I missing here?" I threw up my hands.

"You've been visited by our fave djinn. He helped me and Seth find each other again. He must have come to see you. You don't remember? Dude, you wouldn't forget. He floats," Tibby said.

"No," I said. "No wait…" I stopped. Something, I wasn't sure what—it was just out of reach in my memory — "I can't remember shit. This is all well and good because at least I know the cleaning crew isn't having a raver, but what does that have to do with Olivia?"

"I bet it has everything to do with her. Dhameer is a sucker for love stories," Tibby smiled at Seth.

"You're saying a floating glitter guy sent me Olivia?"

"No, not directly. Just that he made sure your paths would cross. I mean, if she's the real deal. Like, thunderbolts and lightning?" Seth asked.

"Uh…" I didn't want to say it, but…fuck it. What do I

have to lose? "Yeah, I knew she was special the minute I met her. I didn't want to admit it, but she's been thunder-bolts and lightening the whole time."

"So it doesn't matter that she dumped you and ran away all through a text?" Tibby crossed her arms.

"If I don't hold it against her, neither can you," I said.

"Well, you only have one choice," Seth said.

"Okay?"

"You gotta go get her. You can't let her go."

"She doesn't want to see me," I said immediately.

"She's scared," Tibby interjected. "I'm not real happy with her, but I would bet this scared her. I would be. I spent a lot of my…" she looked away, "Earlier lives scared. It sucks."

"I don't even want to get into what the hell that means," I said, holding out a hand. "But you think I should go and see her? What if she doesn't want to see me?"

"Then she needs to tell you to your face," Tibby answered. "You both deserve that."

I could tell by her expression that she wasn't going to budge on this. And I was glad. I wanted an excuse, a reason to go to Olivia. I couldn't let her just walk away. Tibby was right. If she was scared, I wanted to help her.

If she'd let me.

"I know you just got here, but…" I stopped. I felt like an ass.

"Oh, we'll just stay here till you get back," Seth said cheerfully. "We didn't figure you'd be here anyway. So we'll have a little holiday." He smiled at Tibby.

I looked at them. "Ewww. You'd better change the sheets," I said.

"Go pack. Go sort out your shit," Tibby threw a sofa cushion from me.

I ran.

I drummed my fingers on the arm of the seat. I'd been able to grab a plane—not mine, but I didn't care. What good was money if it couldn't help you out in a jam? I didn't know what I was going to say.

I'd think of something, and then dismiss it, and here I was, getting ready to land, and I still had no clue what I was going to say.

I'd arranged for a car to be waiting, and I found my fingers kept drumming as we headed for Olivia's.

"Wait here. If I don't go in, we'll be heading back to the airport. If I do, you can leave," I told the driver as I got out.

He nodded, and I took a deep breath and walked up the steps to the front door.

17

Olivia

I heard the knocking at the door. The pounding, really.

Momma just couldn't leave me alone. Of course not.

"I'm coming!" I yelled, pulling on a robe. Damn that woman to hell. For once, I wanted to marinate in my misery.

"Leave me alone, Momma!" I said as I swung the door open.

Xavier stood in the doorway, hands in his pockets.

I opened my mouth, but nothing came out.

Finally, my voice returned. "What are you doing here?"

"I need to see you," he said.

I'd never heard a man sound more miserable in my life. I might sound that miserable, but I'd never heard it on a man.

My mouth opened again, and I didn't know what to

say. I could feel my fingers grip the doorknob tightly. I wanted him to go away. I wanted him to come in.

If he came in, he'd just convince me to ignore it—until the next time.

If he went away, he'd never come back.

Both made me want to scream.

"Come in," I said.

He glanced over his shoulder, giving the nod, then stepped past me. I could see a car at the curb, and a man getting into the driver's seat.

He hadn't been sure he'd be welcomed.

He was so considerate. Now I wanted to cry.

I was going crazy. That's what this felt like—insanity. Nothing made sense, and everything was upside down.

Including me. Most of all me.

I walked around him and headed for the kitchen. If I had to be up, I needed coffee. I could feel him behind me. He had a physical presence even though I couldn't see him.

The coffee pot sat clean and ready. I remembered that I'd cleaned the house up before leaving, so that I could come home to a neat place, secure in the wonderful weekend I'd just had.

Which meant I had coffee ready to go. I checked, and sure enough, the coffee was in the filter already.

I started it, and then turned around, leaning on the counter, and crossed my arms.

"Okay."

"A text?" His hands were still in his pockets.

"I…" I looked down. I didn't know what to say. It was shabby. I knew it. "It was cowardly of me. I know. I just didn't know how else to tell you."

"You didn't even ask me what happened."

I could hear the anger and the hurt in his voice.

"It didn't matter. This isn't you, Xavier! This is me,

don't you see?" I threw up my hands and turned to grab coffee cups, so I didn't have to see the hurt I'd caused.

"You're you," I said to the cabinet, "and this sort of thing will probably happen to you until you die. I don't blame you—I don't think you want to be with them. I figure if you didn't want to be with me, you'd just tell me. There's no reason for anything else."

"Right. So what made you text and leave?"

Did he always sound so cold? Or was I just sensitive?

Probably, along with a healthy dose of guilty.

I faced him. "Because I can't do it. I want to, I want to make this work, Xavier. But my heart fell to my stomach when I saw that picture. I can't live like that—waiting for the next stomach drop. It will make me a hard, hateful woman. I've had some hard and hateful thoughts. I didn't like it, didn't like what I saw when I was honest with myself."

I crossed my arms again, looking at my feet. "I felt horrible. I don't want to be that person. I don't want to be the person who brings all that anger and shit into your life, into my life." I looked up at him then.

"We both deserve better, Xavier. It's not your job to manage me and my issues." I kept my gaze steady.

"We can work through this together." He didn't look away either.

"But it's not something for us to work on," I said. "This is my thing. You're not at fault here. It's all on me."

He didn't speak right away.

avier

J watched her. She was upset, and I could tell that me being there rattled her. "Olivia," I said carefully. "Livvie, I…" I took a breath. "I love you. I know it's way too soon, and I sound crazy, but I'm not. I love you. I've been trying to ignore it since practically the minute we met, but it doesn't go away. It only gets stronger. Whatever you're afraid of, we can get through this together." I reached for her hands.

She tucked them under her arms.

Shit.

On a stick.

I backed away. "Don't push me out, don't push me away."

Her head dropped, and she didn't respond.

When she looked up, her face was shining with tears. "I am not what you deserve," she started.

That pissed me off. "How do you know what I deserve? I can tell you, I am pretty damn happy with you!"

"When I get crazy, and jealous, and yell and scream at you because some drunk woman grabs at you? Or when people ignore me and pretend you're available? You want to be around me when I'm dealing with that?"

"Yes! I want to be around you, period! Everyone's got shit they deal with, Livvie. I sure as hell do. I don't want any other guys anywhere near you. I'm more possessive than I've ever been in my life. I don't like it. That was the shit my mom's asshole boyfriends used to say right before they beat the shit out of her! They did it because they loved her so much, they couldn't stand to see her in the same zip code with another man! So they beat her for her own good!" I threw up my hands and walked away, too frustrated and upset to be still.

"You think that doesn't scare the hell out of me? To

hear shit in my head that sounds exactly like the abusive assholes I spent my childhood hiding from? You'd be wrong if you thought anything else!"

I looked at her then, her eyes wide. I could see how hurt she was for me, in addition to everything else.

I wasn't making this better.

Without warning, I heard the voice of one of the counselors I'd had at the Y when I was in high school, and I'd been suspended for fighting again.

"You cannot be anything for anyone, much less yourself, until you deal with your demons, Xavier. You have to deal with all the negative things that piled up inside of you before you can deal with anything else. Until you do, that anger, and all the other negative feelings will get in the way of every single thing you do, forever."

I'd scoffed at him, but later that year, I started seeing him every week, because my anger had reached a point where I wanted to hit someone until my own hurt went away. No matter how many fights I had, the hurt never went away.

It had taken some time, but I'd finally listened to him.

Looking at Olivia, I knew she needed to deal with her hurt. I loved her, and I thought she loved me, but until she got through her own shit, she couldn't be with me. Or with anyone else, I thought with some satisfaction.

No one else would do for her but me, but even if she tried, all her negative stuff, as my counselor had said, would still be piled up inside, getting in the way. Until she dealt with it and got through it, she'd never get better. No matter what.

"Listen," I said.

She could hear the difference in my tone and watched me carefully.

"I get it. You have things you need to handle. I understand. So I'm going to go now. I wanted you to know I love you. I wanted to tell you that I'm here if things change. My door is always open. I can't promise you how I will feel….but…" I looked down because I could feel tears in my eyes, "No matter what, if things change, come see me. Please, Livvie."

I almost held my hand out to her and stopped myself.

"I'm just going to go call my car, okay?"

She nodded one small, tight nod. Her whole being was wrapped as tightly as she wrapped her arms around herself.

This was killing me, but it was the right thing. She'd need to come back on her terms, with her own issues handled. I wanted to fight whatever dragons she had going on in her head, but I couldn't. Those were up to her.

I walked out to the front of the house, wanting to hear footsteps behind me as she changed her mind.

The house was silent.

When the car arrived ten minutes later, I opened the door and looked back toward the kitchen. I couldn't hear a thing, and she wasn't coming out.

I shut it behind me and hurried to the car before I broke down.

18

_X_avier

_I_ took a deep breath. It had been a long time since I'd done this kind of thing. I used to sit and record myself when I was younger, when I struggled with imposter syndrome, and worried about making weird faces when I sang.

But now, I just wanted to make sure I got it right.

Marcus nodded at me from outside the booth. "Rolling," he mouthed.

"Hey," I said, looking at the camera. "XTC coming at ya. I haven't done this for a long time, but I want to get this out—I need to—and I thought I'd share it with all of you. I've been working on some new stuff for the tour that's coming up. This is a song that came to me recently. It's a little different, and I want to see what you guys think. I know you'll tell me if it's shit," I grinned at the camera. Once I put this on social media, if people hated it, they'd let me know in about six seconds.

"So if you're not in the mood for sappy and emotional, stop the video right now. I don't want to hear the bitching later that you expected something different. This is…well, here it is."

I dropped my head, waiting for the simple beat Marcus and I had chosen for this. I saw him nodding slightly as the music filled the booth. I looked up, closing my eyes. *Let me get this right,* I thought.

"*I sit where you sit,*
a couple of seats
Don't know if I wanna
Wanna meet n greet
Or run fast on fuckin nervous feet
I don't know jus don't know
X, X, X—Xs and Os."

I stopped, letting the music fill me, closing my eyes, thinking about Olivia watching this. I wished I could see as she watched, as she listened. I'd seen her with some of my other music. Now, this would be her song.

"*X, X, X—Xs and Os*
Where does it go?
Neither one knows
When we age when we grow
No one no one wants to show
But I do
With you
X, X, X—Xs and Os"

How I made it to the end, I didn't know. While I sang, I could see all the things we'd done, the fun we'd had, the time we spent together—it was like a movie playing in front of me. It made me feel like someone had sucker punched me from about ten different directions.

I closed my eyes, letting the music die away. Then I looked at the camera and gave a peace out. Marcus moved something on his board, and then I heard him.

"We're done, man. Got it in one. That was amazing, X."

"You think so?" I felt more nervous about this than anything I'd done in a long time.

"Hell, yeah. This is totally sick. She'll love it."

"Is it that obvious?" I asked.

"Well, I met the 'O' part of that song," he came into the booth, clapping me on the shoulder. "I know where it comes from. I saw you guys together."

"I don't know what else to do. I don't exactly have the best rep with successful relationships."

"You know she watches your videos?"

"That's how I met her," I confessed. "I saw her watching them."

"That must have been weird," he walked out of the booth.

"It was. But it was great," I said quietly.

Please let her watch it.

19

*O*livia

*O*ne month. I'd made it a month.

It had been the longest month of my life. It was like the sun went away.

 *wo months later*

Momma slammed my office door open.

"Well, hello," I looked up from my desk. "What can I do for you? Other than calling the handyman to repair the wall?" I raised my eyebrows at her.

"You need to come with me, right now," she said.

"I have work," I spread my hands out, indicating the mass of papers on my desk.

"That can wait. Let's go." She didn't wait for an answer and walked out the door.

"Momma!" I got up, grabbing my purse and following her.

She was marching out the door to our office before I caught up with her.

"What is going on with you?" I asked.

"We're going out for a while."

"Where?"

"Get in the car." She yanked the door to her car open and got in without saying another word to me.

I thought she was pissed. Every word, every action, screamed that. But she wasn't talking, and normally, Momma yelled at me. She didn't keep her anger in. That wasn't even close to her style.

She didn't speak but drove angry until we got to my hairdresser. "Get out, and go get your hair done," she said.

"Why?"

"Stop arguing, and do as you're told, for one damn time in your life," Momma snapped.

If I didn't know better, I'd say Momma had been drinking from the decanter she kept for some of our clients.

"All right," I said. She kind of scared me at the moment.

"I'll be back in a bit."

"Okay," I shut the door, and she peeled away from me.

"What in the world?" I asked out loud. There was no answer.

Watching her car recede into the distance, I walked into the salon, where Anna, my stylist, greeted me with open arms.

But when I questioned Anna, she had no idea why Momma had made the appointment. So we chatted about nothing in particular. She asked me if I was dating, and I could tell that she'd seen the pictures of Xavier and me on our last night together.

I'd done a lot of deflection about that in the three months since Xavier had left my kitchen and my life. Laughed off all the questions, changed the subject, and made light of it.

My heart didn't crack open anymore.

Not much, anyway.

Anna was polite and kind, and when I said I wasn't dating anyone, she let it go.

Momma marched back in as Anna was drying my hair. She had a garment bag in her hand.

"When you're done, Olivia Anne, you go and get changed."

Momma put the bag down on a chair behind us and marched out again.

"What is going on with Miz Marguerite?" Anna asked.

"You know as much as I do," I said. "She's been in this mood all afternoon."

Anna finished and whipped the cape off me. "Go change before your momma explodes," she whispered. "I've never seen her like that."

I took the bag to the bathroom and pulled out the clothes.

It was a dress the same color as the dress Xavier called my mermaid dress. No sleeves and a silver circlet at the top held it up. There were jewelry and shoes in the bottom of the bag in a shopping bag.

What the hell?

I knew, however, that I wouldn't get anything out of Momma, so I got changed, and touched up my makeup. Wherever I was headed, if this dress was any indication, I needed to look good.

Anna exclaimed as I came out, "Olivia, you look delicious!"

I smiled. "Momma has good taste."

"She always does. Look, girl, you're all set. She took care of it. No, don't," she waved her hand as I reached into my bag to get her a tip. "Once this is all over, you will come back and tell me all about it. I'm dying over here!"

I laughed. It was the first time I'd laughed freely in…I couldn't remember how long. "That makes two of us. Thanks for getting me all spiffed up!"

She squeezed my hands, and I went out to face Momma.

Momma looked me over and made a noise that gave me no indication whether she was pleased or not, or anything at all.

"Let's go."

She turned her back on me again.

"You're going to have to talk to me at some point, Momma."

She didn't answer, just got in the car.

I got in with her. When I'd buckled my seat belt, Momma held out her phone out to me.

"What?"

"Watch this." She shook the phone a little.

I took it and saw that there was a video ready to—oh, God. I handed it back, feeling the pain in my heart.

"No, Momma."

"Don't you no me, young lady! I've left you be because you're supposed to be a grown woman, but this has gone on long enough. Now you act like a grown-up, and you face it. Hit play, Olivia." She gave the phone back.

My heart raced. I could feel it throbbing in my neck. My hands were sweaty all of a sudden. Why was she making me do this?

I hit Play.

Xavier was there, in a studio, looking right at the camera. He looked sad, and tired.

Had I put that there? The crack in my heart widened.

He started to speak.

"Hey, XTC coming at ya. I haven't done this for a long time, but I want to get this out—I need to—and I thought I'd share it with all of you. I've been working on some new stuff for the tour that's coming up. This is a song that came to me recently. It's a little different, and I want to see what you guys think. I know you'll tell me if it's shit," he grinned at the camera.

"So if you're not in the mood for sappy and emotional, stop the video right now. I don't want to hear the bitching later that you expected something different. This is…well, here it is."

He dropped his head, and the music started. Then he looked at the camera again and began to sing.

"I sit where you sit,
a couple of seats
Don't know if I wanna
Wanna meet n greet
Or run fast on fuckin nervous feet
I don't know jus don't know
X, X, X—Xs, and Os."

"X, X, X—Xs, and Os.
Where does it go?
Neither one knows
When we age when we grow
No one no one wants to show
But I do
With you

X, X, X—Xs, and Os."

The tears rolled down my face and splashed onto my lovely dress as I looked up at Momma. "When did he do this?" I whispered.

"About two months ago," she said, thawing for the first time since slamming the door into my office. "I'm not sure I can condone his poor language choices, but the sentiment is one that I approve of."

I looked back down, listening. He was singing to—he was singing to me. I could see it, tell in the way he looked at the camera as he sang the words that were about us.

"X, X, X—Xs, and Os
Where does it go?
Neither one knows
When we age when we grow
No one no one wants to show
But I do
With you
X, X, X—Xs and Os"

He sang the chorus for the last time and gave the camera a look that made me melt right into the seat.

This was for us. He'd done this for me, two months ago, and I'd never seen it.

I scrolled down, looking at the comments.

Other than a couple that called him out for being whipped by some chick, they were overwhelmingly positive. People loved it. They loved the way he sang, the real feeling in his words, his eyes. He got a few marriage proposals. A few proposals that were less than honorable— and instead of making me see red, I laughed.

Of course, he got less than honorable proposals. He'd put his heart out there, and I'd never seen him more appealing, or sexy. And I'd seen the guy in his full-on naked beauty.

"When did you see this?" I asked her.

"Last night. I Googled him because I wanted to see how he was doing. He's not doing anything, other than touring. But that video popped up, and I watched it four times in a row, and when Lloyd came in, I was crying. Honey, that man loves you. At least, he did when he made that video. He hasn't taken it down, or said anything to indicate that his feelings have changed." Momma held up a hand, stopping me from speaking.

"I know your objections, and I understand. But honey, you've been seeing the doctor, and you're working through things. I think you need to give him—give yourself— another chance."

I shook my head, feeling very small. "No, Momma, I broke his heart. That's what he said." Even though she was right. I had been seeing a therapist to deal with all the emotions that had gone off the rails for me. It's why I could laugh when I read the indecent comments on Xavier's video.

"He also said if you changed your mind, if things changed for you, that he wanted you to get in touch. It's time to get in touch, honey."

"Momma, I don't know if I can."

She took my hands in hers. "Yes, you can. This is the man for you, Olivia. I had my doubts at first. He really needs to watch his language, but I don't suppose that any such thing will happen at this late stage of his career. I supposed I could get used to a foul-mouthed Yankee as a son-in-law. Because he loves you. He put himself out there for you, and now it's time for you to do the same."

"Where are we going?" I pulled my hands away.

"You are going to the airport. He's playing in Atlanta tonight, and I called around, called in a few favors, and you have a front row seat to his show."

"No, Momma," I said weakly.

"Nonsense. You're not living, darlin'. You're doing all the things you're supposed to, but you're just existing. I know you're afraid, but you're not happy without him. And he's not happy without you, the last time anyone heard from him."

"Does he know I'm coming?"

"No. So if he's moved on, he can pretend not to see you. And you can leave. I'll pick you up if you end up flying back tonight. I won't let you go through this alone. But if he's still there for you, I'll give you the week off," she grinned at me, and I saw how young it made her look.

"What does Lloyd think of this?" I asked.

"He helped me plan it," she said, starting the car and pulling out of the parking lot. "Watch that video again, darlin'. That is a good man, and he loves you. Even if he's never said it, he loves you."

"He said it," I said softly.

"What?" She shrieked at me. "You never told me that!"

"I didn't want to," I admitted. "You would have told me I was stupid."

"You were. Sorry, darlin', but I don't lie to you. However, you've come through your stupid phase, so it's all going to be fine."

I clutched my purse and looked out the window as she sped along to the airport.

Was I really going to do this?

As I watched Momma drive away from the terminal, it looked like I was.

What if I was too late?

*X*avier

 looked in the mirror. I looked good, well, as good as it was going to get. I knew that something in me had died a little each day I didn't hear from Livvie. I didn't know if we counted as friends anymore, but I thought of her as Livvie. I'd woken up reaching for her more than once.

My manager, Troy, came in.

"You 'bout ready, man?"

I nodded. "Let's do this."

"That's right," he clapped me on the shoulder, but he didn't say more.

Tibby had found him, and interviewed him herself. This was the kind of guy I needed. He was calm, and a problem solver. I knew that Tibby told him about Olivia, and the whole world knew about the video. Everyone assumed I was with the woman who'd inspired the song, and that was why I'd been hiding away—because she and I were living it up together.

I preferred they thought that rather than the truth of the matter.

I steeled myself. If this were like the rest of the shows, the crowd would start chanting 'X's and O's' pretty early on. For fans that loved all my rap, even my really angry shit, they were all over 'X's and O's'. It was getting easier to sing it—I didn't see her all the time when I did.

The lights went down, and I ran out. The crowd screamed, and I smiled and waved.

The music of the first song began, and I went right into it, looking into the crowd, scanning the front rows. I liked to look them over since that was mainly who I'd be seeing for most of the show. A mix of men and women, some only boys and girls, trying to be grown. Swaying, singing along with me.

A flash of the sea went through my line of sight so fast I thought my eyes were playing tricks on me. I looked back. Shit. A girl—no, a woman in a mermaid-colored dress.

She'd ruined that color for me. Shit—I stopped, nearly stopping in the middle of the song, but I managed, through habit, to keep singing.

Was that—?

Olivia was in the front row.

In a mermaid colored dress.

I shook my head, forcing myself to continue, but I kept my eyes on her for another moment, to make sure she was real, that I wasn't seeing the thing I wanted to see.

When she smiled, small and hesitant and nervous, I nearly dropped the mic.

It was her. She was here.

Somehow, I made it through the song. Then I held up my hand.

"Hey, hey, I want to change it up a little. I'm going out of order so I can sing something that has to go on right now."

The crowd screamed, and I could hear various titles being shouted out, X's and O's among them.

"Let's go into X's and O's," I told Zed, my DJ.

"You sure, man?"

I usually never changed set order. I nodded. "One hundred percent. It's all good," I added. *I hope,* I said to myself.

I walked back out to the front of the stage. "I'm gonna do a little song you might have heard," I said as the music started.

The crowd, recognizing the opening beats, went into even louder screaming.

I focused on Olivia, standing in front of her, not moving, or bouncing around like I normally did. This was for her. She was here. I needed to show her that not only was the door open, as I'd said, but I wanted her to come in. Forever.

*"*X*, X, X—Xs, and Os*
Where does it go?
Neither one knows
When we age when we grow
No one no one wants to show
But I do
With you
X, X, X—Xs, and Os

"*Look look looking at you*
    I can see the future
    But do we see the same
Or I am standing here
Just calling your name?
I gotta know…
X, X, X—Xs, and Os

"*X, X, X—Xs, and Os*
    Where does it go?
Neither one knows
When we age when we grow
No one no one wants to show
But I do
With you
X, X, X—Xs, and Os"

Tears ran down her face, and her smile got wider. Watching her as I sang was one of the most intense things I'd ever done.

I'd have to do this more often if she'd let me.

The crowd got quieter. I think the people around her figured out I was singing to Olivia, but at the moment, for the first time in a long time, I didn't care what my fans thought. All that mattered was that Olivia heard me. I didn't know if I'd get another chance, and I didn't want to waste this one.

"*Come with me take my hand*
    Cross over my line in the sand
Show me show me
You understand

Let me show you
I want to know you
X, X, X—Xs, and Os

"W here we gonna go
Don't ask cuz I don't know
But what I tell you's true
I wanna go wanna go
With you
Me, me, me and you

"X , X, X—Xs, and Os
Take me take you
Take me as I am
I'll take you like Peter Pan
To Never Never Land
Forever and ever
Hand in hand
X, X, X—Xs, and Os

"X , X, X—Xs, and Os
Where does it go?
Neither one knows
When we age when we grow
No one no one wants to show
But I do
With you
X, X, X—Xs, and Os

X, X, X—Xs, and Os
           Where does it go?
Neither one knows
When we age when we grow
No one no one wants to show
But I do
With you
X, X, X—Xs, and Os. "

I walked to the edge of the stage and held out my hand to her. She looked at me for a moment, a moment that seemed to last forever, and then stretched out her hand in front of her as she came to the stage.

One of the security guys leaped forward, but I waved him off. Her hand came to rest on mine.

"Come up here," I said quietly, keeping the mic away from my face. "Please."

She opened her mouth, and I spoke again.

"You've come this far," I said. "Come all the way."

"Yes," she said.

For a moment, the crowd, the stadium, everything—it just fell away. It was me, and her, and she was holding my hand, and all that I wanted was there, within my reach.

"Hey, give her a boost, would you?" I looked at the security guy hovering. "Can you get one on each side, and lift her up?"

Another guy appeared out of nowhere, and together, they lifted her up to me.

I put my arms around her and buried my face in her shoulder, loving the smell of her that I could smell even through all the normal show smells.

"God, I've missed you. Are you back to me?" I said to her hair.

I felt her nod.

"Good thing," I grinned. "You'd have to dump me again, in front of all these people. Who love me," I pulled back from her. "Can I kiss you? Please?"

"In front of—"

I stopped her with a kiss. I lifted her off her feet to bring her closer. The energy from the crowd around me felt like it was all over—thunderbolts and lightning. She wrapped her arms around me, and I knew that not only had she walked back in the door, but slammed it behind her.

I was never going to let her go. Not that she'd want to.

"I love you," I said.

"I love you, Xavier."

I kissed her again. "Now that you have your shit in order, you think I could go back to making a living? Some people gotta work."

She burst out laughing.

I eased my hold on her, which wasn't easy. Then I held up a finger to the crowd, pulling the mic back up to me with my other hand. "Hang on," I said, winking.

I led her from the stage, the cheers and noise from the crowd surrounding us. "Stay here. Don't disappear. I want to see you the rest of the show, and then after the show. Okay?"

She nodded. "What about after that?"

"I want to see you the rest of my life."

Olivia grinned. "I'll need to cancel my ride home," she said.

"Damn straight." I kissed her again, and we parted, laughing. "Now let me get back to work, woman!"

I ran back on stage, and while I know I was happier than I'd ever been, I could swear I'd never heard the crowd so enthused.

It was the best show of my life.

Only after I was done, and Olivia and I were walking across the stage towards the exit that led to my bus, did I notice the gold and silver glitter all over the stage.

"Holy shit," I said.

"What?"

"C'mon, let's get out of here. I have a story to tell you." I tucked her under my arm as we walked out.

Together.

EPILOGUE

*F*rom **StarShot website**:
        The bad boy, XTC, missing in action until his tour opened, gave his most successful tour ever. Over the past four months, he's sold out every show. He treats his fans to more encores and requests than ever before. Gone is the sullen, angry rapper, although he belts out those works with the same energy he's always had. The big difference is the insertion of the song X's and O's throughout his show, never at the same time.

X's and O's, written by the rapper himself, was debuted on his social media site in a simple video that showed the star singing in his New York studio. Sorry ladies, but this tour puts to rest all the rumors that came to life when the video dropped. He's taken, very taken if his actions at the Atlanta show are any indication.

He may be getting older, but like a good wine, he keeps getting better.

Update: XTC's manager, Troy Nottingham, released a statement today: At the conclusion of the Up-n-Down tour, XTC and Olivia Meroux will be married, and taking an extended honeymoon. The tour will finish as scheduled but there are no further appearances scheduled for XTC for the remainder of the year.

WANT TO SEE HOW IT ALL STARTED?

Dhameer is the constant in the Djinn Everlasting series. Like Tibby, Xavier, and Bryant, there's a reason why he does the things he does, and why he follows the rules and guidelines he does - rules that frustrate all three of the humans we see him granting wishes to!

Read his origin story here! Click the link below! If you are unable to click it, please visit www.lisamanifold.com/djinnnews, and that will get you the story as well!

SEE HOW IT ALL BEGAN...
READ DHAMEER'S STORY IN HEART OF THE DJINN

CLICK HERE TO DOWNLOAD

ABOUT THE AUTHOR

Lisa Manifold is a USA Today Bestselling Author of fantasy, paranormal, and romance stories. She moved to Colorado as an adult and has no plans of living anywhere else. She is a consummate reader, often running late because "Just one more page!" Lisa writes the things she does because she really, really wants to live in a world where these kinds of stories happen.

She is a fan of all things Con, and has an entire room devoted to the costumes created for Cons. She serves on the board of Rocky Mountain Fiction Writers as the Independent Published Author Liaison, and in 2016, was named the RMFW Independent Writer of the Year.

Lisa is the author of the fae paranormal romance series The Realm, the Grimm fairy tale retelling Sisters of the Curse series, the Heart of the Djinn series which follows a free-lance djinn, the Aumahnee Prophecy urban fantasy series, and the forthcoming urban fantasy series The Dragon Thief.

She lives as close to the mountains as possible with her husband, sons, and three attentive dogs.

Connect with Lisa online:
www.lisamanifold.com
Lisa@lisamanifold.com

TITLES BY LISA MANIFOLD

The Realm Series

Heart of the Goblin King

To Wed the Goblin King

Realms of the Goblin King

Rise of the Dragon King

The Companion Tales, Volume I

The Companion Tales, Volume II (2018)

The Aumahnee Prophecy

with Corinne O'Flynn

Marigold's Tale (Prequel)

Eamonn's Tale (Prequel)

The Gim Crackers (Aumahnee World Novella)

The Portal Keepers (Aumahnee World Novella)

Watchers of the Veil

Djinn Everlasting

Three Wishes

Forgotten Wishes

Hidden Wishes

Sisters of the Curse

Thea's Tale

One Night at the Ball

Casimir's Journey

Do you like being in the loop? Sign up for Lisa's newsletter!
Shenanigans, book recs, and the latest news abound!

www.ingramcontent.com/pod-product-compliance
Lightning Source LLC
Chambersburg PA
CBHW020232260626
47156CB00002B/640